Doppelganger Danger

Blue Moon Sacramento

Alex Gates, Steve Higgs

Contents

One month ago... Infidelity. March 19th, 1837hrs.

CLAIRE BALZAN LAY ON her stomach perpendicular across the bed. Her feet angled upward and pedaled the air. She had long, toned legs, and she knew how they affected men—at least how they affected her husband, Simon. She also knew that he leaned against the bathroom door and watched her. So, she danced her bare legs back and forth, teasing him.

Inviting him.

Claire wore a skimpy black dress that hardly covered her backside. She glanced over her shoulder at her Simon, biting her lower lip and batting her eyes at him.

"We're going to be late," he said, sauntering toward her, unbuttoning his shirt, and peeling it off.

"I'm craving you, though, not whatever five-star restaurant you reserved."

Simon fiddled with his belt. "You can have me any time you want. We can only get this reservation once every four months, and they charge an expensive deposit. You wanted to go somewhere nice and fancy—somewhere we could never afford—for our fifth anniversary." He whipped the belt free of the loops and dropped it on the floor. "Well, we can't afford it, but we made the reservations. If we're going to spend the money, don't you think we should at least enjoy the food?"

Claire rolled onto her back, hiked up the dress' skirt, and dropped her knees sideways, away from each other. She dragged the tube-top down to her belly, exposing her breasts. "You can enjoy me as your meal."

Simon worked the button on his trousers. It stuck. The waist fit him too tightly. He squirmed, sucked in his gut, and pulled the waistband together to build slack. The button slid free.

As he scrunched his pants to the floor, his phone vibrated in the pocket. Reflexively, with no conscious thought, he removed the device.

"Ignore it," Claire said.

"It's from an unknown number. I think it's the restaurant."

Claire sighed and groped her breasts and moaned softly, putting on a heavy-handed show to entice her husband into bed with her.

His brows furrowed. He leaned toward the phone's screen. "What the... Claire." Simon tore his gaze from the device and regarded his wife with pure terror and fear and pain. He stuttered, working his lips and his tongue, but stumbling over the words in his mouth. With his thumb, he swiped at the puffy skin beneath his eye—a tic he often performed when anxious.

Claire adjusted her dress, pulling the fabric back over her exposed bits, and she sat upright. "Simon, what's wrong? Did they cancel our reservation?"

Her husband placed a hand over his mouth, gripping his lower lip, and pulling down. He shared his attention between the phone and Claire for a few seconds, as if comparing whatever he saw to her.

"What is it?" she asked. "You're making me nervous. What's wrong?"

"Who is he?" Simon asked. He whispered it, though, as if he resisted forming the question. He covered his mouth again and shook his head.

"Who is who?"

"Him." Simon tossed his phone at Claire.

It landed beside her heavily, burying into the plushy comforter like a meteor striking Earth.

Claire stared at her husband, refusing to look at the phone—at whatever horror had transformed her fun, confident husband into a shell. She ignored the device plunged into the sheets, hopping off the bed and rushing to Simon. She grabbed his hands in hers, and she leaned her head against his chest. He smelled like Old Spice deodorant and Bleu de Chanel cologne, with a hint of fresh-cut grass and dirt beneath it all. Simon landscaped for a career, mowing lawns, trimming trees, and installing sprinklers.

For a quick second, Simon allowed Claire to hug him. Then he raised his chin to stare at the ceiling, and he slipped her away from her hold. He pulled up his pants and brushed past her to the bed, leaned over, and lifted the phone from its crater.

"Who is he?" Simon asked, turning up the volume and extending the phone toward Claire.

A naked woman sat atop a man, and she rocked back and forth on him, moving up and down. He held her breasts, and she screamed with pleasure. "Oh, God. God. Oh, God."

Claire immediately recognized the man as her therapist, Robert Woods. She also, though unbelievingly, recognized the woman.

At first, Claire had no thoughts in her head, let alone words to offer her reeling husband. She placed her hand, the meaty part between her thumb and index finger, into her mouth and bit down hard. Tears stung her eyes. She dropped the phone to the floor, shaking her head back and forth.

The woman in the video was Claire.

"Who is he?" Simon remained calm, which terrified Claire.

Why hadn't he exploded? After what she had witnessed in the video, why hadn't he reacted more aggressively, more violently?

Because he was a good man.

"I don't know," Claire said, her voice quiet and muffled behind her hand.

"He's a stranger?" Simon asked.

"No." Her face melted. Tears trailed down her cheeks, and her nose leaked, and her lips quivered. She had never experienced so much horror or terror in her life.

"No?" Simon asked. "You know who he is, then?"

Claire placed both her hands over her face and pressed, pushing away the headache charging toward the area behind her eyes. She wiped away the tears, smearing her makeup. She sniffled and breathed, calming herself, hoping to clear her mind.

"I would never do that."

"You would never do what?"

"Simon, you know me. I would never cheat on you. Never. Ever. You're my dream, remember?" The dam broke once more, and tears streamed down her face. "Please, believe me."

"Claire," Simon said, his voice curt, "you're on video fu..." he trailed off, biting his lip. Simon's parents despised vulgarity, and he adopted their perspective on foul language. He murmured. "You're on video… having sex with that man. What do you expect me to believe?"

"That's not me. I would never do that. I wouldn't. I wouldn't. I wouldn't. Never, Simon. Never." Claire stepped toward her husband, reaching out for him with a trembling hand.

He moved away, shaking his head. "Don't touch me. Just, don't, okay?" Simon sat on the edge of the bed and cupped the back of his skull with both hands. "Just give me a second to process this."

From the bluetooth speakers placed on their dresser, Whitney Houston sang about loving someone always. Outside the open window, a dark purple filled the dusk sky. The sun had set. Claire and Simon stood in the twilight, waiting for the darkness to shroud them.

The moaning played again from Simon's cell phone. He watched the video for a few seconds, pausing it and staring at the screen. "You have that same mole on your shoulder, and that one near your belly button." He pinched the screen and separated his fingers, zooming in on the paused video. "I know you have those panties. You wore them for me."

"Simon," Claire said. "I wouldn't."

He looked at her, his eyes red. "Please, just stop. Stop lying. I'm pretty sure that's your therapist. Dr. Woods, right? It doesn't matter, though. I don't care who he is. I want to know why. Why, Claire? I thought I was enough for you."

"You are," she said, kneeling before her husband and grabbing his legs, resting her head on his thigh. "You've always been enough. You always will be."

"Why, then?"

"That's not me."

"Stop lying. You watched the video. That's you. That's you, Claire. That's you." The moaning played from the phone once again, filling the room with the dreaded sound. "That's you." Simon finagled his legs away from Claire without kicking her or harming her, and he escaped off the side of the bed, heading to the bedroom door.

Claire remained on her knees, scooting around to face her husband. She leaned sideways, resting her head on the comforter. "Simon, please, trust me. You have to believe me."

Her husband stared at her for an eternity, saying nothing. He was the greatest man she had ever known, and she could never risk losing him. She would never jeopardize the integrity of their marriage or their friendship.

"Simon."

He raised the phone to his face and tapped the screen, watching the video once more, this time in its entirety.

Claire didn't count the seconds or minutes it lasted, but to her, the sounds emanating from the phone carried on for a hellish eternity. The woman moaning and panting. The man grunting like some animal, then near the end of the video, gasping. "Claire. Oh, Claire. Claire."

Each uttering of her name slapped her across the face, clubbed her in the gut. She shook her head and muttered, "No. No. No," in a whisper. "Simon, it's not me."

Her husband of five years to the very day stared at her with heavy eyes. "Goodbye, Claire," he said, turning away from her.

His footsteps padded down the hall, and shortly after, the door leading into the garage gently closed.

Two weeks ago ... Bankrupt. April 11th, 1222hrs.

CLAIRE SAT IN AN empty conference room in the hospital. She had the day off, but Marie Stump, Claire's nurse manager, had called her in to discuss something urgent. They had scheduled their meeting for 1230hrs.

As Claire waited, she scrolled through her phone, constantly checking Simon's social media accounts for any updates. He hadn't called or texted her in two weeks, though she had messaged him non-stop—texts, voicemails, emails, and private messages on Instagram and Facebook.

Radio silence had answered her.

In the conference room, alone with her thoughts, Claire switched over to Simon's contact. She drafted a quick text message, deleting it, drafting something new, deleting that. She stared at her screen.

Why wouldn't he respond to her? Simon didn't have a history of passive aggression. He had never implemented the silent treatment. If a problem existed, he tackled it head-on. He didn't shy away from conflict, rather he embraced it and solved the issue.

Claire had struggled with that communication method at the start of their marriage. Her parents had failed to model healthy relationship habits, preferring to ignore and bury any issues until they bubbled over and exploded into a critical, offensive, blame-based argument. Once they exhausted themselves without compromise or agreeing on who was right and who was wrong, her mom and dad shut down and refused to speak to each other for hours, sometimes days—one time, they went two whole weeks without saying a single word.

Simon had refused, from day one, to point fingers and accuse one person of wrongdoing. Compromise and sacrifice were pillars to a successful marriage, but even they stood on the foundation of communication. He insisted they build their relationship on two truths—trust and communication.

"So why aren't you responding to me?" Claire asked the empty office.

The door clicked, opening, and Marie Stump entered the room. She was a middle-aged lady with short, black hair and pale skin. She approached the table and pulled out the chair nearest to Claire, sitting on it. The woman sighed, setting a folder on the table. She looked up and offered a broken smile.

"Thanks for coming in," Marie said.

Claire nodded, saying nothing. She clenched her fists, her jaw, her shoulders, sitting rigidly.

"Have you heard from Simon?"

"No," Claire said, breathless. Since Marie had entered the room, Claire had neglected to breathe. She exhaled, and the stress in her body slightly loosened. "Not yet."

"I'm sorry."

Claire nodded as an awkward, tense silence ensued.

Marie cleared her throat and opened the folder. "It's been brought to my attention, by a worried coworker, that you have... that you stole Adderall from one of the hospital's medicine cabinets."

The accusation made Claire feel like a little girl, taking the blame for something she never even dreamed of doing. Getting yelled at by her mom. Getting chastised by her dad. Grounded and forgotten. She sat in the large conference room, feeling tiny and empty and... and shattered.

"Claire?" Marie said.

"Yeah?"

"I understand you had a past addiction to Adderall."

Claire's face scrunched, and she squeezed her eyes shut, not wanting to cry. She had cried so much recently. Her head constantly throbbed, and fatigue riddled her body.

"Did you have an Adderall addiction not too long ago?"

"In nursing school," she said. "Five, six years ago. I haven't used in half a decade. I attend monthly meetings. I have a sponsor and a therapist."

"Your husband, he recently left home, right?"

Claire pawed at her eyes.

"I'm not saying you relapsed, Claire. What I'm saying is that maybe you were tempted. You stole the pills and brought them home… just in case, you know?"

"I didn't steal a thing."

"Please, Claire," Marie said, constantly peppering her name into the conversation, treating her like a little girl. "This conversation will be more productive if you're honest with me."

"I didn't steal any pills."

Marie reached into the folder, grabbing a white leaf of paper, and flipping it over. It showed a black and white, grainy image of Claire going through a cabinet filled with prescription drugs. Marie placed another image before Claire. This one showed the same woman—Claire, presumably—holding a bottle filled with pills in her left hand.

"There's a bottle missing from our inventory."

"Marie," Claire said, nearly speechless and incapable of removing her eyes from the photographic evidence of her stealing Adderall.

"We're going to suspend you without pay while we investigate the matter."

"I didn't steal any pills," Claire said. "That's not me. I didn't steal pills, and I didn't screw someone who's not my husband. That's not me!"

"Please, calm down."

"No!" Claire exploded from her chair, toppling it over. "My life is falling apart. I don't know why. I don't know who that is in the picture. I don't know who's destroying my marriage and my career. But it's not me. I'm not doing it. It's not me!"

Marie collected the two photographs, stacked them neatly together, and set them back in the manilla folder. "Claire, once we've completed the investigation, we'll determine whether you can return to work at this hospital. Even if you're not fired outright, before you ever work here again, you will have to enter a rehab facility and show proof of completing their program."

Claire crumpled to the floor, sitting on the ground and hugging her knees to her chest, shaking her head back and forth.

"That's the best-case scenario," Marie said. "Depending on the investigation, you might not only lose your job here, but your nursing license. You could spend time in jail. Claire, this is an extremely serious offense."

"That's not me."

"Claire, stop denying it. We have video evidence. You used your key to unlock the cabinet. You're wearing your badge—it has the smiley face sticker in the corner. Denial won't help you. Admit what happened. Return the bottle of pills. If it's still full and not missing a single capsule, I'm sure we can work something out between you and the hospital. Maybe you can keep your job. If anything, you won't lose your license. Not this time. But you have to work with us. Help us."

Claire's mouth fell agape, and her eyes remained wide, barely blinking, and she stared at the floor. "I didn't screw him. I didn't steal any pills. I swear on my life, on my marriage—"

"Well, Claire," Marie said, "don't swear on your marriage. We know how much water that held." With that, the nurse manager collected the folder and stood. "We'll be in touch. But until further notice, you're not allowed in this hospital. Do you understand?"

Claire understood nothing about anything at all. She sat on the floor and hugged her knees and wondered when she would wake from this nightmare.

"How will I eat?"

Marie was nearly at the door. She stopped. "What?"

"How will I eat, or pay for rent, or buy gas?" Claire asked. "I need money. I need this job."

Marie's broad shoulders raised and fell, and she left the conference room without another word.

Claire and Simon had shared a bank account, and he managed their money, paying the bills and making financial decisions. Claire had downloaded their banking application onto her phone, but she had only ever logged into it once. Without a job, she needed to know how much they had in the account. She needed to know how long she could survive.

Luckily, the cloud had saved her password into her phone, and it allowed her access through facial recognition. She navigated to their checking account.

Her heart plummeted into her stomach, sitting heavily. The balance showed zero dollars. Claire navigated back to the home screen, switching over to the savings account. Zero dollars. Sweat beaded on her forehead, despite the pumping air conditioning within the conference room.

Had Simon emptied their accounts? Why? Why would he do that without confronting her first? Sure, he managed their finances, but her nurse's salary provided a sizable chunk of their money. He should have left her something.

Claire switched back to the home screen again, searching through the tabs and options for another account. Maybe Simon had moved it over to his business profile, funneling all their cash into something she had no access to.

Again, why? Forty, fifty percent of what they earned belonged to her. He couldn't just make it vanish.

Claire exited from the banking application and swiped to Simon's contact, calling him.

The phone rang five times before catching voicemail. She hung up and called again, and again, and again.

Eventually, the hospital security arrived at the conference room and escorted her from the building.

One week ago ... Discovery. Tuesday, April 19th, 0637hrs.

ROBERT WOODS RAN ALONG the Sacramento River early every morning before work. The dawn had always helped orient him to the oncoming day, and exercising each morning cleared his mind and provided him with a burst of energy not even a bottomless pot of coffee could replicate. He always ran the same trail, preferring predictability.

Through Robert's routine, he had become incredibly familiar with the route and the landscape. So, even in the twilight, the time where night and day tugged at each other, he had noticed the bloated disturbance dead on the bank of the river.

A large, muscular officer approached Robert. He had one hand on the butt of his gun, and the other swayed back and forth in an exaggerated arc as he strolled toward the scene. When he arrived, he curled his nose and glanced around the area. On his left breast pocket, he wore a name tag. T. WILSON.

"You called this in?" Officer Wilson asked, nodding beyond Robert at the corpse lying on the beach.

"I did."

"What's your name?"

"Robert Woods."

"Like the football player?"

"I don't watch football."

"Well, anyway, what do we have here?" Officer Wilson stomped forward, crouching beside the waterlogged corpse—a naked man in his late-twenties. "You found him like this?"

"I never touched him," Robert said.

Officer Wilson sucked on his teeth for a second before picking at them with his fingernail. "Ate a spinach breakfast sandwich this morning on a seeded bagel. Seed stuck in my tooth every which way but out. I tried rinsing and picking, but I can't get it. I'm going to have to grab some floss and wire this sucker out."

Robert did not know how to respond. "I'm sorry," he said.

"Yeah, me, too. It's a real annoyance. Distracting. Anyway, what do we have? A young, white male. Wedding ring. No possessions beyond that, though. No identification." The large officer shifted in his squatted stance, facing Robert. "You do this to him?"

"What... what? No. No. I found him and called it in."

Officer Wilson narrowed his eyes and glared at Robert for a few terrible seconds before breaking off a wide smile and chuckling. "I'm messing with you." The man stood, brushing off his knees. "I'll have to secure the scene. Call forensics. You know the drill, huh?"

"No."

"Well, since you found the body, I'll have to take a statement from you. Can you do that now?"

"Sure. Yeah." Robert glanced at his watch, which continued to track his run, though he hadn't run for over thirty minutes now. "I don't need to bc at work until eight."

Officer Wilson waved away the statement. "I'll give you a doctor's note. I'm sure your boss will understand if you're late." Moving away from the corpse, the officer returned to Robert. Behind them, the river carried onward, always moving and running. "What were you doing out here this early? Sun isn't even up yet."

"I run every morning. Have done so for years."

Officer Wilson bit his lip and glanced at Robert's aging body. He poked a finger into Robert's gut. "You're a little flabby. You think running would have... I don't know, hardened you."

"I don't have the greatest genetics. My grandpa was obese, as was my dad. Both died from heart attacks. I struggle with my weight, especially when I'm not careful with my diet. Running helps me stay healthy without having to kill myself at the gym or experiment with depriving diets. Besides, I enjoy being outside this early."

"Who is he?" Officer Wilson asked.

"Who?"

"Him." Wilson pointed to the corpse.

Robert gulped. "I don't know."

"You said you knew him. That's why you called it in."

"What? I never said that."

The police officer stretched a smile all the way across his face, chuckling. "I'm only giving you a hard time. On a serious note, you have identification on you?"

Robert reached into his zipped pocket and removed his driver's license, handing it to the officer. Wilson compared the picture to the man, dividing his attention between the card and Robert.

"What's a good number I can reach you at?" Officer Wilson removed a notepad from his breast pocket, the one with the name tag secured to it, flipped it open, and pulled out a pen.

Robert shared his contact number.

Officer Wilson noted it, and he copied Robert's identification information onto the pad. When he finished the process, he snapped shut the booklet and returned it to his pocket, along with his pen, handing Robert his license. "Thank you, Mr. Woods. You can go on your way, but expect a detective to follow up for an official witness report. Also, they'll want to ask you a few more questions."

"I can go?" Robert asked.

"Unless you're confessing to a murder and disposal of a body, in which case I'll arrest you and take you to jail."

"No," Robert said, his balls now sitting in his stomach. He hadn't so much as violated a speeding law in his life, but something about speaking to cops—especially beside a corpse—made him more than uncomfortable. And Officer Wilson didn't ease the pain of the encounter.

"Well, you're free to go."

Robert walked rather than ran away from the scene. He believed if he ran, the cop would chase him and arrest him. When he turned the corner, though, and T. Wilson disappeared from sight, Robert sprinted back to his house.

He had lied directly to the cop's face. He had known the man. The corpse belonged to Simon Balzan, Claire Balzan's husband.

When Robert reached the last leg of his run, he slowed again to a walking pace, catching his breath as he removed his phone from his pocket. He called the burner phone, her secret number, and he received an out-of-service message. Silently cursing, he debated whether he should risk calling her personal cell phone. She had warned him to never contact her on that number. Never. No matter what.

Robert glanced up at the sky. He had no choice but to get a hold of her.

"Hello?" Claire answered.

"Claire, it's me. Robert Woods."

"Dr. Woods?"

"I told you, call me Robert. Or Bobby."

"What?" she asked, obviously confused. "Why are you calling me so early?"

"I know you said to never contact this number, but—"

"When did I say that? Dr. Woods, what's going on?"

"Claire," he said, nearly shouting her name to catch her attention and shut her up. "Claire, I found your husband."

"You found him? What do you mean?"

"Did you do it? I said nothing to the cops. I swear. But I have to know. Did you do it?"

"I don't know what you're talking about. Did I do what?"

"He's dead."

"Who's dead?" Claire asked.

"Simon. Your husband."

A few seconds ticked away. Robert walked up his driveway, unlocked his front door, and entered his house. He went straight for the kitchen, turning on the coffee machine.

Once the pot was brewing, and Claire had said nothing, he asked, "Are you there?"

"Simon is dead? What... I don't understand."

"I was running this morning, and I found his body on my normal track. I'm certain it was him, Claire. The cops will identify him soon, and I'm sure they'll contact you. I didn't tell them anything, though. I didn't say a word about... well, you know."

Claire breathed into the phone, not saying a thing. "Know what?"

"Our affair."

"That never happened. I would never cheat on Simon. Never."

"Did you kill him?"

"What?" Claire asked. "What did you say?"

"Did you kill Simon?"

"No." Her voice was timid and reserved—on the edge of slipping and falling.

"A detective will contact me to ask more questions about Simon. They'll identify his body, connect him to you, and they'll connect you to me. Do you know what that means? You're a suspect. I'm a suspect. This could ruin me."

"Ruin you?" Claire asked, laughing. "Ruin you?"

"I didn't kill Simon, Claire. Did you? I have to know if you want me to protect you."

"Get bent," she said, disconnecting the call.

Robert moseyed over to the kitchen sink, staring out the window, and watching the sun rise. Little did he know, Robert Winston Woods would never witness the morning spectacle again.

One day ago ... Missed Meeting. Monday, April 25th, 0601hrs.

Claire Balzan sat in a donut shop an hour before her meeting with August Watson, Sacramento's newest and fastest rising paranormal investigator.

Watson had a growing reputation for digging out the truth in a case, rather than accommodating his clients to prove their supernatural claims. That's why Claire had contacted him over the myriad of hacks roaming the white pages. He could help her, provide her with a grounded, reasonable explanation.

Claire palmed a warm paper coffee cup purchased from the donut shop—her ticket to sit in their cafe and wait. She stared at her left hand, at her wedding ring. The diamond sparkled and reflected the early morning light.

She thought of Simon.

He had died believing she had cheated on him, that she had broken the sacredness of their marriage. His death hurt to the point of being numb.

For the past seven years, she had confided everything to Simon. She had spilled her soul to that man. Now, when she needed him the most, when she needed to speak to him and share her worries and fears, she couldn't. He was gone. Claire had no one but herself, and her mind was a toxic soil that withered and destroyed any positive thought.

No husband.

No job.

No money.

What did she have in the way of optimism? Of hope?

A homicide detective had knocked on Simon's and her door a few days ago—Claire couldn't remember how many days ago. Time had turned into a murky mess—distorted and impossible to discern. It made it nearly impossible to sleep, eat, or do routine tasks, such as brushing her hair or teeth, showering, changing clothes, or cleaning.

The homicide detective for the Sacramento Police Department had wavy, thick, and perfectly styled hair. Detective Quinn, but please, call me Daniel or Danny, looked like a Hollywood star, with his striking blue eyes and chiseled face and superhero physique. He moved and spoke with an unwavering confidence, as if he knew that everything he touched turned to gold.

"Claire Michelle Balzan," he had said, sitting on her couch without invitation. He adjusted his body, sinking deeper into the cushion. "Good morning."

Claire, anything but confident, shied over to an armchair opposite of where the detective sat. She folded into it, crossing her arms over her chest, one leg over the other. "Can I help you?"

"I'm here to ask a few questions about your husband's untimely death. Simon Jackson Balzan, correct?"

"Yes."

"Very good."

"Date of birth, May 9th?"

Claire bit her lip and nodded. If she spoke, she would sputter and cry, and she did not want to cry in front of the pompous man sitting in her living room.

"Two weeks until he turned thirty. Dirty thirty. What did you two have planned?"

"What?"

Daniel shrugged. "What did you two have planned for this thirtieth birthday? A trip? A dinner? A wild night meeting all his sex fantasies?"

"No," Claire said.

"No? No to all of those?"

"He... Simon, he was simple. We were supposed to go to dinner the night of our fifth anniversary. He wanted to take me somewhere nice, but I said no at first. He convinced me by saying it was part of his birthday gift. Anniversary and birthday dinner. He really didn't care about himself, though." Claire crunched her face and exhaled. "He just wanted an excuse to spoil me."

"To spoil you, huh?" Daniel asked, removing a notepad and a pen. He scribbled in it, speaking to the pace of his writing. "Spoil you." The detective lifted his face and smirked at Claire. "Well, husband of the year, two weeks after he spoiled you so rotten, washes onto the Sacramento River bank." He popped his lips and adjusted his seated posture again, angling forward. "I heard a rumor, unsubstantiated as all rumors are, that you weren't a one horse kind of gal. You like to experience the gallop of different breeds. Do you know what I mean?"

The video flashed through Claire's mind—her other self-riding Robert Woods, bending her body back, groaning with pleasure.

"That's not true," she said.

"No?"

"No."

"The good doctor himself said differently."

"Robert?"

Daniel's face beamed. "Dr. Robert Woods. I had him on my fantasy team a couple of years back. He did okay for me. I didn't win the championship, though."

"What?"

The detective snickered. "Did he play tricks on your mind, manipulate you into his bed?"

"I didn't sleep with him."

"They can do that, you know? Shrink your head, make you susceptible to their charms and whims. A pretty girl like you, why wouldn't the man want to, I don't know, hypnotize you into doing as he pleased you to do?"

"It didn't happen like that," Claire said.

"How did it happen then?"

"It didn't happen at all."

The detective noted what she had said, again reading as he wrote. "Didn't happen at all. Okay, then. I believe you." He said it like he believed her about as much as he believed a convicted murderer of their innocence. "Can I ask you about work? You're a nurse, right? At Sutter?"

"I'm suspended."

"Suspended? Ouch. For what?"

Claire licked her lips. The detective wanted her to admit to the crime she hadn't committed. "They have me on camera stealing drugs."

"Do you have a history with drugs?"

Claire nodded.

Daniel clicked his tongue and shook his head. "That's not good. Adderall?"

"Yes."

"Adderall—and maybe I'm wrong, as I've never had a drug—but Adderall stimulates the user, right?"

"It does."

"In my experience, death often zombifies the surviving family. It makes sense you would lean on a drug to help spur you into action." Daniel winked at her. "To get you back in the saddle."

Claire dug her fingernails into her arm. "I didn't know he was dead."

"Oh, sorry," Daniel said, grinning. "Of course not. The hospital suspended you... with pay?"

"Without."

"That's a bummer. Luckily, you had money in your bank account, right?"

Claire knew exactly where Daniel led his line of questioning, but she had no choice but to follow him. "No."

"No?"

"Simon transferred all of it into another account. I had nothing in either the checking or savings account."

Daniel grimaced and hissed, as if burned. "That hurts. That made you angry, didn't it?"

"Mostly sad."

"So, what then? For two weeks, you lived with no money at all?"

"We have a full pantry of food. I Googled how many payments I could miss until the utilities turned off—a couple of months. So, I manage for now."

Daniel clicked his pen open. "I manage," he said, writing the note. He cleared his throat. "Your husband was shot in the back of the head. The bullet didn't exit his skull, but bounced around inside the noggin. He died immediately. Mrs.—" The detective sucked in his lips and sighed, shaking his head. "I'm sorry for that oversight. Ms. Balzan."

Claire flinched when he removed the R from the word.

"Did you kill your husband?"

The question nearly shocked her as much as the removed letter. She curled inward, as if punched in the chest. "No," Claire whispered.

"Excuse me? I have a bad ear. What did you say?"

"I didn't kill my husband."

"Honestly, I didn't think so, but I thought I should ask."

"Do you know who did?"

Daniel tapped on his skull. "I have an idea or two. I'll stay in touch with any updates, and you... you will update me on anything you learn. Do we understand each other?"

Detective Quinn had sauntered out of her house without a care in the world.

Claire sat in the donut shop, staring at her wedding ring. How much time had slipped away as she relived that terrible interview? Removing her phone from her pocket, she glanced at the clock. 0613hrs. Only twelve minutes.

Apart from the clock, she also noticed a voicemail from her sister-in-law, Jessica. Simon's family had mostly avoided speaking with Claire since the discovery of his body. They strongly suspected she was involved in his death, but they, like their son, were decent people who held their tongue and minded their business until the light exposed the truth.

"I'm going to kill you," Jessica started the voicemail. "I'm going to find you, and I'm going to kill you for what you did to my brother. The truth is out now. You can't hide anymore. You can't deny what you did anymore. Pray, Claire, pray that the cops arrest you before I find you."

Claire played the voicemail again.

Jessica, of Simon's entire immediate family, had always been the most volatile. She was the oldest child at thirty-three, and she had a mean, protective streak, often chasing away Simon's previous girlfriends. Claire always chalked it up to their mom passing away from cancer when the children were young, and Jessica assumed the matronly role for the family. It didn't matter, though. She played the Balzan patience game well enough. But when push came to shove, Jessica always retaliated.

So, what had set her off this morning?

Claire opened up the Internet browser from her phone, crossing her fingers that the data plan would still work. The donut shop didn't offer free Wi-Fi. She wasn't sure when the phone bill was due, or when the phone company would cut off her services. Luckily, Google opened, though.

Claire stared at the empty search bar, wondering what to type.

Claire Balzan.

Enter.

A block of updated and trending news results filled her feed.

"Desperate Housewife Murders Husband and Therapist," the titles read in one flavor or another. The headlines remained consistent in detailing the fact that Claire had cheated on Simon with Robert, murdered her husband, and murdered the therapist.

Murdered the therapist.

Claire opened an article and skimmed the words. Robert Woods was found by his secretary, Trisha Berry, murdered in his home. Apparently, he had missed all his appointments last Wednesday and Thursday. After missing his first appointment on Friday, Trisha swung by his house. Through a window, she noticed his body lying in the kitchen. According to reports, he allowed Claire Balzan into his home, and she stabbed him sixty-seven times.

Claire glanced up, darting her attention around the donut shop. A television mounted to a top corner mutely played a commercial. What if they had the station on a news channel? What if the program splashed a picture of her face across the screen?

"I'm innocent," Claire muttered.

But was she? What had Daniel Quinn mentioned during his home visit?

"Did he play tricks on your mind, manipulate you into his bed? They can do that, you know? Shrink your head, make you susceptible to their charms and whims. A pretty girl like you, why wouldn't the man want to, I don't know, hypnotize you into doing as he pleased you to do?"

What if she had no memory of the affair, of stealing the drugs, of the murder because Dr. Woods had hypnotized her?

What if she had killed her husband?

Claire's face melted, and her mouth unhinged as she fought against sobs. She spared a few seconds to calm herself, then she thought.

Why would Dr. Woods convince Claire to kill him? He wouldn't, meaning she didn't do it. Not only that, she hadn't murdered her husband, and she never had an affair or stolen drugs or anything.

Then who had done it?

Claire rubbed her eyes and massaged her temples. Her phone buzzed on the table, startling her. An unknown number. Law enforcement, most likely Detective Quinn. Was he calling to track her phone and pin her location? Did he already know where she was?

Claire jumped to her feet and scanned the donut shop. No customers to witness her being there, apart from the employees. She put on her sunglasses and lowered her head, shielding her face as much as possible.

She exited the shop, disoriented and unaware of where to go or who to go to.

August Watson was her answer, but she couldn't risk meeting with him in public. What if he believed the evidence stacked against her? What if he turned her into the police? No. Claire couldn't risk that. She had to find another way.

Present Day ... Second Thoughts. Tuesday, April 26th, 1137hrs.

MY FIST HOVERED IN mid-air, mere inches from knocking on Raymond and Tammy Brooks' front door. In my left hand, I held an envelope filled with a brief note and a small wad of cash, along with a grocery-store bouquet.

Five years ago, I—August Allan Watson—murdered their nineteen-year-old son, Aaron Brooks.

I worked as a cop in the small town of Galt, California, and I responded to a call stating that a kid at the park had a gun. When I arrived, he pointed his weapon at me, and I fired my weapon at him.

Except nothing is ever that simple. Aaron had only held an airsoft gun. I had reacted out of fear, and my emotional response had ended a life.

The Galt Police Department and a judge deemed my shooting justifiable. They wouldn't press criminal charges against me, fire me, or suspend. Instead, they offered me paid time off until a psychiatrist recommended I could return to work.

I never returned to work, though. I quit and drowned myself in liquor for three straight years, destroying everything in my life—a coping mechanism, I guess. I had taken Aaron's life, so I deserved to lose mine. However, a few incredible friends and the love of my parents dragged me back to functionality. I sobered up, and I have remained sober for two years. I recently created a business investigating the paranormal, which has picked up a little steam and momentum.

I visited by Aaron's parents' home as a healing exercise for myself and hopefully for them, too. Over the past years, I had never so much as written them an apology letter. Why would they want to hear from me? What could I say to them that wouldn't cut them deeper, make them angrier? So, I had said nothing—at least until a string of circumstances, including a lovely woman, convinced me to swing by their house and knock on their door.

Except, I couldn't knock.

I stood on their front porch with my fist raised to eye level, and I couldn't will it forward to rap on the wood. What if they were home? I understand that's the point, but I had consciously shown up at their house at 1137hrs on a Tuesday. Secretly, I didn't want them to open the door. Secretly, I wanted to knock, stand there for twenty seconds, and leave. Standing there was hard enough. Seeing them, speaking to them... that bordered on impossible.

So, what would I do if I knocked, and they were home and they opened the door and they recognized me? How would they respond? Would they interpret my presence as taunting and disrespectful? Would Raymond attack me? Shoot me? Would Tammy break down and sob?

It all overwhelmed me. I doubted I could mentally or emotionally handle any of it.

Yet, I remained standing on their front porch, hand suspended and ready to knock.

Like someone reaching out their hand and dragging me from the depths of drowning, my phone vibrated in my pocket. I exhaled relief, and the tension and anxiety melted from my body. I had to take the call, no matter who called. I had to accept it. Convincing myself of that truth, I placed the card and the bouquet on the doormat and turned around, rushing back to my car.

Once safely inside, I answered the phone. "August Watson, Blue Moon Investigation Agency. How can I help you?"

"Yeah, can I order a large pepperoni pizza? Hold the pepperoni and add pineapple and ham. Also, do you have a barbecue drizzle? If so, soak that pie in some sauce." Fred Rogers, my assistant-slash-secretary, chuckled, finding himself hilarious.

I stared at the Brooks' front door. In my mind, I still stood there, having just knocked, waiting for them to answer. In my mind, they opened the door. We all recognized the pain in each other's faces, and we fell into each other and cried.

"Hello?" Fred asked.

"What's up?"

"You grabbing lunch?"

I glanced at the clock on my dashboard. 1140hrs. "It's not even noon."

"It'll be noon by the time you get here. I'm starving, bro." Fred was a retired NFL athlete. He had the stature of a small giant, and he consumed as many calories as a baby dinosaur.

"What do you want?"

"I don't care. What are you feeling?"

"I'm not hungry."

"You need to eat more. You're looking old, which means you're skinny, and not in a good way, either."

"Do you want me to grab you something?"

"Swing by that sandwich shop I love."

"You love all sandwich shops," I said.

"Exactly! Chicken breast. Add bacon and avocado."

"Text it to me. I won't remember."

"Aye, aye, captain," Fred said.

"Was that it?"

"What?"

"Why you called? You wanted food?"

"Oh, no. I started talking about pizza and I got hungry. I really called because an interesting case came through earlier in an email. I haven't responded yet, mostly because you haven't updated me on that case with—" Fred clicked his tongue and ruffled a few papers. "With Mr. Dupree. Vincent Dupree. You tackling that?"

I turned the key and started the car. It was a Honda Civic hybrid, so the engine didn't roar into life, but sort of purred into existence.

Vincent Dupree had walked into the office yesterday. According to him, his dead wife—who was very much dead, and there was a body and documentation to prove that—haunted him. Her ghost claimed him as responsible for her death, and she would have her vengeance once she gained enough power in her spiritual form. Whatever that meant.

"Yeah," I said. "I need to contact him and schedule a date to walk through his home. We agreed on an appearance fee, along with an hourly rate, if I decide to take on the investigation. So, money, you know? That's always promising."

"I do like money."

"What's your case?"

"A girl named Miette emailed this morning. Vague details, but she thinks her life is in danger, and the police don't believe a word she's saying. She didn't know where else to go, but she heard about Blue Moon through the Living Gargoyle case and thought, why not give us a shot?"

"No details?" I asked.

"She would prefer to meet with you in person."

"Alright." I massaged my neck and pulled into the road, driving to the nearest sandwich shop. "I'm going to call Vincent Dupree and schedule a time to investigate his house for any signs of... of his dead wife. Once that's on the books, I'll shoot—what did you say her name was? Marie?"

"Miette."

"I'll give a Miette a call. Do you have contact information?"

"Just the email."

"Alright," I said. "Send her a response. Tell her to meet me at the office at 1300hrs today. I'll schedule with Dupree after that."

"Done and done," Frank said. "Also, just sent you my order. Thanks, boss."

"Don't mention it."

After we hung up, I drowned in the quiet of my car's cab, losing myself to memory and thought. I had solved three cases over the last week—an enormous accomplishment. Without a full day to catch my breath, I already had two more paying cases in the barrel. Maybe this paranormal gig would work out, after all. One could only hope, right?

The Changeling. Tuesday, April 26th, 1300hrs.

MIETTE VERDIN ARRIVED EXACTLY on time. She carried a few extra pounds, but she walked with an undeniable attractiveness. Miette wore no makeup, and she had hurriedly pinned up her hair. Her eyes sagged on her sunken face. Despite the obvious signs of exhaustion, she smiled at me with a pure radiance. I found myself constantly entranced by her natural beauty and electric aura.

"Miette?" I asked, standing from the seat behind my desk.

"Yes."

"You may sit." I gestured to a chair placed near my desk for clients.

"Do you care if I stand? I'm just... I haven't slept well in a few nights, and I'm not eating, so I'm fatigued and shaky. Strangely enough, though, I have this wild energy burning through my body. It's what keeps me up at night. When I sit or lie down, I can't keep up with my thoughts. Does that make sense? I'm sorry. I'm rambling."

I returned to my chair and leaned back. "You're fine. You're in a precarious situation, and I understand the mixed feelings you're experiencing."

"It's like a concoction of every known liquor spiked with methamphetamine and cocaine. At any moment, I might collapse from exhaustion or scream and rip out my hair or, most likely, explode." She chuckled, shaking her head. "Kaboom!"

"If you choose to explode," Fred said from behind the reception desk, eating chips, "could you make it into the hallway? I prefer this tiny, dirty place absent of blood and guts."

Miette turned her head and offered him a quick, unenthused grin before returning her attention to me.

"Can you run me through what's going on?" I asked.

Miette untied her hair and shook it out, running her fingers over her head and tightening her knot again. "Okay. But it's messy."

"I specialize in messy."

"This random girl followed me on my social media accounts. Vanessa Brown."

"Do you know her from somewhere?"

"Not that I remember. She doesn't look familiar. When I asked my other friends about her, they didn't know who she was. Our only mutual friend is my boyfriend. I asked him about Vanessa Brown. He denied knowing her. I asked why he followed her. He shrugged. Didn't know."

"Does she take provocative photos?" I asked, understanding the male mind and why they might follow a random woman.

"No. Normal stuff. Reading. Eating. Out and about. She followed him, so he followed her. That makes sense to me, because I did the same thing. Vanessa followed me, and I followed her back. What harm, you know? Maybe I met her at a party or in a bar, or anything, and she found me, but I have no recollection of her."

"Sure," I said, not sure where Miette carried this story.

"Well, she DM'd me."

"Direct message," Fred said. "I know he looks early thirties, but you're going to have to treat August like an eighty-year-old man. He's a little behind on the times."

Miette smirked at me. "Vanessa directly messaged me on Instagram. 'Hi,' she said, adding a little smiley face emoji. 'How are you?' I felt terrible at that point. She definitely knew me and expected that I knew her, but I didn't. I don't. I do not have a single idea who she is."

"Did you write her back?" I asked.

"Not at first. I typed her name into Google, hoping to draw her Facebook or LinkedIn account. Something, you know? Nothing popped up other than her Instagram, which she created only a month ago." Miette cocked her head, as if expecting me to react.

"Okay," I said.

"Okay? Okay. Well, she has over three thousand followers, right?"

"Sure."

"When she posts a picture, guess how many likes?"

I shook my head. "Three thousand."

"Like, maybe, three. One. Two. Three." She counted with her fingers to emphasize the number. "Three likes. The most she has... seven likes. Three thousand followers and seven likes."

"Oh, fishy!" Fred said, popping his head over the high counter.

"It has a foul stench, for sure," Miette said. "So, I wrote her back. 'Hi, yourself.' I added one of the goofy-faced emojis with the crossed eyes and tongue poked out. 'I'm sorry, but how do we know each other?' Send. I'm not kidding you. I have the read receipts to prove it, too. Thirty seconds later, she responded. Thirty seconds. As if she had stared at her phone, refreshing her page, waiting for me to reply. Do you know what she said?"

"I don't."

"Close," Miette said. "She said, 'You don't.' She said that I didn't know who she was. I didn't write back. What would I say? Who are you? What do you want? Why are you following me and my boyfriend? I called Justin, my boyfriend, and told him she messaged me, and I messaged her, and she responded, and of course I read the brief conversation. He said she had also messaged him." Miette plopped into the client seat beside my desk. "Justin broke up with me. He wouldn't give a reason, he just... ended things. Eight months. Gone. Like that. I called him back. No answer. Texted him. No response. Nothing. Don't you find that strange?"

"What exactly?" I asked.

"Him ending things with me when they were going so well, right when this Vanessa chick arrives on the scene? It's not a coincidence."

"That's what you brought to the cops?"

Miette chuckled. "God no. They already think I'm crazy. Imagine what they'd think if that was my distress call."

"Please, continue," I said.

Miette nods. "Next thing I know, Vanessa sends me another message.

"'Hi.'

"I say, 'Hi yourself.'

"She says, 'How are you doing?'

"'Not good,' I say.

"You know what she says? 'You're not doing as bad as you will be doing.'

"I asked her what that meant. Nothing in response. I'm obviously a little freaked out at this point. So, I stare at Google for a second, wondering what to do. I figure out a way to reverse search images. I downloaded Vanessa's profile picture and uploaded it to this website. It brought me to the original image. It belonged to the Myspace page of a girl named Vanessa Brown."

"Myspace?" I asked, snickering. "I had one of those."

"We get it," Fred said. "You're old."

"Yeah, but Miette isn't. How old are you? Twenty?" I asked.

"Twenty-two."

"And I'm assuming Vanessa appears the same age as you?"

"Precisely!"

"But she has a Myspace."

"Strange, right? Myspace still exists, too, but mostly as, like, a music platform. Anyway, the picture was uploaded to the original Myspace—the one from the early 2000s. That weirded me out, like it gave me the heebie-jeebies. So, I typed in Vanessa Brown's name into Google again. This time, I didn't care to find another social media account. Instead, I looked for any mention of her. I found something on the second page. Are you sitting down for this?"

I glanced at my lap, confused by her question, as I obviously sat. "Yes."

"Good. Obituary."

"Same girl?" Fred asked.

"Same flipping girl," Miette said. "Same picture used in the obituary as on the Instagram account direct messaging me."

"That's when you went to the police?" I asked.

"Shoot no," Miette said. "Those morons don't listen to a word unless you're pounding on their door, bloody, getting chased, about to be killed by a serial killer. They react. That's their go to."

That throwaway remark socked me in the stomach. I had reacted, and in the worst possible way, to Aaron Brooks.

"Anyway, I get home from work one day and find my apartment off. Different. I couldn't figure it out, though. Then, it hit me. I don't know how I noticed it, but I did. Luckily, I freaking did. My wall calendar—which I never look at, because why, you know? I have a phone and a computer and an iPad. Anyway, someone had flipped my wall calendar to May and circled a date. The fifth. They also drew a face in the circled square. Straight line for a mouth, two X's for eyes—like a dead person. That's it. That's when I went to the cops."

I tapped a pen against the desktop and pondered the whirlwind of words she had thrown at me. What did I do with her story? Technically, it didn't fall into the realm of the paranormal. On the surface, it sounded like a simple catfishing scam. Except, potentially, the scammer had threatened Miette, if a face drawn on a calendar counts as a threat. I could see why the police had disregarded Miette's report, but I could also understand her fear.

"That's not all," Miette said.

"What do you mean?"

"Vanessa sent me a text message."

I scrunched my face. "How?"

"I don't know how she gained my cell phone number, but she did. She sent pictures of me. Nude pictures. Ones I had sent to Justin, and ones I had intended to send to Justin, but never did. She said if I kept calling Justin, or trying to contact him, she would release the images."

I glanced at Fred. He had recommended we listen to Miette's case. As interesting as it was, it had nothing to do with the supernatural. "I'm a paranormal investigator, not a private detective. As intriguing as your case sounds, I'm not sure it fits within my niche."

"Tell him," Fred said, crumpling his empty bag of chips and tossing it toward the wire-mesh garbage can, missing.

Miette popped her lips. "Vanessa claims I stole her life. She says I'm an imposter, and she's the real me. She said I'm a changeling. I showed up at her house when she was a little girl, and I ate her and turned into her and stole her life. She said on May 5th, her birthday, not mine, she would expose the truth to the world. I don't know what that means, but I don't want to find out. Can you help me?"

"You're a changeling?" I asked, now mystified by her story.

Miette's magnetic smile cut across her face. "I am. I stole that other girl's life, and her parents could never tell the difference." She snickered, and her humor bubbled over to full, keeled over laughter.

It was contagious—magical. Fred and I also laughed.

When we settled down, I said, "Well, before I agree to anything, let's make sure you can afford my rates."

Girl in the Window. Tuesday, April 26th, 1457hrs.

ALINA AND I ARRIVED at Vincent Dupree's mansion in Wilton. We came to a stop before a closed electronic gate. Dr. Dupree hadn't provided me with an entry code, so I pressed the call button and waited.

"Do people with money really have nothing better to do than hire someone like you?" Alina asked, tapping her middle knuckle against the passenger window and staring outward at the vibrant trees shading the entry gate.

Alina Mylene Moore was a sixteen-year-old girl who had forced her way into interning with me, mostly because of her aunt, Maya Adler. Maya had convinced me to bring on her niece, though she hadn't warned me or prepped for the spitfire teenage girl. Alina dreamed of a career in the FBI, investigating serial killers and doing all the fun, glamorous tasks shown on television. To gain the experience and piece together the background, though, she needed an investigative job where she actually investigated rather than sat at a desk and flipped through reports. Hence me, the sucker, hiring her—or rather, allowing her to volunteer her time. Only after school, though, and through legal means. We had drawn up a work permit, signed by her educators and her parents. The more I learned about Alina, though, the more I questioned the legitimacy of those signatures.

Either way, however the coin spins or the cookie crumbles, she sat in the passenger seat of my car, ready to investigate a malevolent spirit.

"What's that mean?" I asked. "Someone like me?"

"Well, I mean, I haven't really seen poor people hiring your services. It's always long driveways and big houses and deep pockets. You think the rich folk are just... bored? They have too much spare time and too many thoughts, and their imagination gets the best of them?"

"James Connors didn't have much money," I said.

James Connors had bought my services to investigate a rabid Bigfoot he had spotted. Turns out, he hadn't slept too often or that well since his wife's untimely death, and he had undergone sleep-related hallucinations.

Alina rolled her eyes and shook her head. "In my family, we used to scrape the mold off our bagels—and that's all we would eat for the day, if we ate at all. James, an old, retired, white gentleman, has never scraped mold off his only meal of the day. Maybe he's not rich to Dr. Dentist here, but he's rich compared to most of the world."

"I don't get what point you're trying to make. This is one of your crusading missions? You'll die on this hill?"

Alina snickered. "What hill? That rich people are boring and they know it, so they hire people like you to spice up their lives?"

The young woman often portrayed the youthful trait of arguing for the sake of arguing—speaking for the sake of hearing her own voice vomit words.

I pressed the call button again. "Why isn't this working?"

"Dr. Dentist forgot to leave you a gate code?"

"Dr. Dupree," I said, removing my phone and scrolling back through my texts. "And he never shared it."

"Call him."

I was way ahead of her, dialing Dupree's cell.

"Hello," he answered in a bored tone, emphasizing Alina's observation.

"It's August Watson," I said. "I'm at your gate, but it's closed and the call button doesn't seem to work."

"Oh, sorry about that. The thing hasn't worked since they installed it. Shelly—my wife—continually nagged me to have someone out, but I never did. Never will, I suppose. Anyway, I'll get you the code."

He recited four numbers, and I punched them in. The gate opened.

"I'm in," I said.

"I'll be standing out front to greet you."

Dupree's driveway snaked about a quarter mile. A canopy of trees created a majestic tunnel for us to drive through.

"How's Glacia?" Alina asked.

Glacia Vasquez was a recent client and a potential love interest. After I had cleared her inherited home of the supposed ghosts haunting it, we had scheduled a double date. The events of that date turned, well, nearly murderous. Glacia ended up in the hospital with a severe concussion, where she currently remained.

"Awake," I said. "I was with her this morning. She seemed tired, and she mentioned she had a pretty gnarly headache, but I think they'll discharge her this evening."

"Then it's back to Oregon?"

I popped a knuckle and nodded.

Glacia lived a state away in Oregon. She had only come to California to deal with the haunted house, which her late grandmother had willed to her. She wished to rid it of the ghosts so she could sell and not have the inconvenience of managing it from five-hundred miles away.

"Back to Oregon," I said, hugging my car around the last corner, which had hid the mansion—a plantation-styled home. It had a man-made lake in the front yard, a dock, and a paddleboat.

Dr. Dupree leaned against the railing of a wraparound patio. He stood no taller than five-eight, and I doubted he weighed much more than a hundred-forty pounds. He sported a thin mustache and a receding hairline.

I pulled into the designated parking area and switched off the ignition.

"I'm sorry," Alina said.

"About what?"

"Glacia. She was special."

"I know. Apparently, she thinks we would've never worked because I'm in love with your aunt."

"She's not wrong."

"Why does everyone say that?"

Alina snickered. "You can't see the way you look at her."

"I look at her like I look at you."

"Ew. Gross," Alina said, opening her passenger door. "You're disgusting. I'm living with you, remember? Don't say that to me." She slammed the door and crossed the driveway to Dr. Dupree.

I wanted to sit in the car and chew on that exchange, but I had zero interest in allowing Alina to have a private conversation with the dentist. Hurrying out of the vehicle, I caught up to them.

Dr. Dupree remained standing on the porch, gripping the railing. He beckoned us up the steps. "Good afternoon. Beautiful day, huh?"

It really was. Mid-seventies. Slight, cool breeze. Golf weather, my dad always called it.

"Gorgeous," I said.

"I'm sure you're not paying us to discuss the weather," Alina said, brash and to the point as ever.

"He's not paying you at all," I said.

Dr. Dupree chuckled, pushing himself off the wooden railing and moseying toward the front door. "I suppose the young lady is correct. Please, follow me."

He led us through a double door entry. The ceilings in his home were all over ten feet, the spaces vast and populated with sturdy, expensive furniture and large pieces of expensive art. We entered his study, finding seats—him behind a large oak desk, Alina and I in plush leather armchairs beside a floor-to-ceiling bookshelf.

I reached into my back pocket and removed a stick of cinnamon gum, folding it into my mouth. "Dr. Dupree," I said. "We spoke yesterday at my office."

"Yes."

"Correct me when I'm wrong, if you will."

"Of course."

"Your wife died during a hiking expedition."

"She fell off a cliff."

"Again, I'm sorry for your loss." I closed my eyes and saw Aaron Brooks in my mind. "Death has a way of wedging itself uncomfortably into life."

"What?" Alina asked. "What does that mean? Who says stuff like that?"

I shook my head, freeing my mind of the ghost that haunted me. "Anyway... the rescue party found her body."

"What remained of it," Dr. Dupree said. "She fell quite far."

"Now she has returned?"

"Yes," he said, grabbing a trinket off his desk—a small globe—and fiddling with it. "She broke every dish in the kitchen, tossed knives into the ceiling, wrote threats on the walls with ketchup and mustard."

"Do you know what she might want?"

"Revenge," he said. "She blames me for what happened."

"How do you know that?" Alina asked. "Does she speak to you?"

"She leaves notes. Some of them have inside jokes only we knew, memories only we shared. Some notes detail how she wants to kill me, how she wishes to avenge her death."

"Has she hurt you?" I asked.

"Not yet. She claims her spirit doesn't have enough strength yet."

"What?" Alina asked, scrunching her face. "How does that make sense? How does a spirit get stronger?"

Dr. Dupree glanced at me, as if I knew the answer.

I looked at him, expecting the doctor to respond.

Alina chortled. "Well, nobody knows. Great. In short, we have the ghost of your dead wife threatening to kill you." The girl crossed an arm over her chest, planting her other elbow atop it and resting her chin in her hand. "We have ourselves a genuine mystery, don't we? A real *Scooby-Doo* hijinks."

I entertained zero notions that Dr. Dupree's late wife had returned to haunt him. Instead, someone—much like with Glacia's situation—donned the appearance of a spectral being, and tormented the poor widower.

Rescuers had found his wife's remains. They produced a death certificate. She had died. So, who acted like her ghost? Why? Who knew inside information about Shelly and Vincent's marriage? That question burrowed me further into the rabbit hole. What if Dr. Dupree orchestrated this entire affair? Unlikely. What did he have to gain? Why go through the hassle of hiring me? The simple and lazy answer was attention. Maybe his story would find its way to the local news station.

I doubted as much, though. Dr. Dupree seemed like a sad, lonely man, but not a sad, lonely man who craved the public's attention. He seemed like a sad, lonely man who missed his wife.

"I apologize for my curtness," I said, exploring another route—one similar to Glacia's haunted house, "but with your wife deceased, that leaves you the only person standing between a benefactor and your will." I glanced around his office, highlighting the heftiness of his will.

Dr. Dupree shook his head and smirked. "No will. Like the call button on the gate, Shelly bugged me about drafting a will. But we're in our mid-forties. We don't have kids. Both our parents have passed, and the both of us are only children. I figured a will was the least pressing thing—other than the gate, of course—in our lives."

"No family at all? Cousins?"

"It's a crazy coincidence we always laughed about. Both my parents came from households with only children. They only had me. Shelly came from the same background. The only child to parents who were also only children. No aunts. No uncles. No cousins. Parents have passed, as have our grandparents. We vetoed the idea of children. Why waste time and money on a will?"

I chewed on my cinnamon-flavored gum, absorbing that information.

"I have a bag in my car," I said after a few seconds. "In it, there's an EMF meter which can detect otherworldly entities." Not true, at least in my experience, but clients expected certain things, and I bought the bells and whistles of the trade. I also carried crucifixes, wooden stakes, silver knives, iron horseshoes, among other supernatural defenses. "If you don't mind, I'll grab it and walk through your home to see if I can't find anything... abnormal."

Most likely, the faulty device would come up with a faulty reading. The manufacturers designed them that way. I never trusted what the EMF meter showed, and I doubted it would have registered a ghost if one actually existed.

"Of course," Dr. Dupree said. "The house belongs to you. Please, do as you need to rid this place of..." he trailed off, licking his lips.

I knew he meant to say her, as in his wife, but he couldn't convince his tongue to admit that he wished for Shelly's presence to leave their home. The man longed to have his wife back, alive, warm in his arms, and a secret part of him enjoyed her ghostly, murderous spirit.

"I'll do what I can," I said, standing from the leatherback chair and leaving Alina to supervise the man.

As I leaned into my Honda Civic to grab my bag, my phone buzzed. Maya's name flashed across the screen.

"Hey," I answered, sifting through the contents of the backpack until I happened upon the EMF meter.

"What's up?"

"Working."

"Nice. Nice."

Silence for a second.

"Why are you calling me?" I asked. "Shouldn't you be writing your article? Isn't it due tomorrow?"

"Blah," she said. "Blah, blah. That's all I can write. Blah. Inspire me, my muse. Light a fire beneath my firm, round booty."

"I'm working."

"What's the case?"

I shut the car's back door and turned to face the house, staring up at the second story. A woman stood in the window, staring down at me. We made eye contact for a quick second, and she slipped away from view.

"Gussy," Maya said. "You still there?"

"August," I said, correcting her. Only mom could call me Gussy.

"What's the case?"

"Dead wife has come back to haunt her husband. Apparently, her spirit blames him for her death."

"Juicy."

"I have another juicy case, too."

"Do you?"

"I do."

"Can you share?"

"Not now." My attention remained fixed on the upstairs window. "Write your article. Get the job. Once you're staffed at *Here & Now*, you'll know the shareable details of all my cases."

"Deal. Oh. Gussy?"

"It's August."

"I'm sorry about Glacia. She told me she's heading back to Oregon."

"Stop calling people. Put your phone away. Finish your article." I hung up, emphasizing my point.

I scanned the second story, which had six large windows overlooking the driveway.

Was that Shelly, Dr. Dupree's late wife? Was that the ghost? Who had I seen upstairs?

I opened the car's back door and reached back into my backpack, grabbing a canister of pepper spray and a pair of handcuffs for good measure.

They had come in handy before, and after witnessing what I had witnessed in the window, they might come in handy again.

The Discovery. Tuesday, April 26th, 1519hrs.

This case played eerily familiar notes to Glacia's inherited haunted house case. To further propel my dodgy mind down the rabbit hole of love and attraction, Maya and I had ended our phone conversation about Glacia and her decision to return to Oregon.

I exhaled, vibrating my lips, leaning against my hood, and glancing at my cell phone. Magically—though I didn't believe in magic or the paranormal—Glacia's contact showed on my screen. I had last spoken to her at the hospital earlier that morning. She had surprised me by gifting her Nana's house to me, the one I had extrapolated the familial ghosts from. She had also said she planned on heading back home.

I popped a knuckle, shifting my gaze to the second-story window. No ghosts peered downward at me.

"Hello," Glacia answered.

I was barely aware I had dialed her number, and her answering the call shocked me into silence for a moment.

"Hello? August, you there?"

"Hey," I said, speaking through a wall of nerves.

"What's up? You off work?"

I shook my head, silently answering her question.

My track record with women, dating back to the beginning of my adolescence, reported as awkward, shy, and disastrous. I had one girlfriend in high school who cheated on me, breaking my heart. According to her, I was too nice. Funny enough, Alina had provided the same critique a day or two ago regarding Maya. The young girl said I was too safe for someone like Maya—too boring.

However, according to other feedback, I'm quite the first-date catch. I'm more than handsome, and I keep my demons at bay by working out far too hard and far too often. My physique rivals that of a Hollywood celebrity. My most common critiques from female friends concerning why I can't seem to snag a long-term girlfriend are closed off, safe, nice, and too romantic. I understand the first concern. I am closed off, mostly after the shooting incident. Discussion leads to reliving, and reliving leads to... well, not pleasant thoughts or emotions. So, I choose to close myself off to the world and repress my memories and feelings. Healthy, I know. The last three critiques, though—safe, nice, too romantic—I don't understand. Why do women, at least the women I find myself attracted to, prefer dangerous, mean, and selfish?

Anyway, August Watson and women haven't had the most swimming relationships beyond first dates, which more often than not, when I oblige, turns out swimmingly. That's a complicated way of saying sex is awesome, but I'm not and never have been a one-night-stand guy.

Glacia and me, though, we went together like a bee and honey. Even my awkward, less than flattering moments seemed more endearing than disastrous. If I had a chance at love, a real shot at the elusive relationship, it was with Glacia. But she had eyes and ambitions set on returning to Oregon.

"August?"

"Hey," I said.

"You okay?"

"Yeah, sorry. I'm working on this case—another haunted house. Well, a husband believes his wife has returned from the grave to haunt him. I'm at his house, and I got to thinking about you." I miss you, flashed through my mind, and it stayed there, locked in the safety of dark, dead silence.

"You were thinking about me?" Glacia asked, flirty.

A better man than I may have piggybacked on her inviting tone, flirting back. Not me, though. Not me. I often struggled with spoken words, and I always struggled with women. To combine the two equaled definite disaster. Or, at the very least, missed opportunities.

"How are you feeling?" I asked. "Have they discharged you?"

"An hour ago. I'm at Nana's... packing my things."

"When do you leave?"

"Tomorrow morning, first thing."

I popped another knuckle. Despite the mildly warm temperatures of spring, I was burning up and sweating.

"You want to come over tonight?" Glacia asked. "I feel like our date the other evening was interrupted and cut short."

I held my breath, unsure of how to answer, or how I would naturally answer. In situations like these, words often popped out of my mouth before I could consciously shape them. "I don't think that's the best idea." I also doubted that was the best thing to say for either of us.

Glacia remained quiet for a few seconds, leaving the door open for me to explain myself.

Great. Here came a stuttering train wreck of words.

"It's not that... I don't want to see you again. But, I... I like you." My balls launched into my stomach as I admitted the last part, tightening as if someone squeezed them in a death grip, attempting to pop them. My stomach burned with fire.

"You like me? Do you think I'm pretty?"

"Beautiful."

"Do you like my body?"

I gulped and nodded. "Yes."

"Do you think I'm sexy?"

"I do."

"Well, if you like my body, and if you think I'm sexy, let me know."

I chuckled at the recited song lyrics.

"I like you, too," Glacia said. "I think you're pretty, and I like your body, and I think you're sexy. So, August Watson, paranormal investigator, why should we complicate this? You're always so adamant about the supernatural not existing because we can't see it or prove it. Well, we can't see love, can we? But sex—we can see each other, and we can prove that an attraction exists between us. No?"

I swallowed my tongue, and it stuck in my throat, walling off any words and suffocating me to boot.

"Why don't you come over tonight?" Glacia asked. "We'll enjoy a good meal, then we might even eat some actual dinner." She snickered, as if her little innuendo was the funniest thing ever. "Let's enjoy each other's company while we can, rather than complicating this by discussing long distance and feelings and... yeah. Besides, I bought you a housewarming gift."

"Okay," I said.

"Really?"

"Really."

"You're such a slut," Glacia said. "See you when you're finished with work." The line disconnected.

After regathering my wits, I entered Dr. Dupree's house through the front door, finding him and Alina sitting in his study.

She was bragging about her perfect teeth with adamancy.

"'Freak of nature,' the hygienist said. That's a direct quote. Braces couldn't get my teeth this straight. Also, I eat candy like I might die tomorrow and it'll save my life. Guess what? No cavities. Ever. I have maybe flossed three times in my entire life, but don't tell my dentist that." Alina laughed at herself. "Whenever I'm sitting in that chair, though, reclined back with those bulky sunglasses, the hygienist oohs, and she tells me to keep up the good work. That my flossing is im-maculate. Can you believe that? Immaculate. I never floss. It's a joke. A scam. Big Pharma, you know? Capitalism. I won't dive into those deep and treacherous waters, but do you think ancient civilizations flossed, I mean, other than to loosen a piece of meat? No way. Not a chance."

Dr. Dupree's eyes widened with hope when I entered the room. He about leaped from his chair. "Mr. Watson," he said, cutting Alina off.

The girl frowned, glancing back at me. "Where have you been?"

She worked as an unpaid intern. I had no obligation to answer her question, so I ignored her, keeping the conversation between Dr. Dupree and myself. "I'm going to start upstairs, if that's okay with you?"

"Please, do what you need to do. The house is yours." He cleared his throat and his eyes flickered to Alina. "Will she assist you on the walkthrough?"

I smirked, knowing he was politely asking me to take her away from him. "She'll help, yes."

After exiting the office, but before walking up the stairs, I pulled Alina aside, speaking quietly to prevent Dr. Dupree from overhearing our conversation.

"I saw her," I said.

"Who?"

"His wife."

"His wife is dead. You saw her ghost?"

I licked my teeth and shook my head. "I saw whoever is impersonating her, or maybe I saw her."

"Why do you keep saying her? She died."

"According to Dr. Dupree, they found what remained of her after the fall."

"Stop it. You're better than that, Investigator Watson. You're much better than that."

"I'm opening every door right now. What if she lived? What if she planted evidence to prove her death? What if she returned to haunt her husband?"

"Why? Why go through the trouble?"

I scratched my cheek and shook my head. "Money. Revenge. I don't know. Either way, I saw a lady upstairs, whether it was his wife or someone impersonating his wife—"

"Or a spirit."

"It wasn't a spirit."

"You said you were opening every door. Considering all possibilities. How do you know you didn't see her spirit?"

"Spirits don't exist."

"How do you know?"

"Do you have evidence of one?"

"Do you have evidence of them not existing?"

"Yes," I said. "Ample evidence, in the fact that there is no evidence." I ran my hands through my hair and peered up the stairwell. I reached into my back pocket, removing the pepper spray canister and handing it over to Alina. "In case things go sideways."

"I hate this stuff."

"Me, too, but it's effective."

"What's the plan?"

"Stick together. We'll go into the room where I noticed her, look for clues there. If we're lucky, we'll find her lying under the bed."

"You scared?" Alina asked.

The question took me by surprise. I hadn't thought about that, hadn't even considered it. Whenever I worked a case, dating back to my time in law enforcement, or I responded to an emergency, adrenaline pumped through my veins like an enhancing drug, driving me forward. I wasn't afraid of fighting, though, or of getting hurt, or even dying. I was afraid of failing—of losing the suspect and allowing them to continue their spree of terror.

"Are you?" I asked.

"I asked you first."

"A little, yeah."

"Me, too." For the first time since meeting her, Alina looked her age—like a sixteen-year-old girl. Small and helpless, balancing the lines of childhood and adulthood, but not entirely sure which side she should stand on.

I should have said something reassuring or inspirational. Hone your fear, and use it like a weapon. What does any of that mean, though? We're all afraid, aren't we? We all fear the unknown, and what is a day if not unknown? But we all put on our pants and drink our coffee and pretend like we're not scared out of our minds, and we go on with our day, living on a thread of hope that we keep our jobs and homes, and that our families stay safe and we can fall asleep and wake up to pretend everything is fine and dandy the next morning.

I sighed and popped my pinky knuckle.

"That's a gross habit," Alina said.

"It's how I cope with my fears." I ascended the stairwell, pausing at the top to orient myself to the driveway. I snuck down the hallway to the room I had spotted the woman in.

It was empty of any living person besides Alina and me. Someone had neatly made the bed. The wall shelves, nightstands, and dresser held a layer of dust, as did all the books and pictures and random trinkets set atop their surfaces. A cobweb stretched across the unmoving fan blades, and another nested in the room's corner.

"A little over a year since his wife died," Alina said, scanning the time-capsule room. "According to him, he hasn't ventured upstairs since her death. In fact, he has used none of the house beyond his study, the living room, and the kitchen. Sleeps on the couch, I guess."

"He told you that?"

"I asked what he does with all this space. He said he avoids it. I asked why he won't sell it or move out. He said he's not ready. He said he's not ready to live in it, and he's not ready to live out of it."

I understood that. Death has a way of stopping life in its tracks, even for those who survived the deceased.

My life went on pause for five years after I murdered Aaron Brooks. For three years, I drank until in a state of unconsciousness. It was the only way I could sleep. Once I sobered up, I found other ways to take my mind away from the gunshot, from the airsoft BB bouncing along the asphalt, from the halo of blood. I exercised and worked and drank coffee until my body and mind quit on me, entering a self-induced coma. Otherwise, my mind raced with terrible thoughts as I lay awake in bed, and my dreams crossed into nightmares. So, I rented my apartment to have a place where I occasionally crashed. Other than that, I lived in my office or in the gym, avoiding everything that needed addressing. Healthy, I know. But I understood Dr. Dupree's state of stagnancy—of not ready to live in, but not ready to live out of his home. That made sense to me.

"Well," I said, crossing the room to the window, looking downward at my car parked in the driveway, "that's our clue then."

"What?"

"Signs of life. We look for signs of life upstairs. If he hasn't come up here in a year, well, there shouldn't be any disturbances, right?" Once again, my mind jumped back to Glacia's haunted house.

Her mom and uncle had camped out in the attic, sneaking in through a nearly hidden, broken window. They had wanted their mother's house, now worth a fortune, and they felt slighted it had gone to Glacia.

"He has no family, huh?" I asked.

"Neither did his wife."

"Why would someone want to pretend to be his wife's ghost? What do they get out of it?" I turned away from the window, facing Alina.

The young girl looked through the closet, shaking her head. "If we're assuming it's not his wife's spirit and an actual person... I don't know. Who would and why impersonate the poor man's dead wife a year after her tragic accident? It makes no sense. There's not a motivation there."

"There's always a motivation, and it's our job to find it."

My eyes fell on the bed, staring at it. The pillows appeared collapsed. The comforter wrinkled. Used. Laid in, though only across the top, as if someone had come in there to sit down for a second and scroll through their phone or—

I looked at the nightstand.

"Or read."

"What?" Alina asked

A Moleskin notebook lay on the nightstand. A clean streak cut across the dusty cover. I picked it up, held it as if intending to read it, and my fingers fit perfectly with the clean lines.

"Someone laid on the bed and read this notebook." I turned to the first page within the Moleskin. Shelly Welch was scribbled across the opening flap in big, sprawling handwriting, accentuated and decorated with hearts and smiley faces and little flowers that dropped their petals down the page.

"What is it?" Alina asked.

I flipped the page and read the first entry, written in neat, careful block lettering.

Dear Journal,

Today was my first day as a freshman in high school...

I looked at Alina. "It's something, and someone has recently read it. I think we take a turn at skimming through the pages. Maybe it has an answer. If not, maybe it has a more direct clue to our ghost." I extended the journal to the girl. "You want to do the honors?"

"What?"

"You want to read it, see if you can't find us a direction to walk?"

Alina frowned at the journal. Then she snatched it from my hand. "Shouldn't we tell Vincent?"

"Dr. Dupree. And we will. Maybe he read it. But if what you told me is true, I think someone else did."

We concluded our search of the upstairs, taking our time and doing a thorough enough job. I didn't notice anymore disturbances among the vacated spaces, and I didn't see anyone hiding under the beds. Also, I never used the EMF meter. When we returned downstairs, I briefed Dr. Dupree on our discovery.

Alina handed him the journal. The old man looked at it like a devout Christian regarding their first Bible. "That was her maiden name," he said. "Welch. I never knew this existed. I've never seen it before today."

I knew what came next, so I interrupted him before he could ask to keep it, read it, bask in his late-wife's words. "With your permission, we would like to read through those pages and see if there's any clues we can look into. I think within those pages, we'll find something about the spirit harassing you."

Dr. Dupree clutched the journal to his chest like a child refusing to share a toy. After a second, he sighed and nodded his head.

Saving Water. Tuesday, April 26th, 1831hrs.

I DROPPED ALINA OFF at my apartment, where she temporarily stayed. Her father had run off with another woman, and her mother had just run off, leaving their young daughter homeless and having to fend for herself.

Maya had agreed to take in her niece, but both Alina and I insisted that could wait until she finished her article on the voodoo doll murders, which would launch her career in investigative journalism... or so Maya claimed. It would at least secure her a full-time position as a writer at *Here & Now*, the region's supernatural tabloid.

Alina had one more night in my apartment, which she would most likely spend alone, as I planned to spend the night with Glacia.

I also planned to shower at Glacia's house—well, I guess my house now. If the evening went as teased, we would hopefully save some water by sharing a shower. While at my apartment, I packed a pair of clothes and a toothbrush. Sharing a shower was one thing, sharing a toothbrush was something completely different.

"Hey," Alina said as I walked out the front door.

I paused, gripping the frame and glancing over my shoulder.

The girl sat cross-legged on my bed. She had a laptop off to the side, and Shelly's journal in her hands. "Remember, Glacia likes you. Don't wait for her to kiss you. If you really want my advice, when she opens the door to let you in, grab her, pick her up, and kiss her. Right then and right there. No hesitation."

Heat rushed into my face. I cracked my neck, immensely uncomfortable by a sixteen-year-old girl offering me sex tips. "Read the notebook and don't worry about me."

"I'm not worried about you, dummy. I'm worried about her. Glacia. I'm worried about her having to spend an entire night with you, playing board games because you're too awkward and chicken to make a move. In that situation—that very predictable situation involving you—she's bored, thinking of her ex-boyfriends, and you're sweaty and fidgety, touching everything but her."

I'm apt to let my curiosity to get the best of me, often controlling my words before logical thought could involve itself in shutting me up. So, I asked a question I instantly regretted asking. "How do you even know any of this?"

Alina cocked her head and furrowed her brow, scowling at me.

Please don't answer, I thought. *I don't actually want to know.*

"How do you think I know?" she asked.

I sucked on both lips and shook my head, ready to leave my apartment and never return.

"Through lots of sexual experience with lots of different men."

"Okay, I'm leaving."

"Wait," she said, chuckling. "Kidding. I watch a lot of movies. One of my guilty-pleasures, and I hate admitting this because it makes me sound girly and I hate sounding stereotypically girly, is romantic comedies. Also, Maya doesn't care who she's talking to, as long as she's talking to someone. I've heard stories, and I've heard opinions, and I've heard off-hand advice that no aunt should offer their niece."

Not knowing where to take the conversation from there, not wanting to take it anywhere other than in reverse, I stepped into the hallway and closed the door.

Glacia opened her front door fifteen minutes later. She wore knee-high white socks and an overly large white T-shirt cut to ribbons and with two eyes and a mouth drawn on it.

"Boo!"

I back pedaled a step, not out of fear, but from shock.

"I'm a ghost," Glacia said, switching balance from one foot to the other. "What do you think?"

Alina's unwarranted advice crashed into my head. *Grab her, pick her up, kiss her.*

"A sexy ghost," I said, stepping toward her, grabbing her and picking her up.

Glacia gasped and giggled, wrapping her legs around me as I carried her into the entry, kicking the door closed behind me.

"Do you like it?" she asked

"What does a guy have to do around here for a ghost to haunt him?"

Turns out, I made the right decision not taking a shower in my apartment. We played our role in conserving water.

Once dried and halfway dressed, we shared a folding chair in the kitchen. She drank red wine, and when I kissed her again, I could taste the alcohol on her lips. It was the closest I had come to drinking in two years.

"Are you okay with this?" she asked.

"With what?" I kissed her again, savoring the taste of the wine.

"Me drinking."

"I'm enjoying how it tastes on your lips far more than drinking it. I might indulge to the point of drunkenness, if you allowed it."

Glacia rolled her eyes. "Stop being so cheesy."

"I'm not the one who wore a ghost costume inside the once haunted house."

"But you liked it."

"I did."

We fell into a comfortable silence, waiting for our pizza to be delivered. I only had one thing on my mind, one topic that riddled my thoughts and prevented me from sparking a conversation, mostly because I wished to avoid the subject.

After a minute or two, Glacia broke the quiet. "What are you thinking about?"

"Hmm?"

"You're quiet, and you have that look on your face, like you're solving a problem."

"I don't have any look on my face. That's just how my face looks."

"What are you thinking about?"

I kissed her again, stealing some more liquid courage from her lips. "You."

"Me?"

"You."

"What about me?"

"You and me."

"Us?" she asked.

"Yeah."

"Sharing a shower?"

"Yes," I said, grinning.

"What else?"

Could I ask her to stay in California? To leave her home and her career and her life in Oregon for me, a man she met a few days ago? Every relationship had the honeymoon stage. What if she uprooted herself, moved down to Sacramento, and four months later, we discovered we had nothing in common? We were incompatible.

"You know what else I'm thinking about," I said after a moment.

Glacia touched my face, holding my chin up toward her. "Let's not ruin this moment, okay? Let's think about right now. Let's only think about tonight. If we think any further ahead..." she trailed off. But she didn't have to finish her thought.

If we thought any further ahead, we would set ourselves up for nothing but pain.

"Those in Heaven don't want to return to Earth, I imagine," Glacia said. "So why would we?"

We took full advantage of our Heaven once again, right there in the kitchen.

The doorbell rang, and Glacia rushed to her purse, grabbed a handful of cash, opened the front door completely naked, threw the crumpled money at whoever delivered the pizza, told him to leave the pie on the ground, and returned to me.

There wasn't any furniture in the empty house, so we slept together in a bed of sheets thrown on the floor. She had traveled with one pillow, and we shared it. In the night, between one of those indiscernible hours between two and five, Glacia woke me again. I didn't mind, though. I hadn't slept so soundly in five years, not since before the incident. It didn't take long for me to slip back into sleep, either. The entire night felt like a dream.

When I awoke the next morning, Glacia was gone.

The Ghost. Wednesday, April 27th, 0234hrs.

Most nights, Vincent Dupree drank wine and watched a movie from his recliner—a gift a few years back from Shelly—until he passed out. That night, he had ventured upstairs, into the guest room where August Watson and his spitfire intern had found the journal. He searched under the bed and in the closet and the drawers for another journal, another trace of Shelly, finding nothing but dust.

Vincent had sprawled across the bed and watched the ceiling fan slowly run in circles, working hard against the heat and mild humidity built up in the upstairs bedroom. For a while, he considered opening the window and allowing a fresh breeze in, but that consideration slipped away as the ceiling fan rotated around and around, hypnotizing him.

He awoke to a pressure on his chest.

The moonlight broke through the bedroom window, highlighting a woman sitting atop him. No, not a woman. His wife. Shelly sat on his chest, hunched over so her hair fell like curtains around her face. She breathed heavily, raggedly, gasping.

Vincent held his breath, unsure of how to interpret the moment. He thought he should feel terror, but he only felt excitement. His wife had always rivaled his height and weight. He could have attempted to wrestle her off of his body, but he didn't know if he physically had the strength. Also, Vincent didn't want her—ghost or not—off his body. He enjoyed her warmth and tangible, living weight.

"Shelly," he said, whispering her name. For a second, he almost reached up to touch her, but he withheld. What if his hand passed through her face, brutally reminding him she was dead, that only the spirit of her had returned to him? He preferred to believe, even momentarily, that she was actually with him.

"I'm getting stronger," Shelly said, her voice airy and distant. "Soon, I will avenge my death. Soon, you will join me in Hell."

A cloth covered Vincent's mouth. He inhaled, and the room tilted. The ceiling fan rotated around and around. The spirit had vanished, as had the pressure on his chest, and he slipped into a dreamless void of unrestful sleep.

The Third Case. Wednesday, April 27th, 0913hrs.

"So…" Fred said, holding onto the end of the word as if holding the last note in a song.

I hadn't yet heard from Alina that morning. She attended school and wouldn't come into the office until after 1400hrs. But she hadn't texted me, either. I figured she had found nothing in the journal. That allowed me to focus my attention on Miette Verdin and her dead stalker, Vanessa Brown, who claimed Miette had stolen her life.

I scanned my notes.

- *Vanessa Brown followed Miette on social media and directly messaged her. Vanessa also followed Miette's boyfriend on social media accounts.*

- *Vanessa Brown has a Myspace account, which shares the same photograph as her Instagram account, which shares the same photograph as a young woman's obituary picture.*

- *Someone, presumably Vanessa, messed with Miette's home (a circle around a dead face drawn on the calendar).*

- *Vanessa learned Miette's cell phone number and sent her threatening texts.*

- *Vanessa claims Miette stole her life—that Miette is a changeling. The circled date on the calendar was Vanessa's birthday, not Miette's, and Vanessa would expose the truth on May 5th.*

I reread the notes, pausing at the first bullet point. Vanessa had messaged Miette on Instagram. Why hadn't I secured Vanessa's Instagram handle from Miette when she was in my office? I went to the social media platform—I didn't have an account, so I had to search through the profiles as a guest. I typed in Vanessa Brown.

That's when Fred broke the silence with his drawn out 'So.'

"So, what?" I asked, sipping coffee and massaging my temples.

"How did it go?"

"What?"

"Don't pretend like you don't know. Last night, with Glacia. How did it go?" Fred's giant puppy dog head poked over the reception counter, and he grinned at me with a knowing look in his eyes.

"I woke up to her long gone," I said. "I called her, she sent me straight to voicemail with a follow-up text stating it's for the best."

"What's for the best?"

"I don't know. That she ignores my calls. That we don't speak anymore. She went back to Oregon, and I stayed here, and that's that."

"Did you guys... you know?" Fred formed a circled with his left hand, and he crudely poked his right index finger in and out of the circle. "Did she hit it and quit it? I mean, can you blame her? You're more of a one-night-stand guy, you know?"

"How did you even know I spent the night with her?"

"A little birdie."

"Alina?"

"I can't reveal my sources."

"Why is Alina telling about my dating life?"

Fred shrugged. "We talk. We're cool like that."

A terrifying thought struck me. "You didn't tell my mom I had a date last night, did you?"

Fred and my family had grown considerably and unfortunately close over the past five years in my absence. He was a fill-in son and brother, keeping them updated on my wellbeing, as well as filling in for me at family events. He showed up to dinners and game nights and birthdays. It was, for me, quite uncomfortable.

"I told her you—"

My phone rang, cutting him off. Low and behold, my mother called, most likely wanting updates about last night. Who was the lucky girl? Were we serious? When would she meet her? What does she look like? Does she have a Facebook? What's her name? When is the wedding and when will the grandchildren come?

"Fred, stop talking to my mom," I said, answering the phone. "Hi, Mom."

"Gussy," she said, gushing. I could hear the morning birds chirping in her voice. Her excitement bled through the receiver and tickled my ear—but I wasn't ticklish.

In fact, I hated the sensation. I lifted my gaze to Fred, looking at him like I might look at a man who ripped his pants in a humid elevator, partly disgusted, mostly furious.

"What?" he mouthed, grinning like a fox.

"How did your date go last night?" Mom asked.

"Not well," I said, not removing my attention from Fred.

"No?"

"Poorly, in fact. She drove back to Oregon this morning. When I called her, she ignored the call and asked for me not to contact her again."

"Oh, Gussy." Excitement melted into disappointment. "Are you okay? Should I come by later to check up on you? I can bring your favorite dinner over. Macaroni and Cheese mixed with baked beans."

I curled my lip. That dish hadn't landed on my top fifteen meals since I was twelve-years-old. Back then, I had also enjoyed Doritos on my ham and mayonnaise sandwich and Fruit Loops for breakfast. A fancy restaurant included Taco Bell or Denny's. Now the thought of that cramped my stomach into a digestive train wreck.

"No, thank you," I said. "I think I'll be okay."

"Well, Cambria, the woman from church, raved about you. She said you two really hit it off, and she would love to see you again. And Gussy, I think you should date a good, Christian girl. I think that would be good for you."

There was a lot to unpack there, as with most of her 'I think you should' sentences. I found myself stuck on the 'good Christian girl' comment. Cambria may have attended the same church as my parents, most if not all Sundays, but she wasn't any Virgin Mary. In fact, Cambria, on the very morning I met her, directly after the church service, pulled me aside and groped my more sensitive areas. How would my mom respond had I shared that bit of information? Probably in favor of Cambria.

"I'm not interested in her," I said, sealing my lips as soon as I heard the words wriggle themselves free of my mouth. Why had I said that?

"What's not to be interested in? Do you not find her attractive?"

"It's not that—"

"She's extremely beautiful, intelligent, and a successful young woman."

"I believe you, Mom."

"Not only that, but she loves the Lord. She attends church regularly, and she's involved in the community."

"I'm sure she is," I said, once again speaking before I could help myself. How did my mom have the unique ability to crawl under my skin and dig all these throwaway comments out of me?

"What does that mean?"

Only that I'm sure she's very involved in the community, I thought. *That she is very charitable and generous with her time, among being generous with other things.*

I scratched the top of head, hating myself for thinking those thoughts about Cambria. For all I knew, Cambria was an incredibly nice, lovely woman.

"Gussy," my mother said.

"Yeah."

"What's that mean?"

"Nothing. I'm sure she's friendly and charitable. I didn't feel a connection to her, though. That's all."

"Well, I think I set you two up for failure at church. You had family surrounding you. Imagine how intimidated she must have felt. I'm sure she was nervous and not herself."

Very much so, I thought, coughing back a fit of laughter. *Very nervous.*

"Even without family around," my mom said, "you could have intimidated her. I'm mean, you are a very handsome, charming boy, who had attended church to see his mother. That can throw a wrench in a woman's confidence."

Uh oh, I thought, realizing too late where my mother steered this conversation.

"I reserved a table for you two on Friday night at Kru. Have you ever been there?"

Kru was a nice Japanese restaurant in Sacramento.

Before I could answer, she continued speaking. "You can pick Cambria up from her house around six o'clock. Your reservation is at seven. Show up early, though, and buy her a drink, or walk around Sacramento."

"I had a date last night," I said. "What if she would have stayed? What if it would have worked out? I couldn't have gone on a blind date with Cambria this Friday, now could I?"

My mom went into a defensive explanation of why she had reserved the table, even though she knew I had spent the evening with Glacia. As she spoke, my phone notified me of an incoming call. I pulled the screen from my ear and checked the caller. I didn't recognize the number.

"Mom," I said, cutting her off. "I have a client calling me on the other line. Cancel the reservation. I'm not going."

"But Gussy, there's a cancellation fee."

"You and dad can enjoy a delightful night out, then. Love you. Bye." I switched over to the new caller. "August Watson, Blue Moon Investigations."

"August, it's Sarah Herling, from the law office next door."

My cheeks blushed.

Sarah had created her own firm a few months ago, about the same time I created my business. She worked as a defensive attorney, representing people falsely accused of a crime—or people who she believed were falsely accused of a crime. Not only did she work a lot for a little pay, making herself somewhat of a martyr for the oppressed, she was knock-out gorgeous. So why had she called me?

"Hi," I said.

"I think I need your help with my latest client."

The room shifted as her call found perspective. Why would she have called on a personal errand? Of course she meant to discuss business—whatever overlapping business a defense attorney and a paranormal investigator shared.

"Are you available to speak for a few minutes?" she asked. "I'll lay out the case, and if you're interested, I would like to set up a visitation between you and my client."

"Um," I scraped my teeth across my lower lip, not knowing how to say no to Sarah. I had recently solved three cases, and I already had two more in my lap—two that offered little to no leads and a lot of legwork and time. Could I juggle a third? "Though I'm a private investigator, I only investigate paranormal circumstances."

"I know. That's why I called." She cleared her throat in a soft, petite manner. I could almost imagine her making a small fist, holding it to her lips, and gently excavating the phlegm and saliva from her esophagus with a lightly forced cough. "Last night, a woman named Claire Balzan—" Sarah's words blended and her voice faded into a constant, ringing hum.

Claire Balzan. Why did the name sound so familiar? I ran through my mental files, searching for the name, and I found it in the cabinet labeled unresolved.

Claire Balzan had contacted me on Saturday. She had left a voicemail at first, sounding terrified. When I called her back, she refused to hold a conversation over the phone, insisting we meet in person at the donut shop near my office. I agreed to meet her Monday morning—two days ago. She had flaked. Yesterday morning, as I visited Glacia in the hospital, Claire had called me again. What had she said that left me so cold and sweaty at the same time?

She financially ruined me. She destroyed my marriage. I'm scared... so scared of what she'll do next.

Who? I had asked, staring out the room's window at the parking lot.

Me.

The call ended, and I hadn't heard from her since. Now Sarah Herling, defense attorney, contacted me about Claire Balzan.

"She was arrested?" I asked, blurting out the question, unsure of what Sarah said over the past handful of seconds, unsure if I had interrupted her. "For what?"

"Two counts of murder."

I already sat at my desk, reclined in my chair, so I couldn't take a seat to process the information. To change elevation and hopefully view this news from a new perspective, I stood and paced. "Claire contacted me on Saturday, then again yesterday morning."

"I know. She told me—another reason I reached out for your help."

She financially ruined me. She destroyed my marriage.

Who?

Me.

"Claire mentioned nothing about murder," I said.

Is that why she wanted to meet? She didn't want to broach such a conversation over the phone?

"They arrested her on two counts of murder. They have direct evidence linking her to the crime scene. Video evidence. By all counts, purposes, and appearances, Claire is guilty."

I stopped pacing, standing in the middle of the room, staring out one of the two windows that mirrored each other in my office. This one overlooked the brick wall of the neighboring building. If I peered downward, I had the lovely view of a couple of dumpsters and an occasional homeless man named Gerald.

"Mr. Watson, are you there?" Sarah asked.

"August, please. And from what I understand, based on my few conversations with Gio, you only take on clients you believe are innocent."

Gio was her Fred.

"That's correct."

"Evidence ties Claire to the murders. No alibi. Does she have motivation?" I asked.

"Very much so."

"Yet, you believe her innocent?"

"It's a gut feeling. But that's why I chose this line of work—to listen to the people without voices. I believed her story, despite everything stacked against her." Sarah chuckled then, a nervous, icy laugh. "I believe there's something paranormal at work."

"Paranormal?" I asked.

Sarah said nothing for a few seconds. Then she sighed, throwing caution and sanity to the wind. "A doppelgänger. I think Claire has an evil twin."

Visitation. Wednesday, April 27th, 1129hrs.

SARAH SCHEDULED FOR ME to visit Claire Balzan in the county jail at 1130hrs as a legal consultant.

I sat in the visitation room, hands on the cheap table, waiting to meet with my latest client and thinking of my other two cases.

Vincent Dupree's late wife's spirit haunted him, threatening to murder him when it got enough power to do so. He had even seen the apparition twice, the most recent encounter last night when it had woken him by sitting on his chest. He claimed the spectral entity resembled his wife perfectly.

A stranger named Vanessa Brown accused Miette Verdin that she had stolen her life—that she was, in fact, a changeling. Vanessa planned to expose Miette for who she was on May 5th.

Now Claire Balzan claimed an evil, supernatural twin, a doppelgänger, had ruined her life.

The coincidence of my three congruent cases didn't go beyond my noticing. They all spelled a certain, obvious theme. Identity. Vincent Dupree's late wife had returned as a ghost. Vanessa claimed Miette Verdin was a changeling who had stolen her life and would now get revenge. Claire insisted the crimes attributed to her were really the fault of a doppelgänger. Three cases all hinging on some kind of mistaken identity.

What were the odds?

Slim to none, I thought. *Zero to impossible.*

Movement in my periphery caught my attention. I turned to peer out the glass walls.

A female guard escorted a young lady, no older than thirty. Even in her orange jumpsuit, Claire Balzan was gorgeous. It wouldn't have surprised me to find her mugshot trending on social media. The Sacramento County Jail Beauty turned into a Beast.

The female guard—who unfortunately looked squat and square compared to Claire opened the door. She led Claire to the chair across the table from me, guiding her cuffed hands to a ring welded onto the metallic table.

"If you don't mind," I said, "there's no need for that."

"It's policy," the guard said, unlatching a cuff, sliding it through the ring, and refitting it around her wrist. "You have thirty minutes. I'll be right outside." The woman stomped out of the room, standing guard near the window, though with her back to us.

I broke off a half-smile.

Claire lifted her eyes. Her face was a mask of terror. The fear drenching her features launched a primal, masculine urge within me to save her. To rescue her from the maw of the dragon and reap my rewards.

Neither of us said a word—me shocked into silence by her surprising beauty, by her trembling hands and quivering face. I was a fourteen-year-old boy tasked with the impossible feat of asking the prettiest girl in class to the dance, or on a date. My tongue swelled in my mouth, and my throat was suddenly much too small to squeeze single syllables through, let alone sentences. Once again, my unrelenting charm with the women proved winning.

"August Watson," Claire said, her voice tiny—like a scared toddler not wanting to reach for the hand of a stranger, but not having any other choice.

"We finally meet," I said, shedding a cautious smile.

Claire reciprocated the good humor, despite everything leading up to that moment. Her bright, terror-shattering grin told me all I needed to know of the woman. She was a warrior, and under normal circumstances, she never would have needed someone like me to save her. These weren't normal circumstances, though, and I was the only person qualified to complete the task at hand.

"Did Ms. Herling call you?" Claire asked.

"She did."

"So you know my story?"

"A broad-stroke version. Could you fill me in on some details?"

Claire's right hand twitched, as if she meant to lift it and realized she couldn't. "When I'm nervous, my face gets warm and itchy." Again, she smiled that smile that could snap steel. "It's what I hate most about these handcuffs, believe it or not. They are sometimes too tight and hurt my wrists, but I can deal with a little pain. It's when they're holding my hands behind my back, or flat against this table... and I'm speaking with Sarah or now you, and I'm nervous. My face itches, but I can't scratch it. That's the worst part."

She spoke in a strange staccato, like a heart rate machine spiking and falling. Something about her frenetic pace captured my attention, though, and I could have listened to her speak all day long.

I knew better than to approach her and touch her, which meant I couldn't offer to satisfy her itching face.

After a second of silence, Claire said, "I'm innocent."

"Can you tell me your version of the story?"

Her eyes widened, but she nodded tentatively. "My husband received a video of my therapist sleeping with another woman. A woman who looked an awful lot like me. He believed she was me."

I clicked open my pen and took notes. "Does Sarah have access to the video?"

"She has access to everything. You're welcome to—" Sarah sighed, obviously embarrassed. "You're welcome to use any of it."

"Continue, please."

"Simon, my husband of five years, left me. I tried to contact him. To explain the unexplainable. To convince him I hadn't cheated. It wasn't me in the video. He never answered my phone. A couple of weeks later, they found him dead."

"Who did?"

"My therapist."

"The one in the video?"

Claire nodded.

"He found the body?" I asked.

"Robert Woods. Yes. That's why they didn't arrest me at first. Robert found the body, and they suspected he played a role in Simon's death. They actually suspected we worked together. Maybe they still do."

"Did they arrest Robert?"

"It's pointless to arrest a dead man."

"He's dead?"

"Murdered. His secretary found his body after he didn't show up to work for a couple of days."

A bell rang in my head. Ding, ding, ding. "I read about that," I said.

"It was on the news and the paper. That's how I found out at first. Apparently, detectives found my hair at the scene of the crime—at the scene of both crimes. Not only that, they have me on camera murdering Dr. Woods."

She had referred to him as Dr. Woods. I noted that. Was she being extra cautious of what she said, choosing her words wisely? I didn't get that impression. She spoke too quickly. My bet, she called him Dr. Woods out of habit. Did someone having an affair with another person refer to them professionally out of habit? I doubted as much. Either way, I noted it and continued listening to her.

"They have me on his security camera, just like they have me on camera at the hospital stealing drugs from the locked cabinet. Just like they have me on camera sleeping with Dr. Woods." She lowered her chin and stared at her shackled hands. "I don't know how to say this without sounding completely insane, but despite their footage, that's not me. I'm innocent. No affair. No theft. No murders."

"No alibi," I said, not to incriminate her, but to state a fact of her arrest.

"No alibi," Claire agreed.

I massaged my shoulder. "If you can think of an alibi—anything that might take you away from either murder—we can start building a defense in your favor. Did you speak to a friend that night? Go to a bar? See a movie? Do anything outside of your house?"

"I don't know which night my husband died, and I don't know which night Dr. Wood was murdered, either. The police will tell me one thing, then they change the details of their story in the next interview."

"They're testing you," I said.

"Either way, I wasn't out doing much during that time. I had recently lost my husband and my dream job, then I learned my husband was murdered and that I was the prime suspect. I have spent most of my evenings with a bottle of wine in the bathtub or in bed. When I'm not crying, I'm sleeping."

I leaned back in my chair and crossed my arms. If Claire expected Sarah and me to help her, to prove her innocent, she needed to cooperate a little. She needed to provide us with a launching pad, no matter how small and defective it was. In my mind, proving she wasn't at the scene of the murders while the murders occurred seemed like the most legitimate way to go about that.

"I'm going to look through the documents and evidence Sarah has about your case, see if I can't find anything useful. I'm also going to pinpoint the exact dates and times the murders occurred. In the meantime, I need you to do something for me."

"Anything," Claire said.

"Make a list of everything you did over the past month. I mean everything. What websites did you visit? What TV shows did you watch? Where did you eat? Who did you talk to? Where did you go? I need names, times, dates. Can you do that?"

"I can."

"Good. We'll meet again in two days. Friday."

"That works for me. I'm pretty available these days." Claire smiled—a natural, unforced, genuine smirk that sent me in a tizzy.

I stood, collecting my notes.

"Mr. Watson?"

"August."

"August, do you think I committed these crimes?"

I paused a beat, not wanting to lie to her with a quick, placating answer. "I don't know."

"Do you believe something supernatural, like a doppelgänger, couldn't have done it?"

I frowned and glanced through the glass wall, reaching out and tapping on it with my knuckles. The guard turned to me, saw me standing, and removed her keys from her belt to unlock the door.

"No," I said to Claire. "I don't think a doppelgänger committed these crimes."

Delegation. Wednesday, April 27th, 1308hrs.

I STOOD BEFORE MY office entrance, glancing over my shoulder at the door behind me on the opposite side of the hallway. Sarah Herling's office.

At some point this afternoon, I needed to swing by and update her on the interview with Claire. Not that there was much in the way of updating. Still, a little is better than nothing, and often in these investigations, a little goes a long way. Besides, Sarah had some documents I wished to pour over.

First things first, though. Feed the beast.

Fred had called me during the interview. When I called him back, he begged for me to stop somewhere and grab him some food. I had also worked up an appetite, so I grabbed us sandwiches from a local shop with farm-to-fork ingredients. Since Fred manned the office, intercepting walk-in clients, answering phones, and responding to emails, he was more or less anchored to his spot. More so now than ever since we had a consistent stream of inquiries.

I opened the door and stepped inside. The acrid, muggy air curled my nose. The unit we rented had no air conditioning. It sat three stories above a restaurant, and the small space absorbed the worst odors seeping up from that restaurant.

"Why don't you open a window?" I asked, dropping the to-go bag on the reception counter and crossing the room to the alley window, unlatching it and pushing it upward.

"It's just my farts. Daphne made a bean and Brussel sprouts dish last night, and my stomach has paid the price."

"My nose has paid the price. What's wrong with you?"

"What's wrong with me? What does that mean? You want me to hold it in?"

"Yes. Most definitely."

"Must I enlighten you on the plethora of research detailing the negative side effects of holding in your gas?"

"There's no evidence of that."

Fred peeled the foil off his hot sandwich and bit into his lunch.

"It would explain his bad breath," Alina said from behind me.

I wheeled around and backed against the wall, half-startled by her presence. "Where did you come from?"

"That's a long, gross story," the girl said. She sat in the client chair placed before my desk, scrolling through her cell phone. She wore denim shorts and a long-sleeve, button-down shirt. "So I'll avoid telling it. Fred's gas, though atrocious, at least escapes through the correct side of his body. Holding gas can often lead to building pressure within the body, blah, blah, blah, which may cause releasing that pressure through his breath." Alina lifted her eyes, looking at me like an impatient professor looks at a student who refuses to learn. "So, we can either smell his farts as God intended, or we can smell his literal crap breath."

I popped a knuckle, not knowing what to say or how to respond. As thoughts trickled back to the forefront of my mind, they spilled into my mouth and burst off my tongue. "Why are you here?"

"Me?" Alina asked, pointing at herself.

"You."

"Why am I here?"

"Yes."

She narrowed her eyes and looked at me from the side of her face. "Because I intern here." The girl spoke each word slowly, as if rolling it around her mouth before spitting it out.

"From 1400hrs to 1700hrs you intern here." I glanced at my watch. "You're an hour early."

Alina's face shed her confusion with a bright smile. She chuckled. "You're the worst boss of all time. In the work permit, the one you, my mom, my dad, my teacher, and myself signed, agreeing on the days and hours of my work, it explicitly says Wednesdays are minimum days at school. We get out at 12:30."

I turned to Fred. The big man already shoved the last of his sandwich into his mouth.

"You knew she was here?" I asked.

He shrugged, speaking behind a wad of food. "I watched her come in."

"We talked about the latest Marvel movie for, like, fifteen minutes," Alina said. "He saw it last night. Finally. It's only two weeks old now. Anyway, he loved it. Me?" She rolled her eyes. "Not so much. Those movies are eye candy at this point. Attractive people wearing fun suits doing awesome things. So, entertainment value, sure. It was fun. Ten out of ten. Movie value, though, like overall." Alina rocked her head back and forth, as if weighing the strength of the film. "Six out of ten, and honestly, I think that's generous because I'm partial to Marvel movies, and I could never rate them below a six. Even when they're bad, they're fun. That counts for something, right?"

I couldn't remember my original question. Why had Alina spiraled about the Marvel movies? "I've never seen a Marvel movie," I said.

Alina gasped, dropping her phone into her lap and clutching her chest. "You what? August. I knew your film knowledge was low, but I didn't know you were a complete moron. I mean, Marvel movies are like Harry Potter movies, or like *Stranger Things*. Everyone has seen them."

"I don't even know what *Stranger Things* is," I said.

Fred coughed, choking on the last of his food.

Alina's eyes couldn't have gone wider had someone hung hooks from the ceiling and held them open.

"We have three cases on the table," I said, spurring myself toward my desk and sitting. I laid out my sandwich, pouring my chips on the paper wrapping. "We need to solve one or two of them before we can justify taking on any other cases. We have to accept more cases to make more money. In short, we have to solve cases to accept more cases to make more money. Does that make sense to you two?"

"No," Alina said. "Can you explain how economics work? Maybe in a way a two-year-old will understand."

"I don't think it's wise to choose which cases to work first, isolating only one while leaving the others in a queue." I thought Dr. Dupree's dead wife threatening to avenge her death, of Miette receiving a perceived threat, and of Claire sitting in jail. To put off any of the cases meant to choose who deserved to be saved the most, when all of their lives hung in the balance. "I think we should all focus on one case, but keep everyone up to date on any discoveries." I glanced at Fred. "Except for you."

"Oh, thank goodness," he said, relief clear in his tone.

The big man had accepted a secretary-like role within the company. He manned the front desk. He organized the paperwork, finalized the reports, balanced the books—clerical tasks. Despite his incredible stature, Fred more than feared the supernatural or any threat of danger. He hated going out in the field, and only did so when I asked him to, though he never missed an opportunity to let me know I owed him afterward.

"Wait," Alina said. "I'm only a dumb, sixteen-year-old girl who doesn't know a fart from bad breath, but we have three ongoing investigations you want to parcel out evenly. But if Fred doesn't receive a case, that leaves two of us to handle three investigations equally." The girl spoke obnoxiously slowly, as if to emphasize how she struggled to understand the math.

"I'm consulting on the third case, so I'll leave most of the legwork to Sarah Herling."

"Oh, nice," Fred said.

"Lawyer next door?" Alina asked, glancing at the big guy.

"Yeah."

"She's cute."

"Yup," Fred said, shifting his attention to me and grinning.

"You think he has a chance?" Alina asked.

"Nope."

"I'm not interested," I said.

"Okay," Fred said.

"Sure," Alina added.

I rolled my eyes and refocused our discussion. "As for you, Alina, since you've had the journal for almost a day, I'm going to leave you to continue working on Dr. Dupree's case. By the way, he called earlier, stating he had another encounter last night. Follow up, will you?"

"Sure. What will you do?"

"I'll continue looking into Miette's changeling situation." I popped a knuckle.

"That makes sense," Alina said. "Speaking of the journal, though, I found some juicy intel within those pages."

I bit into my sandwich. Unlike Fred, I opted not to speak through a mouthful of food, so I hand gestured for Alina to proceed.

She straightened her posture, sitting upright, leaning over, and rustling through her backpack set beneath her chair. When she came back up, she held Shelly's journal. Shelly Welch, with hearts and flowers circling the name.

Alina tucked a strand of hair behind her ear and opened the journal, flipping through the pages. "Okay," she said, clearing her throat and reading. "Today I received a letter in the mail. That was exciting, because the mail is never for me. It's always bills or spam, at least that's what Daddy says. Anyway, the letter came for me. It said Shelly Welch on the envelope, but it had no return address. I think that made my mom nervous, because she refused to let me look at it until she did. She read the entire thing and then she showed it to Daddy. He read the entire thing two times. When he finished, he looked at me with sad eyes and said, 'Sorry, Bug. You can't read this today.' I was mad at him, but I was also really sad. Who had sent the letter? Why had they addressed it to me? What did it say? I asked him those questions, and he said he couldn't answer any of them. He walked into the kitchen and clicked on the stove. Then he put the corner of the letter to the blue flame and dropped it in the pan." Alina looked up at us.

"That's it?" I asked.

"What do you mean, 'That's it?' The rest of the journal tells us nothing but who she had a crush on, what the latest gossip was, which teachers were the worst, and who she lost her virginity to. Believe it or not, Vincent Dupree. They were high school sweethearts. I thought that was touching. Anyway, the mysterious letter was the only out-of-the-ordinary entry."

"It tells us nothing," I said.

"It tells us her parents were hiding something from her," Alina said. "What would a mom and a dad want to hide from their fourteen, fifteen-year-old daughter? Allow me to rephrase the question. They received a letter with no return address—so, not a government- or medical-issued letter. A private letter. Why would her father burn it?"

"To protect her," I said, leaning forward and planting my elbows on my desk. "Who would a father want to protect his teenage daughter from? A toxic love interest. Vincent, maybe?"

Alina shook her head. "No mention of any past relationships, handsy uncles, or creepy stalkers in the journal. Also, had Shelly suspected it might be from Uncle Chester or ex-boyfriend Punchy, she probably would have mentioned that in the journal—that she suspected the person it had come from. But she had no clue who the sender was."

I stared at my desktop, at the sandwich and the chip crumbs, thinking hard for too long.

"Holy smokes," Alina said. "I know you've lived a privileged life, but you have to know this answer."

Fred spoke up, filling the quiet space with his thoughts. "I didn't have the greatest childhood," he said. "Little to no parental presence to keep me in check. When they were present, they abused me. My mom wielded her tongue like a barbed whip, especially toward my sister, but also toward me. My dad swung his belt like one, primarily at me. When I was with them, I hated them. I hated them for what they did to Halle—my sister—and I hated them for what they did to me. I hated them for what they didn't do, and what they would never do. Love us like parents should love their children." Fred cleared his throat. "Halle and I went to a foster home when I was in middle school. We remained there for a couple of years, never hearing from our parents. In fact, our foster parents wanted to adopt us. When they began the proceedings, my biological mother caught wind of it, and she contacted me. She claimed she was sorry, so sorry for how she had treated us, and that she had changed, and she wanted to do better. She wanted a second chance. I had an abusive mother, and I had a loving, gentle foster family. When it came time to choose, guess who I chose?"

"I would choose my mom every single time, too," Alina said with confidence—without hesitation. Her eyes swelled with tears, but they didn't break down her face. "Despite everything she has done to me, I would choose her every single time."

"I chose my biological parents," Fred said, nodding his agreement. "Shelly's dad read that letter, and he knew who it was from, and he knew if Shelly read it, she would go back to a dark, terrible place. So, he burned it."

"Shelly was adopted?" I asked.

"Purely speculative," Alina said. "But if I had put money on something, guaranteeing a payback, I'd put everything on her being adopted."

"Do you think Dr. Dupree knows?"

Both Fred and Alina shook their heads, but Alina spoke. "I don't think Shelly knew—or she confirmed none of the suspicions she harbored."

I massaged my temples. "Alina."

"Yes?"

"Get in contact with Dr. Dupree. He said Shelly was the only child of parents who were also only children. I'm guessing he meant her adopted parents." I put adopted in air quotes to emphasize we had no proof of that claim. "Mention nothing to him about that possibility. Instead, I want a list of all Shelly's friends and colleagues. Once you have that list, contact them one by one. Ask them about Shelly's circle of contacts. Cross reference the names with Dr. Dupree's list, and add any new ones. Continue down the list, getting ahold of different people and asking them about her correspondences."

"What am I looking for?"

"Someone to mention a long-lost family. Adoption. A new friend, perhaps."

"Why? Where will that get us?" Alina asked.

"Ghosts or vengeful spirits don't exist," I said. "But greedy family does. If we find someone related to her, we maybe identify the ghost."

Alina licked her teeth. "Okay. I'm on it, then."

"Thanks."

"What's the third case?" She asked. "We have the Changeling. The ghost. What's the third?"

"Doppelgänger." I briefed her and Fred on Claire Balzan's story, neglecting my lunch throughout the explanation. When I finished, I bit into the sandwich.

"Weird," Alina said.

I chewed and swallowed, downing a sip of water. "What's that?"

"It sounds oddly familiar to a Stephen King novel. *The Outsider.* I read it, and I watched the television series. I loved both of them. Anyway, in the story, the cops arrest the main character for murdering a little boy. However, he has an airtight alibi, and he maintains his innocence. Except, of course, eyewitnesses saw the character near the crime with blood all over his clothes. Turns out, the Outsider committed the crime."

"Spoiler alert!" Fred said.

"You haven't seen it?"

"It's on my list, but I haven't watched it yet."

"Dude, read it, don't watch it."

"I don't read."

"What? Like, you can't read, or you choose not to?"

"Of course I can read," Fred said. "You think August would have hired me to run the clerical aspect of this job if I couldn't read?"

"I don't know. He's a weirdo. I can't predict what he will and won't do."

"Hey," I said, raising my hands to calm them down. "How did the novel end? Did the character kill the kid?"

"Earmuffs," Alina said to Fred, and the big guy covered his ears with his giant hands. "No. It was some Mexican bogeyman creature that could absorb someone's blood and take on their appearance."

"That's not helpful," I said, taking another bite of my sandwich.

We all sat in silence for a while. I finished my lunch. Alina scrolled through her phone. Fred hid behind the reception counter, sitting before the computer, most likely playing Hearts or Solitaire. When I finished eating, I balled up my trash and threw it away, standing and heading toward the door.

"I'll be back later," I said.

"Where are you going?" Alina asked.

"To meet with Sarah about the doppelgänger."

"Hey," Alina called out before I could shut the door.

I paused and glanced back. "Yeah?"

"How did it go with Glacia last night?"

After a second of frustrated hesitation, I shut the door and crossed the hall.

All Hands on Deck. Wednesday, April 27th, 1352hrs.

"Rewind it a few seconds," I said.

"Why? So you can see her naked again?" Sarah asked, snickering, rewinding the video of Claire Balzan grinding on Robert Woods.

She straddled the much older man. Claire was close to thirty, and Robert flirted with sixty. His saggy breasts and bulbous stomach directly juxtaposed Claire's body. His bulldog face created a distorted reflection of her smooth, angular features. Young women sometimes chase rich, elderly men, and they have the impressive capabilities to overlook the nature's toll, as long, of course, as they can drink real champagne and eat caviar and fly private jets. Dr. Woods had enough money, but he wasn't yacht-wealthy. Claire and her husband, though not financially well off, were both young, attractive people with a promising life. Even if Dr. Woods had compensated her for the sex, why would she engage? It didn't feel logical.

Except, there she was, in full, living color, rocking back and forth on Dr. Woods. Claire's blonde hair and her blue eyes. The face belonged to the woman I had met with earlier in jail. Through the obviously acted moans, the voice also belonged to her.

Once again, for the fifth or sixth time, the video ended.

"Same moles there and there," Sarah said, pinpointing a mole on Claire's naval and one on her shoulder. "In our meeting, she mentioned that, not wanting to withhold any information. She showed me... rather, she told me where to look to confirm the matching moles."

"It's her," I said, my voice numb and barely existent.

"She denies it." Sarah scrolled through her saved files and enlarged another video.

It showed an empty hospital room. Sarah pressed play.

For a few seconds, the room remained gray and vacant. Then the lights flashed on in an explosion of white. The screen settled, showing a blonde woman walking to a cabinet. With her left hand, she inserted a key, twisted the lock, and opened the door. Once inside, the woman removed a bottle of pills, closed the cabinet, and locked it again. When she turned around, facing the camera, she was unmistakably and inarguably Claire Balzan. The light turned off, and she exited the screen right.

"That's her," I said. "If that's not Claire, I'll eat my hat."

Sarah glanced at me and grimaced. "Eat your hat? Who says that? Are you ninety?" She returned her attention to the computer screen, minimized the hospital video, and clicked on another thumbnail.

That one expanded to show a sizable kitchen with a minimalist style. Robert Woods stood at the counter near the sink, chopping vegetables. Over the sink was a window. I wondered what it overlooked. A vineyard? The river? His backyard? His neighbor's front yard? I only considered it for a second, because he flinched when Claire snuck up behind him and touched his waist—as if he did not know she was there, in his house with him.

The video didn't have sound, but the two had a brief, unheard conversation. Dr. Woods set his knife down, rounded the kitchen island, and opened the refrigerator door. He removed two eggs and brought them to the stovetop, turning his back to Claire to crack them and drop them into the frying pan. He never saw her pick up the vegetable knife.

From behind him, she wrapped her right hand around his waist, grabbing his crotch.

His shoulders stiffened in response, and he dropped his head back, staring at the ceiling.

Claire worked her hand, hiding her left behind her back, clutching the knife he had set on the counter. She kissed his neck.

Dr. Woods turned to face her. He kissed her on the mouth, and he groped at her breasts, her butt, her crotch. Claire went along with it, puffing out her chest, leaning into him, moving with his body and his hands.

Then, like a snake lurching to attack, her left arm wheeled from behind her back. The blade of the knife disappeared into Dr. Woods' neck. Claire ripped it free, and blood sprayed and splashed across her face and torso, across the white cabinets, on the tile floor. The frying pan steamed, most likely boiling the droplets of blood that had landed in with the eggs, like ketchup or Tabasco. Dr. Woods grabbed the wound, but his blood continued to pump through his fingers. Claire stabbed him again, straight on, driving the blade into his cheek. Into his jaw. Into his forehead. Into his ear. Into his nose. Into his eye. Into his cheek. Jabbing and slashing at his face until he no longer had one.

The doctor slipped in his own blood and fell to the floor hard, without grace. His skull bounced off the tile. He never moved again.

Claire faced the camera, looked directly at it, and she grinned.

Sarah ended the video, pushed back her chair, and faced me, crossing her arms.

"It's obviously her," I said.

"She removed the knife from the scene. No one knows where it's at now. Forensics found a few strands of her hair at the crime scene. Not only that, but they found her hair on her husband's corpse."

"Video evidence of her committing a murder," I said. "They found her DNA at the scene of the murder."

"Yup."

"Motivation?" I asked.

Sarah exhaled. "Dr. Woods sent the video to Simon, her husband. The detectives learned that pretty early on. Because of the video, her husband left. In her state of despair and with no one to turn to for help, she revisited an old addiction—Adderall. That cost her a career as a nurse. Also, Simon controlled their finances. He emptied their shared account, leaving her with nothing. So, she had no husband, no job, and no money. Detectives think she contacted Simon, met with him, and murdered him for leaving her and taking all the money. After that, she went to Dr. Woods and murdered him for sending the video to Simon."

"That's what the detectives think?" I asked, popping a knuckle.

"That's the picture the evidence has painted for them."

"What do you think?"

Sarah stared at me for a long time before shying her eyes away and glancing at the computer screen. It showed the end image of the murder—Dr. Woods lying in a puddle of his blood in an otherwise empty kitchen. "Would you call me gullible to say I don't think she did it?"

"No," I said, feeling the same way.

I had met with Claire. I had spoken to her. Not once did I sense anger, let alone murderous rage. I sensed a great deal of confusion and frustration, as well as sadness. But after meeting with her, I doubted she could kill a rabid dog.

Now, murderers were sly and manipulative, and they knew exactly what to say so anyone would believe their sob story. With that in mind, I still couldn't fathom Claire murdering her husband and her therapist in such a brutal manner.

"If not her, then who?" Sarah asked.

"The Mexican bogeyman," I said, thinking of *The Outsider.*

"What?"

"Nothing." I reached into my pocket and removed a stick of cinnamon gum, popping it into my mouth. "It was something my new intern, Alina, said." My mind raced with questions. Where did we go from here? How did we prove the innocence of someone so obviously guilty? Where did we even begin? "I gave Claire some homework."

"You did?"

"I told her to record a time and date of everything she did, no matter how big or small, going back three weeks. I don't know how anything she comes up with will hold up against video evidence of a murder, but it's a start."

Sarah tapped her chin with her index finger. "You don't have to do this."

"Do what?"

"Help me with this case." Sarah was probably in her late-twenties, same age as Maya, but she looked younger at that moment. Twenty, perhaps. Closer to Alina's age. A child struggling to keep her head above water without exhausting herself and drowning in the choppy, stormy sea of life.

Which had always proved the crux of my existence—a girl in need of saving. I couldn't help but throw out a lifebuoy and play hero. I never had fancy, charming words to woo the fairer sex. Instead, I had always been awkward, stuttering through sentences. To overcome my unfounded anxiety, I spoke to women through gestures and actions.

The Claire Balzan case potentially saved two women, and that feat was too grand for me to ignore.

"I want to," I said. "I really do."

Sarah chuckled—a laugh meant to ward off nervousness. "Thank you. I mean that. I had to cut back Gio's hours because I can't afford to pay him anymore. I can't afford to pay myself."

"You don't have to explain yourself. Okay? I have a good team across the hall. Maya often lends her unique thoughts to these things. With all hands on deck, we'll figure this out."

"Okay," Sarah said, inhaling and hiding the frightened child that had plagued her face before. "I usually hate this kind of thing, you know?"

"What's that?" I asked.

"Asking for a man to help solve my problems—problems I don't need a man to help me solve. I hate contributing to the stereotype that women need men to save them."

My face burned as I realized I thrived on that stereotype. I was the man who waited in the shadows for a woman to call on him to save her. Truthfully, though, I think most men fit in that same box. We want to feel powerful, especially around women, and we want to feel like we can protect and provide for them. What better way to feel that sense of pure masculinity than saving them? I also jumped at any chance to save another man, though for different primal reasons. I wanted to feel superior to them. To prove I was the alpha. Those motivations brought me to law enforcement, then again to private investigation. It was my core identity to help other people who couldn't help themselves.

Maybe I was right for feeling that way, maybe I was wrong. I didn't know. I only knew that, at the moment, Claire Balzan and Sarah Herling needed my help, and I fully intended to help them.

Finally Finished. Wednesday, April 27th, 1506hrs.

I NEEDED TO TAKE a walk. Too many irons sat in the fire, and the heat was overwhelming me. Cool, fresh air sounded enlivening and necessary. So, instead of crossing the hall and rejoining Fred and Alina in the office, I opted for the stairwell.

Sunny and seventy-four degrees. Not a cloud in the bright-blue sky. A cool wind whispered through the city.

As I walked and basked in the afternoon warmth, I allowed my mind to drain—a practice my father had taught me as a kid.

"Gussy, just walk and observe the beauty of the world. Get out of your head. It's a cluttered, anxiety-ridden place, dark and terrifying for most. Get outside and walk. Think about the sky. Think about the animals and the plants. Mentally describe their colors and textures and scents. Do not, whatever you do, return to your head, though."

The practice—for that's what it was, something I had to work at constantly as escaping one's mind proved difficult—worked like a charm. Stepping out of my office, out of my head and my problems, focusing instead on nature and the world around me, the toxicity poisoning my mind burned away. A decluttering of all the useless junk stored inside the cranium.

Eventually, I wandered into a cafe, purchased a coffee, and sat outside to people watch.

As I settled into the wire-mesh chair, my phone buzzed. I considered ignoring the call. My head already felt lighter, more receptive to new information, and, as I mentioned, I had a lot of irons in the fire. Did I care to add another?

Removing the phone from my pocket, I saw Maya's name on the screen.

"Hey," I answered.

"I freaking did it like a gosh darn champion." I censored her actual language. "I finished the article and sent it over to Jonah."

"How do you feel?" I asked, slouching in the metal chair and smiling.

"Like a bird. Like I can spread my wings and fly. Like all the weight that had anchored me to the world has loosened and fallen off, and now I'm free." She cackled, exaggerating her excitement. "I'm still running on a writer's high. Sorry for the metaphors."

"I'm proud of you, and happy for you. Congratulations. Should we celebrate?"

"Yeah, I'm getting blacked-out drunk tonight. If you want to join, which you should, you can chauffeur me around."

"I'll one-up you. I'll buy your first drink, too."

"Wow. So chivalrous. When was the last time you bought a drink?"

I chewed on my cheek. "Two years ago. It was a week into my sobriety. I bought a bottle of bourbon. I stared at that bottle for three straight hours, thinking of Aaron and of my family and..." *of you*, I thought, but didn't say. "I fought every demon within my head not to drink it, to stay true to my sponsor and myself. In the end, I poured the fifty-dollar bottle down the drain."

"Waste of fifty dollars. You should have given it to me."

"That's what it cost me to quit," I said. "Since then, I've sometimes craved the taste of it, but it's been easy to resist. Those fifty dollars bought me a fight with the devil, and I walked away the winner."

"Now you sound like the writer." Maya snickered. "Speaking of, now that I finished writing The Boy Who Played With Voodoo Dolls—"

"You really went with Fred's title?"

"I liked it."

"Never tell him that."

"He's getting a copy."

"You'll never hear the end. He's going to name every article you write from here on out."

"Good. I suck with titles. And now that I finished that one, I need a new one. Since Jonah hasn't assigned me anything, and he hasn't promoted me—"

"Yet," I said.

"Yet. Since he hasn't promoted me yet—wait until he reads that mother freaking article, though. Anyway, I'm still in the business of finding subjects to write about. Do you have any ongoing cases?"

"Yes," I said, nodding my head. "Three of them, none of which seem solvable."

"Yummy. That's my favorite. Supernaturally themed?"

"We have a ghost."

"Mm."

"Changeling."

"Sexy."

"Doppelgänger."

"Wow. A changeling and doppelgänger at the same time? That's more of a supernatural mystery than the actual mysteries. How did you manage that?"

"The ghost case involves a dead wife haunting her husband—and I believe that's also an impersonation attempt."

"Three for three, then?"

"Yup."

"It seems like you might have a Joker."

"What does that mean?"

"Every Batman has a Joker," Maya said. "Every Superman has a Lex Luthor. Every Spider-Man has a Green Goblin."

"You think someone has noted puny me, and they have coordinated three different cases at the same time to... what? That's more unbelievable than ghosts existing."

"But more believable than you have three doppelgänger cases at once." Maya sighed into the receiver, blowing a gust of static into my ear. "Anyhow, I'm not working tonight. I'm celebrating. Also, we can move my niece into my place. Now that I have the article written and submitted, there's no reason for her to stay at your apartment. I'll house her until we can find or contact her mom. God, I hate my sister so much. Who just leaves their kid like that?"

"I don't know, but I don't think my spine can handle another night's sleep on the sofa. Thank you for taking her off my hands."

"So, you going to tell me or not?"

"Tell you what?"

"About your doppelgänger cases. Do I get to know the juicy details?"

"I'll tell you later this evening, when Alina and I come by."

"Eek," she squealed into the phone. "I'm so excited! When are you coming by?"

I glanced at my watch, confirming the time. "Alina's permit states she has to work until 1700hrs."

"Five o'clock," Maya said, gurgling annoyance.

"Whatever. We'll swing by my apartment when she's off and grab her stuff—it's not a lot—then we'll head over to your place. Alina knows how to get there, yeah?"

"You don't know where I live?"

"Why would I? I've never been over."

"You're an ex-cop, current investigator. You give off serial killer, creeper vibes. I figured you had followed me home before. My bad." Maya chuckled. "I'm just kidding. You think I'd allow my favorite niece to sleep over at your apartment if I thought you would murder her? Calm down, Nancy Drew."

"What does that even mean?"

"I think Nancy Drew was this volatile, expressive woman who let no one ever slight her. So, she's infamous for having this quick temper, but also for perceiving everything as a slight. People say she would snap if they said her name wrong—which to her was always said wrong."

"Did you just make all that up?"

"No. Of course not."

"Nancy Drew is a fictional teenage detective."

"I may have made up a little of it. How do you know who Nancy Drew is, nerd?"

"I enjoy reading."

"Then read my article when it's published. You'll enjoy the rather sexy, long-legged, big-busted heroine and her dopey, aloof, awkward-looking sidekick."

"Did you just describe yourself in purely physical terms—like a bad male noir writer who's never been laid?"

Maya snickered. "Intelligent. Capable. Independent. Strong. Resourceful. Would you see a movie about a woman with those descriptors? Or read a book? 'Female main character is an intelligent and capable woman, resourceful and independent, and strong. She doesn't need a man, because she's a woman.'"

I rolled my eyes. Alina and Maya had a few things in common—their middle name (Mylene), their grating persistence on any topic they wanted to dig into, and their inexplicable ability to talk about nothing for far too long, especially about things they didn't really care about or believe in. They just... talked to hear their voices, or to fill the quiet cracks in life, or to watch their speaking companion squirm.

"No one reads that book or watches that movie," Maya said. "Do you know why?"

"I don't really care."

"It's boring. But… if I threw up a poster of a woman in skimpy clothes that really highlighted her curves and showed off her tanned skin, and I hand her a weapon, who's not seeing that movie? *Tomb Raider. Underworld. Wonder Woman. Black Widow.* All the aforementioned boring descriptors are implied through the woman's sex appeal. Why? People flock toward sex and sexiness, whether they want to admit to it."

I sniffled, running a finger across my nose and staring at the street. I debated disconnecting the call and not entertaining Maya's rant. Instead, my lesser self got the better of me. "Remember a couple weeks ago when you lectured me about how the entertainment industry exploits women for their bodies, or sex, or something along those lines? It's hard for me to follow what you actually believe sometimes."

Maya sighed. "I just want conversation—maybe a little debate. That's all."

"What do you think, though? What's your actual opinion?"

Maya chuckled. "August, you sweet, naïve child. Nobody actually cares about my opinion. They only care that what I say aligns with their opinion. That's the secret to journalism."

I scratched my head and popped a knuckle as my heart dropped into my stomach. "Honestly, Maya? That's where you stand?"

"What's that mean?"

"I mean, what was it, three years ago... you dropped out of medical school and dedicated your life to the truth? To finding and to telling the truth, no matter the consequences. You told me you never had a dream because your parents never taught you how to dream. I thought that was beautiful and haunting. Then one day you came into work at the bookstore, and you said you found your purpose. Your destiny, I believe you called it. For whatever reason, you were incensed with the mainstream media—about their lies and their agendas and their catering to the fanbase. You swore you would change that. You would sift through the lies and filter out the truth. You would present that truth, nothing but the truth, no matter how offensive or hard it was to hear."

"Truth isn't opinion," Maya said, her voice quiet. I think I had struck a nerve.

"Not always," I said. "But you can find your opinions on truth and evidence. Rather than wobbling from one side to the next for the sake of argument, find the truth—not your truth—but the truth. Find it and report it like you promised you would. I mean, that's why we're celebrating tonight, right? You finally finished that article. You submitted it. If Jonah approves, he'll hire you full time. *Here & Now* isn't ideal. That's what you said. But it's a stepping stone." I popped my knuckles again, having to catch my breath. I wasn't used to speaking so many words at one time. It was quite exhausting, and I wasn't sure how Maya and Alina performed such verbal marathons so often. "Don't slip on the stone and fall into the water. But don't get scared to move forward to the next stone and cross that river."

"Your metaphors suck."

"You get what I'm saying, though, don't you? Keep moving toward your goal. You will help thousands, if not millions, of people."

"Sometimes I really hate you. Like a lot." I could almost visualize her pouty lips and wide eyes as she said that.

"See you tonight?"

"Seven o'clock," she said.

"1900hrs. I'll be there."

Moving Out. Wednesday, April 27th, 1706hrs.

FRED AND ALINA FUNNELED out of the office and headed toward the stairwell, chatting about some movie I had never heard of. Their voices faded into mere echoes, then disappeared altogether.

I remained in the leased space, collecting any paperwork I thought I might need later on. If Maya planned to drink herself into oblivion, I would most likely make sure she safely returned from oblivion and into the land of the living. Rather than sitting around staring at walls, I would pick away at the pending investigations. I gathered my thin, nearly empty case file on the changeling mystery and headed toward the door, locking it behind me.

Sarah Herling also filed into the hallway, carrying a briefcase in one hand and a purse slung over her shoulder. Her tawny hair had loosened throughout the day, and it lay in skinny strands across her face.

"Hey," she said. "Calling it quits for the day?"

"Never," I said, securing the deadbolt and sliding my key from the lock. "I'm one of those obnoxious people who can't leave work at work. It's always with me. I just grow tired of the acrid stench that we can't seem to get rid of."

"Have you tried candles?"

"Candles. Air fresheners. Open windows. Those pine trees you hang in cars."

"Ew. Gross."

"Yeah, it was gross. It made everything so much worse."

"Your office sits right atop the kitchen, though," Sarah said.

"The agent never disclosed that information to me. I signed the lease, and the owner of this building laughed all the way to the bank."

Sarah tilted her head and smirked off the side of her mouth. She always looked stunning, but in that simple gesture, her personality bled into appearance. I saw a shy, driven woman with simple humor and exhausted from a hard work ethic.

Before I knew what I was doing or could stop myself, words sprouted off my tongue and blossomed from my lips. "What are you doing tomorrow night?"

Sarah's head straightened, and she pinched her shoulders back, stiffening her posture—a nearly reflexive reaction. If I had to bet, many men had asked her a similar question, and she had practiced that motion many times, turning them away through her rigid demeanor.

Her hesitation allowed me a window to backtrack and find an excuse for the question. "We can get together for dinner, maybe downstairs, and go over the case," I said. Somehow, the proposition made everything worse. "We don't have to, either. We can always meet in your office again. Or in mine. Or anywhere." *Shut up, August.* I barely enjoyed speaking when I had something to say, so why did my mouth continue to move when I so desperately wanted to stop sputtering words? At that moment, I fully understood Maya's and Alina's incessant need to fill the quiet spaces of time. If the silence stretched any longer, I would have to scream—just one long scream—to fill the void.

Luckily, Sarah cleared her throat—a gentle cough. "Yeah."

"Yeah?"

"I've never eaten down there, but I've always wanted to. Is it good?"

I scratched the back of my neck and chuckled. "I've never eaten down there either." I hadn't realized that before. Whenever Fred complained about his hunger, which happened frequently, we always left the building and walked or drove somewhere else to eat, never even considering stepping downstairs and eating at the built-in restaurant attached to our building. "I don't know if it's any good."

"Is it open?" Sarah asked. "I don't know if I've ever seen anyone in there." Her face brightened with a smile, and that shy woman transformed into something different—energetic and spunky. "Why don't we check? It's only downstairs three flights."

"You make a sound argument." I gestured for her to lead the way. "I can see why you're a lawyer."

When we came to the sidewalk, we walked right past Alina and Fred. I glanced at them from the corner of my eye, cherishing the look of utter bewilderment splashed across their faces. Fred's mouth hinged, moving up and down, but no words escaped his lips. Alina squinted at us, as if she couldn't quite believe what she saw.

Sarah and I rounded the corner and entered the restaurant. It had red walls, gold trim and light fixtures, and hardwood floors. It looked more like a lounge than a restaurant, but a few patrons sat at the tables.

"What do you know?" Sarah said, looking up at me. "They're open. Says right here. 4:30. That's probably why I see no one around at lunchtime."

"Perfect for an early dinner."

Sarah giggled, shaking her head and heading toward the door. "Okay."

"What?" I asked, chasing after her.

"I struggle to leave work on-time, as it is. From my inability to escape the office, I see most days that you suffer the same affliction. We're workaholics, addicted to the job." Outside, she stopped and wheeled around, facing me. "Early dinner won't work. How about 6:30 tomorrow night, though? A proper dinner time, and it allows me to stay late and work on my case."

"I thought we were going to work on the case at dinner?"

Sarah smirked. I couldn't get over her bubbly personality. She seemed to smile and laugh like it might save her life. "We will. What? You think this is a date?"

I glanced off to the side at the question, avoiding her gaze. A dozen feet away, leaning against the restaurant's brick wall, Fred and Alina stared right back at me, watching us.

"You're too easy," Sarah said. "I'll see you tomorrow." She offered one last smile before walking away.

I shuffled to Fred and Alina, my hands stuffed in my pockets.

"Well, well, well," Fred said. "Mr. Loverboy himself. Glacia last night, Cambria Friday night, and now Sarah. Wow. Everything I ever said about you not knowing how to behave around women... I gladly eat my hat."

"Thank you!" I said, excited that someone else other than me used that phrase.

Fred patted Alina on the shoulder. "Don't let his recent behavior fool you, Padawan. In the twenty years I've known this man, he's had one girlfriend."

"Oh, don't worry," Alina said, "he's not fooling me. He seems like a one girlfriend in twenty years kind of guy."

"I'm right here," I said, cracking a knuckle.

"Well, feel comfortable in the fact I wouldn't say a word behind your back that I wouldn't say to your face," Alina said.

I exhaled and stared across the street at the passing traffic. "Anyway, Maya submitted her article. We're moving you out of my apartment and into her house. Yay for everyone!"

"Tonight?"

"What do you mean tonight?" I asked. "You have one bag of clothes. It's not like we're moving my entire apartment over there."

"No, but you promised me we could watch the original Star Wars trilogy."

"I never said that."

"Well, you implied it."

"Not once."

"Why are you so lame? It's just a movie."

I narrowed my eyes, confused by her outburst. When I glanced at Fred for some kind of answer, he shook his head, frowning. Without a clue to Alina's strange behavior, I pushed forward. I could have asked her what's wrong, but she would have denied anything was bothering her. Besides, I didn't feel qualified to hound a teenage girl about her emotions. I barely felt qualified to discuss emotions with a teenage boy.

"Fred, see you tomorrow?"

"Nine sharp," he said, grinning. Work began at 0800hrs.

"We have customers these days paying for our services, meaning you have income. Meaning, get to work on time."

"Have you seen the Europeans and how they live? Work doesn't even begin until eleven in the morning. Later. They stay up late and enjoy life. They wake up slow. Look at how happy they are compared to us Americans."

"You sound like Alina. Stop arguing baseless arguments and making up random facts to support them. See you tomorrow at 0800hrs."

"What's so wrong about sounding intelligent?" Alina asked, perking up again. Whatever shadow had fallen over her sunny, energetic disposition passed.

We bid farewell to Fred and piled into my Honda, driving to my apartment, and collecting Alina's belongings. She spoke the entire time, about everything and nothing at all. It was a special skill she possessed to speak about such a broad range of topics without really speaking in depth about anything.

Maya had texted me her address, but I never plugged it into my navigation. Alina directed me there. As we drove from my place to Maya's, Alina once again grew quiet.

"You okay?" I asked, deciding to explore the territories of a friend.

I had only known Alina for a short time, but we had already experienced a lot together. I didn't think it was too far of a stretch to consider her one of my few friends. In fact, I could probably count all of my friends on one hand—not including family. Fred. Maya. Alina... maybe.

"Fine," she said—short, gruff, bitten off.

I popped a knuckle and held my tongue. If she didn't want to talk, who was I to force the issue? I would compliment her desires to remain quiet. Except Alina and quiet had never got along too well.

"Here's the thing, Dummy—since you're obviously too thick to see it."

"Insults are your love language, aren't they?" I asked, turning to her and grinning.

"My entire life I've moved. I lived with my grandma and my other grandma. I lived with my mom and dad. With just my dad. With just my mom. Neither of them could ever afford an apartment for too long, so we constantly moved. We lived in Stockton. Lodi. Sacramento. We were homeless for a second. I lived with foster parents for a year. It just seems..." she trailed off and shook her head, staring out the passenger window. "I lived with you for a few days. Now I'm moving in with Maya. When my mom shows back up, I'll move back in with her until she leaves again. I'm sixteen, and I've never had a home, like an actual home." She brushed her shoulder across her face. "I didn't even like living with you. Your apartment sucked, and it didn't have a TV or any food, but... but it was something. And Maya's will be something, too. Yet, maybe in a day, maybe in a week, maybe in a month, I'll move again."

I fished into my pocket, grabbing a stick of gum, and chewing on it.

How did I respond to that? My parents had lived in the same mansion since I was twelve. They had never left me, had never sent me off to live with anyone else. They had always been there when I needed them. I had no perspective on what Alina felt, and I had no right offering her any advice. No wonder why I only had two-and-a-half friends. I had nothing to offer in the way of help.

Except... maybe I did. I had my time and my money to offer, what little of that existed.

"Glacia gifted her Nana's house to me," I said.

"She told me she would. I said it was a bad idea. You suck at taking care of things. Glacia ignored me. She likes you. I mean, likes you, likes you. I think you're okay enough to hang around, but you're not really the liking type, you know?"

"I don't know, and you don't have to expound on that. What I was going to say, when title goes through, and my lease ends on this apartment, and I have the time to move, well... I'll make you a room. No. Let me rephrase that. I'll give you a room, one which you can make into whatever you want. I'll furnish that room and stock it for you, and you can come over whenever you want and hide in there and watch movies for weeks on end. Maybe it's not a home, but it will be yours—a safe place for you and you only."

Alina turned away from the passenger window and looked at me, her eyes filled with tears. "A projection screen?"

"What?"

"I want a projection screen, not a television. I want it to take up the entire wall. And surround sound."

"I mean, I'm not Bill Gates, so we'll have a budget, but I'll do my best. Sure."

"Why?"

"Why what?"

"Why do that for me? Why do you care?"

I thought of Aaron Brooks lying dead on the asphalt, murdered by me. I thought of my inability to confront his parents and endure their wrath face-to-face. I thought of the three years I had lost to alcohol and my fears, how I had done nothing positive or selfless in that time.

"We're all lost," I said. "We're all looking for a home, or a place where we belong. You helped put me on the right track. You cleaned my apartment, you worked your voodoo magic on Glacia."

"Too soon." Alina snickered at the reference, though.

"You helped me realize the world is a better and happier place when I'm outside my head. So, if this helps repay you, or if it helps to give you some kind of home, I'm more than happy to do this for you. Besides, what else would I do with the extra room?"

"Can I take the master?"

"Not a chance."

As we pulled into Maya's driveway, Alina snapped her fingers. "I al-most forgot to tell you. I'm so sorry. Sometimes I get all jammed up in the head, and I... you know how it goes. I can't think right, or I just lose my train of thought."

"I get it," I said, again remembering my years as a drunk, lost in my all-consuming thoughts.

"Anyway, I spoke to Shelly Dupree's best friend, Tina... what's her last name? It doesn't matter right now. I have it in my notes. Anyway, I learned Tina's name through Vincent."

"Dr. Dupree."

"Sure. Anyway, he also provided me with her contact information. I didn't want to cold call her, so I emailed her. She responded within the hour, asking me to call. We spoke for a while. Tina said Shelly was meeting with someone before her death, but she didn't know who. I asked about another man, and Tina said no. 'Shelly would never have an affair. She loved Vincent.' Tina said his name, not me. That was a quote."

I rolled my eyes.

"I asked her how she knew Shelly met with someone in secret then, if it was a secret. Tina said, 'I know Shelly, and I know when she's keeping something from me.' Tina pushed the issue, and Shelly confessed to speaking with someone from her past. That's it. Apparently, she wouldn't reveal any more information. She wanted to play it safe, or slow, something like that."

"Someone from her past?" I asked.

"I think Fred's and my hunch might be right. She found her biological mom or dad or someone, and that's who she secretly met with."

I cut the ignition to the car and stared out the windshield at Maya's tan garage door. How could we identify this mystery person? I would have to speak to Vincent again to see if he couldn't hand over Shelly's phone records. Maybe his wife had spoken with the unidentified subject over the phone. I doubted that. I'm sure Vincent would have looked, had he suspected anything. Except, did he suspect anything? Had Tina come forward and shared her knowledge with him? I could also ask Dr. Dupree to share Shelly's email login information. It seemed more likely any distant-based conversations had taken place over email or social media than on the phone. Last, I could ask for her credit card receipts and visit every place she had frequented without Dr. Dupree in attendance, ask the staff if they noticed Shelly with someone else, or try to convince them to allow me access to their security footage.

"During my conversation with Mr. Dupree," Alina said.

"Dr. Dupree."

"I asked him if Shelly ever subscribed to one of those family tree websites, where you send them a swab of spit and they insert your DNA into their database, using it to find any ancestors or current but unknown family members. He said she had, about three months before she passed."

My heart jack hammered in my chest. Did we have a lead?

"Did you get her login information?"

"Nope. I didn't. I'm a complete idiot with no clue how to tell east from west, let alone think of asking for her login information."

I shrugged. "Why do you have to be sarcastic?"

"Of course I asked for the login information. Why do you have to ask?"

"And?"

"Dr. Dupree didn't know. He said he would look through some of her old files and see if he could find it. I'm sure it's saved in her browser, though. I asked him if we could swing by tomorrow and try to hack into it. He has to work, but he told me where he left the spare key. If we can access her account, we can confirm any long-lost family she may have found and met up with."

The garage door opened, revealing Maya standing before us with her hands planted to her hips.

Alina released a nervous laugh, almost like a burp. "I think we're in trouble."

Pregame. Wednesday, April 27th, 1809hrs.

Maya brought Alina and me through her garage into the mudroom, which cornered into the kitchen. A cramped space barely big enough for the dishwasher to open fully. She grabbed a hard seltzer from the refrigerator and tossed it to Alina. The teenage girl caught it midair.

"What are you doing?" I asked, stepping toward Alina and snagging the alcoholic beverage from her.

Maya rose on tiptoes and stretched to the cabinet above the fridge, fingering a bottle of tequila from the shelf. She padded over to me, snatched the skinny can from my hand, and returned it to Alina. "We're celebrating," she said.

"I'm sober, remember? She's underage."

"Oh, please," Maya said. "It's not like she's never had a drink before."

"My mom used to serve me boxed wine with dinner," Alina said, cracking the can.

My mouth fell open, and I narrowed my eyes, confused. "Really, Maya?"

"What?"

"Her mom did it, so it's okay with you? That's the example you want to follow. Where's her mom now?" I regretted the question the instant I asked it.

Alina popped her lips. "Good question, Sherlock."

"Listen," Maya said, skirting Alina's missing mother, "in Europe and Russia, they serve alcohol to kids all the time. Like to twelve-year-old kids. I don't even think there's a legal limit for beer. In fact, I'm pretty sure they consider beer a soft drink, like a soda."

"Why does everyone keep telling me about what Europe does?" I asked. "Why do we care? Unless I'm mistaken, Americans fought for their independence against Europe."

"Great Britain," Alina said. "But sure, that's in Europe."

I massaged my shoulders, which had grown increasingly tense. "We're in America, either way. Twenty-one is the legal drinking age."

"But in two years, Alina can fight in a war?" Maya asked. "Does that make any sense?"

"What are you even talking about?" I asked, realizing my mistake. I should have never, not in a million lifetimes, shown up at Maya's house with Alina. The two of them would argue endlessly about anything at all. I sighed, defeated, already exhausted by their shenanigans.

"Listen," Maya said, slightly slurring her words. She was already a little buzzed, which explained her carefree attitude and her eagerness to pressure someone else into drinking with her—it's never fun to drink alone. "Listen, okay, buckaroo."

"Buckaroo?" I asked.

"You're just some dude who Alina stayed with. I'm her aunt. Her blood. You have no voice in the matter. If the girl wants to drink, let her drink."

I glanced at Alina. The girl chomped on the corner of her lip, contemplative. "Just one," she said after a second, raising an eyebrow. "Please, Dad. That's all."

"Just one!" Maya said, skittering forward and hugging Alina. "I love you, kiddo."

"Love you, too," Alina said, lifting the can to her lips and sipping.

I paced out of the kitchen into the nook, sitting at the round table and slapping my work folders before me. I removed a single leaf of skeletal notes, which traced Miette's changeling situation.

"What's this?" Maya asked, moving over to me and swiping the college-ruled paper off the desk. She regarded it for a few seconds. "Your client is a changeling, huh?"

"So she's accused," I said.

"And what exactly is a changeling?"

"A fairy resembling a human, believed to be left as a replacement for a kid stolen by the fae. The child's parents then raise the changeling, who adopts the appearance of the kid they replaced—apparently, humans provide a better and safer upraising than their fae family could provide."

"So, your client is a changeling. She replaced the actual child, though no one knew any different?" Maya asked, drinking straight from the tequila bottle. "And now that actual child has returned, and she plans to expose your client for the fraud she is?"

"That's the gist."

"I thought you had a doppelgänger case?" Maya asked.

"I do."

"You promised to brief me on that."

"You want to know now?"

"While I'm sober-ish and functioning, yes."

I shared Claire Balzan's story with Maya, from the infidelity sex tape to the security video of her brutally murdering Dr. Woods. "Other than her on camera committing the acts, investigators found Claire's hair at the homicides. There's also a clear-cut motivation."

"If it's so clear-cut, why are you investigating this case?"

Much like Sarah had admitted, I whole-heartedly believed Claire was innocent. I had copped for five years before the incident with Aaron Brooks. I had a solid grasp on when people lied, especially regarding a crime they claimed innocence to. With Claire, though, I had this gut-wrenching, sinking feeling that despite all the evidence stacked against her, she was innocent. Maybe that instinct, that innate hunch, was, in its own way, supernatural, which was the most ironic of all.

I didn't believe in the supernatural world. I wanted to—I drastically and desperately wanted to. If ghosts existed, then maybe I could communicate with Aaron and tell him I'm sorry. I think I needed that for my soul, so I clung to the hope that the supernatural existed. Except, I didn't believe it. Most paranormal experiences hinge on a mentally unstable or intoxicated or manipulated or fragile mind. They occur at night, in shadows, when paranoia and fear pinnacles in the human mind. Maybe my desperation, my reaching and hoping mind believed Claire's innocence, clung to my hunch that she was innocent, because I wanted to believe that. So, what difference was there between my hope and someone believing in vampires?

"Hello! Earth to August. You there?" Maya waved her hand before my face.

"Sorry," I said. "I lost myself in thought."

"Why are you accepting this case if she's obviously guilty?"

"Because I don't think she is."

"Do you have a crush on her?"

"No. She's a recent widow."

"You can't have a crush on a widow?"

"I don't have a crush on her."

"Is she pretty?" Maya asked.

I sighed, knowing she would persist until satisfied. "Yes."

"Well, there you go. August couldn't pass up on a pretty girl, even if video and DNA evidence proved her a murderer."

"Pretend, for the sake of conversation, she's innocent," I said.

"Sure. She's innocent. Ms. Pretty Pants, and notice how I removed the R from her title, is, for the sake of a conversation, innocent." Maya pulled another quick drink from the bottle, grimacing and coughing into a fist.

Alina sat across from me at the table, nursing her hard seltzer.

"Where do we start?" I asked.

"What do you mean?" Maya scrunched her face, as if I had asked her the simplest question in the world and it confused her. "Same place you start in any other investigation. Canvassing. Interviewing anyone and everyone who knew Robert Woods."

"And the husband," Alina said. "Simon."

"And Claire's husband. Did they have any enemies? Did they have debts? A drug addiction? Were they acting strange in the past few days of their lives? Et cetera, et cetera."

"You don't think the police have already explored those avenues?" I asked. "I mean, if we're going to convince them that the woman on video murdering another human isn't Claire, we need something unique."

"I don't think the police have explored any avenues for the exact reason you just laid out," Maya said. "They're strolling down Main Street, not even glancing in the rearview mirror. They have video evidence. A murder weapon. DNA. Motive. Open and shut."

"So what would the great Maya Adler do?" I asked.

"Honestly, I would interview—what's her husband's name?" She glanced at Alina, snapping her fingers.

"Simon."

"I would interview Simon's parents. What did they think about Claire? How did they feel about the relationship? From there, branch out to Simon's friends to see what they have to say about Claire. Create a profile on the woman. Was she volatile? Passionate? Jealous? Calm? It won't solve your case, but it might open a few new doors."

I sighed. "You're right."

"Of course I'm right. Also, if you think she's innocent, what's that mean?"

"Someone else did it," Alina said, stealing another drink from her hard seltzer.

"Bingo," Maya said, pointing at her niece.

"Someone else impersonated Claire, planted evidence to frame her for committing the crime, and made sure security footage caught her in the act," I said. "The person planned it, though, beginning with the infidelity, moving to the stolen drugs, and ending in the homicides."

Maya nodded like a proud teacher who had coaxed a slow student into the correct answer. "Who would want Dr. Woods and Mr. Simon Balzan dead? Who hated Claire enough to destroy her entire life? Find that person, and you find your doppelgänger."

I stared at the case file regarding Miette Verdin, the changeling. "Same with her," I said. "I should interview Miette's parents, ask if they suspected their daughter ever... suddenly acted strangely when she was a girl."

"Or went missing," Alina said.

"If she has siblings, they might know even better," Maya said. "Siblings often have better insight into each other than parents have of their children. Speak to any brothers or sisters she has. See if her behaviors ever drastically differed from one day to the next."

"Except, she hired me to find out who her stalker is and get rid of her, not prove she's a changeling."

Maya scratched her chin for a second. "You said she had an ex-boyfriend who cut off all contact once this... Vanessa appeared in their lives."

"Yeah," I said, knowing exactly what to do. "I'll contact him first."

Maya made a fist with her right hand, poking out one finger, counting as she spoke. "Doppelgänger. Interview Simon's family and friends, as well as Claire's family and friends. How did they feel about Claire? Did anyone hate her or hold a grudge against her? Maybe look into Simon's exes before he and Claire got together. Maybe one of them still loved Simon and couldn't let him go." Maya counted a second finger. "Interview the Changeling's ex-boyfriend and see what he knows about the stalker girl. If nothing, interview Miette's family about anything strange from her childhood—a day or two she went missing or sudden odd behavior." She straightened a third finger. "Don't forget to compliment Maya Mylene Adler for how freaking intelligent and witty she is, and that she's a smoke show. I'm halfway to mars right now, and I'm still the most valuable investigator on these cases." The fourth finger lifted. "I'm getting drunk now. My favorite bar has karaoke night tonight, and Mariah Carey is screaming for me to let her out." She smacked the table, raising all five fingers high into the air. "Also, I almost forgot." Maya grinned, proud of whatever she meant to reveal.

"What?" I asked.

"I had to call him and thank him."

"Call who?" I asked as realization donned on me. "No, you didn't. Maya, did you really?"

"I did."

"Why?"

"Because without him, I wouldn't have had a story to write, and I wouldn't have guaranteed myself this promotion."

"Wait," Alina said. "You called Eddie?"

Maya smirked and pinched back her shoulders. "I did."

"What did you say to him?" Alina asked.

"I asked if that prison booty treats him better than I did. He didn't respond to that, so I thanked him for being a selfish, psychotic, murderous butt-head."

"You used butt-head?" I asked.

"I did. Something about the juvenility of the word makes it so much more painful."

"I don't think that's true."

"Well, I used it. I told him I submitted the article which featured him and highlighted his absolute crazy. He said to me, 'You're welcome. I hope it works out.' I nearly jumped through the phone and kissed that sexy mouth of his."

"He's a murderer," I said.

"Doesn't mean he doesn't have a sexy mouth."

I glanced at Alina. "A little help, please."

"He was a moron," the girl said, setting her can on the kitchen table. "I hated his guts. But he was a sexy moron, and I hated his sexy guts."

I dropped my head to the table, surrendering, knowing I didn't stand a chance against those two.

The Dance. Wednesday, April 27th, 1932hrs.

I DROVE MAYA AND Alina to the bar—an old dive with sticky floors and a crowd who, all combined, had thirty teeth. No bouncer stood in a wide-stance with his arms crossed over his barrel chest at the front door. No cover charge to get inside.

A few bikers shot pool and stood around tall tables, wearing their club jackets and eyeing us as we crossed to the bar. A handful of blue-collar men sat at the counter, shooting whiskey and drinking light beer. Only a few women braved the dingy establishment. They danced with cowboys to a country song playing much too loud.

"This is your favorite bar?" I yelled over the music. "This place, where I'm more likely to get murdered than drunk?"

"Stop being a banana," Maya said. "It's the best bar in Sacramento."

"A banana?"

She waved at the bartender. "Nick!"

The broad-shouldered man turned around. He wore blue jeans and a gray Mickey Mouse T-shirt, and he sported a beard any man would be envious of. When he saw Maya, he grinned. The genuine smile shifted his face from bored to handsome. We could have walked onto a movie set, for all I knew, and he played the lead role in some romantic comedy starring Maya Adler and Nick the Bartender. They would, after a string of hiccups and poor timing, fall madly in love against all the odds.

"Maya, hey! How did the article end up?"

"Beautiful! Thanks for your help, by the way."

"Makes sense now," I said. "It is the best bar in Sacramento."

Maya gently elbowed me in the ribs, continuing in a flirtatious conversation with Nick the Lumberjack.

I glanced at Alina, who I only then realized was five years too young to be inside a bar. "Who is he?" I asked.

Alina shrugged. "Nick, from what I hear."

"Who's Nick?"

"That handsome bartender who looks like he could wrestle a bear and come out victorious."

"Thank you for your help."

"Any time."

"We're celebrating!" Maya said, elbowing me again. "Well, they're tagging along for the ride, and I'm celebrating. This is my niece, Alina." Maya ushered Alina forward, introducing her to Nick. "She's only sixteen, so she can't drink!"

"Pleasure to meet you, Alina!" Nick shouted. We all competed with the music.

"This is August, the investigator," Maya said, slapping me on the chest. At least she hadn't repeated the elbow blow. "He's the one from The Boy Who Played With Voodoo Dolls!"

"Oh, very cool! Great to meet you, August."

I offered a lip-exclusive smile and nodded at the bartender, not caring to shred my vocal chords to respond.

"He doesn't drink!" Maya said. "Two years sober."

"Congratulations," Nick said.

"Thanks!"

"So, only you're drinking tonight?" Nick asked.

"Only me!" Maya said. "Unless you care to jump in."

"I'm closing tonight. Sorry."

"Too bad."

Nick frowned and nodded, allowing the implications of 'too bad' to soak in. "The usual?" he asked.

"But a double tonight, baby," Maya said.

Nick made her a margarita, pouring a generous amount of celebratory tequila. We made our way to the corner of the establishment on the opposite side of the bikers. The small, enclosed, dusty space and the lack of proper air conditioning created a muggy environment. My shirt stuck to my chest, and sweat formed on my brow, dripping down the side of my body, and I hadn't done anything more than stand around and walk a few dozen feet.

A scrawny woman, somewhere between the ages of thirty and seventy, stumbled to our table after a few minutes. She carried two cans of beer, placing them on our table. Her blonde, straggly hair lay matted across her sweaty forehead, and she smelled of tobacco, marijuana, and booze—the holy trifecta of partying.

"Hi," she said, her voice a thick southern drawl. "Care to dance, big boy?" The woman touched my arm with her bony fingers, sending chills of revulsion through my body.

"No, but thank you," I said, politely nodding at her.

"He would love to dance!" Maya said, shouting louder than me and overriding my voice. "We came here especially for him. His name is August. He wanted to learn how to dance. So, be patient with him!"

I would have glared at Maya with a look to wither roses, but I feared taking my eyes off the strange woman. She reached out, offering me her hand.

I reluctantly accepted it.

"I'm Patricia," she said. "Patty to my friends. You want to be my friend, August?"

No, I thought. *Nope*. "Sure."

"I think we can be good friends."

"I think you two can be the best of friends!" Maya said. "Go easy on him. He's fragile."

Patty led me to the center of the dive bar. A country song played. I'm not too versed in country music, so I'm unsure about the artist or the title, but it had a beat one might consider two-step worthy, whatever that meant.

Patty, though, she ignored the country stomp, playing the city girl in a club. The woman—who wore a denim skirt, cowboy boots, a cowboy hat, and a flannel shirt—spun around and dropped low, grinding against my crotch.

I had a perfect view of Maya and Alina from where I awkwardly stood, and I glowered directly at them, not coming close to pretending to dance.

Both aunt and niece had their phones out, pointed at me, recording the spectacle.

The song must have been the longest-ever recorded country song. It lasted close to an eternity, one spent in Hell where the seconds dragged on for hours or days.

The woman wriggled and jiggled. She rocked back on her heels and dropped to her knees, crawled across the floor, and jumped back to her feet. It was, for me at least, like watching a reluctant demon get exorcised. Except, the demon exorcised was from my body. Patty's freedom of spirit and the way she moved about without a care in the world unlocked something deep and buried within me.

Without thinking, I grabbed the woman's hand and twirled her in a tight circle, pulling her into me so the back of her head rested on my shoulder. It was a simple gesture, but one I would have never considered performing a year ago, a month ago, a day ago.

The right for August Watson to enjoy a semblance of fun had ended five years ago, on July 18th.

"Thank you," I whispered to Patty as the song's last note finished, steeping the bar into a palpable silence—silence broken by the amused applause of Maya and Alina and a few other spectators.

The woman twisted away from me and grinned, curtsying.

I bowed.

"You owe me a drink," Patty said, her voice whiskey stained.

"Find me when you're thirsty." I returned to the booth, glaring at Maya with feigned anger. Whatever initial annoyance I had felt toward her evaporated under the heat of Patty's stomping feet. "I should kill you, right here and now."

"You were a natural out there," Maya said, chuckling. "You really know how to move."

I worked way too hard at suppressing laughter, failing miserably. The genuine amusement bubbled from my stomach, spritzing into my throat, and spilling off my lips. As I laughed—really laughed for the first time in years—the world slipped away. Nothing mattered in that moment but laughing and feeling happy and alive, almost like I was a kid who cared for nothing but having fun. There's something refreshing and revitalizing in that simple fact. Seeing life like a kid, even for a moment.

"Look what Fred texted back," Alina said, smirking and handing me her phone.

I wiped tears from my eyes—happy tears, of course—and read Alina's text message. Above the block of letters was a video of me standing statue-still while Patty cut loose.

I read Fred's response aloud, so Maya could hear. "He's too advanced with his moves. He's dancing so fast, it almost looks like he's standing still." I responded to Fred's comment with a few more riffs of laughter.

Alina accepted her phone from me, placing it face down on the table.

Maya stared at the dance floor, wearing a permanent grin. "I think someone wants round two."

I turned, glancing over my shoulder. Patty sat at the bar, looking back at me, signaling for me to join her with a single curl of her finger. "I made a promise to the pretty lady," I said, standing again. "Don't wait up for me, kids."

"Hi," Patty said when I sat beside her. "I'm ready for that drink."

"What would you like?" I asked, waving for Nick's attention.

"Whatever you're drinking."

"Water for me, but the bar is open to you. Pick your poison."

Patty bit her lip and hummed for a second, considering her options. "They have a special tonight. Two beers for the price of one. That's what I've been drinking."

Nick arrived, and I ordered the two-beer special. He cracked both cans, handing them over. After I paid, instead of excusing myself and rejoining Maya and Alina, I remained seated beside Patty. Still riding my earlier high, why not sit there and have a light conversation with a stranger? Except, it seemed my verbal skills diminished not only around pretty women, but all female strangers. I had zero words to speak, and no thoughts to think of.

Luckily, Patty broke the silence. "That your family?"

The woman didn't point anywhere, but I knew she meant Maya and Alina. For a split second, I entertained the idea of saying yes to her, of pretending like I had a wife and a teenage daughter, who we had—for some ungodly reason—brought into the dive bar.

"No. Friends. We're celebrating."

"Congratulations."

"You don't even know what for."

"Do I have to? Celebrating is enough reason for congratulations."

"Yeah, I guess you're right."

"What are you celebrating?"

"My friend submitted an important article to her boss this afternoon. She believes it will earn her a promotion."

"I hope it does."

"Me, too."

A silence built between us, but nothing awkward. It was almost comforting—like we both had a million things to say, but we found assurance through the mutual quiet.

"Thanks for the dance," Patty said after a minute.

"Thank you for approaching me. I can't remember the last time I had that much fun."

"Well, share that fun with your friends. Celebrate. You've entertained an old woman long enough."

"The pleasure was mine," I said, reaching out my hand. "Patty, don't be a stranger."

She broke off a smile that shaved years off of her face. Behind her leathered and wrinkled exterior, I saw a vibrant, joyous woman. "You know where to find me."

I returned to Maya and Alina, sitting at their table. For the first time in five years, I felt perfectly content.

Running Out of Time. Thursday, April 28th, 0233hrs.

Vincent Dupree awoke to something cold and metallic shoved deep into his mouth, deep enough that he gagged on the foreign object. A familiar pressing weight sat on his chest. Blackout curtains eliminated any hint of moonlight from his master bedroom, preventing Vincent from seeing much of anything beyond phantoms.

Still, he knew.

His wife's spirit had found substance and weight. She had materialized from the spiritual realm. She sat on him, pinning him to the bed, and she had shoved a gun into his mouth. Vincent's gun—the one he kept locked in a safe on the closet shelf. It required a passcode to open. Their anniversary. 1021. Shelly had known the code. That's how her spirit had grabbed the gun.

Did ghosts kill like this, though? With material human weapons? Or did they kill through paranormal means? Vincent shuddered, as he realized, however it happened, he would die.

That night, instead of drinking wine and watching a movie, falling asleep on his recliner, Vincent had braved another bedroom—his and her bedroom. Though his encounter the night before had terrified him to a degree, it had also excited him. He wanted to experience her weight once more. Her touch. He wanted her to come to him once again, so he had braved prying back the sheets to their marital bed and crawling onto the mattress for the first time in a year. Vincent had fallen asleep there, praying to Shelly that she return to him, even if that return meant his death.

"Please," he said, or rather grunted. The single, pleading word failed to take shape around the barrel of the gun—though whether he pleaded for his life or for death, not even he knew.

"It's almost time for you to die," the specter hissed, removing the weapon from Vincent's mouth. "But not tonight. You have one more day to live."

"Please," Vincent said again, and again his word failed. This time, sobs broke into a thousand pieces. "Why?"

The pressure eased from his chest.

Vincent remained in his bed for a few moments, panting and catching his breath, calming his nerves. Once a semblance of strength returned to his limbs, he stood, though still wobbly, and he cantered to the bedroom door, flipping on the light switch.

Nothing. No one.

His room was completely empty of anything that didn't belong there. Except for his gun. It rested on the nightstand like a stain. He hadn't taken it out of the case, not since the day he bought it three years ago.

Shelly had convinced him to purchase the firearm, though he hated the idea of owning a gun. However, her good friend had experienced a burglary, and Shelly did not want to go through the same trauma. So Vincent had purchased the handgun. He locked it in the case and set in his closet, never even considering removing it from its permanent home.

Only Shelly knew he owned it. Only Shelly knew the code to the safe box.

Vincent grabbed the gun off the nightstand, holding it outward of his body, pinching the handle between three fingers, as if carrying something vile. He placed it back in the safe, resetting the lock, and returning it to the top shelf.

He moseyed back over to his nightstand, sitting on the side of his bed, and staring at his cell phone. It was late, but August Watson had said to call, especially in case of an emergency.

The phone only rang once before August answered.

"I'm running out of time," Vincent said.

Early Morning. Thursday, April 28th, 0412hrs.

I HAD SLEPT POORLY before Vincent Dupree's phone call, and I hadn't slept at all after we ended the conversation. He had sounded like a man who jumped at his shadow, who saw demons in the mirror.

I hated thinking that he had driven himself into madness. What else was there to think, though? That his late wife had actually punched in the security code to his safe, removed his handgun, sat on his chest, and shoved the barrel of the weapon so deep into his mouth, he gagged?

Glacia had a background in psychiatry, with the criminally insane. She would have better insight into Dr. Dupree's behaviors and mental state than I had. If he suffered a psychological breakdown from his wife's death, Glacia would have solid advice for me to heed. Yet, I couldn't call her in the dead of night.

So, I had waited.

In the meantime, I opened the email Alina sent me the day before. It detailed all the progress we had made in Vincent Dupree's case, including a summary of her and Tina's conversation.

Tina, Shelly's best friend, believed Shelly had secretly met with someone in the months leading up to her death. Who? Tina insisted Shelly wouldn't cheat on Vincent, leaving a potential romance out of the question. That brought me back to what Fred and Alina had speculated. Shelly's parents had adopted her, and her biological family had found and contacted her.

Even if that theory proved correct... what did it matter? How did Shelly's biological family connect to Vincent Dupree and the ghost haunting him? They didn't, was the short and simple answer. They couldn't.

Again, my thoughts shifted to Dr. Dupree's mental state. What if his wife actually haunted him, but she haunted his mind? What if he had grabbed the gun from the closet and put in his mouth? What if, just before pulling the trigger, Dr. Dupree had exited from his fugue state, realizing his situation, and he blamed it on her ghost? Was that possible?

As the scenarios and the questions rolled around my head, I drifted into a light sleep, waking a couple hours later when the rising sun broke through Maya's living room window. I reached to the coffee table, grabbing my cell phone.

At a little past 0600hrs, I felt comfortable calling Glacia.

It went straight to her voicemail. After the tone, I held my breath, debating whether I should leave her a message. We would eventually have to talk again, though, considering she had gifted me her Nana's house.

So, I broke the silence right then.

"Hi. Sorry to call you so early, but one of my latest cases has... grown complicated and dangerous. I need an expert opinion from you. Call me back when you can." I ended the call and stared at my reflection from the black television screen.

Vincent Dupree's case had taken a fatal twist. Whether a mental breakdown or an actual threat, he needed help.

Miette Verdin claimed something bad would happen to her on May 5th.

Claire Balzan would face a criminal trial for crimes she insisted she didn't commit.

Three cases, all of them overwhelming, all of them hinging on my investigative success to save the clients.

I ran my fingers through my hair and sighed. Sitting on the couch, staring at my reflection in the television, saved no one. So, I dressed and readied for the day.

I arrived at the office a little after 0700hrs with a bag of bagels and a cup of coffee. Before unlocking the door, I checked across the hallway to see if Sarah was in, but her office lights were off.

Entering my small space, I shuffled to my desk and plopped into the chair, firing up my computer. As I clicked on the internet icon, my phone rang. I rushed to answer it, hoping to see Glacia's name stamped across the Lock Screen.

Instead, Dr. Dupree called.

"Hello," I said.

"Hi," he said, nearly out of breath.

"Is everything okay?"

"I couldn't sleep after what happened last night. So, I spent the night going through Shelly's files. She had her own office space within the house, and I never went in there after... after her death. I couldn't. It's just... it sounds stupid, I know, but that's where she lived." He exhaled, calming his nerves. "She has a book in there with a bookmark in it, somewhere halfway through. It's just, I don't know... she'll never finish that story. She painted, and she has unfinished paintings in the office. She has unfinished assignments from her job. Everything in there is... it's unfinished, and it'll remain unfinished because she has finished her life." Vincent rambled, sounding more like a broken man than ever before.

I listened to him, though; acted as his sounding board.

"Anyway, I braved her office last night. I forced myself to. I found her login credentials to everything—to her email and the ancestry site. Your intern, Alina, asked about them."

My heart fluttered. "She told me."

"It's the same username and password for most of her accounts. Would you like me to send it over?"

"Yes, please. Did you look at it? At the ancestry results, that is?"

"I couldn't convince myself to, if that makes sense. I want to know, but I don't want to be the one to find out."

My computer pinged as the text message from him came in. I opened it. Dr. Dupree had sent the login credentials to a genealogy website. I copied the URL into the search bar, tapped on the login option, and carefully typed in Shelly's information.

The screen loaded. I stared at the homepage for a few seconds, holding my breath with anticipation.

"Mr. Watson, are you still there?" Dr. Dupree asked.

"I'm here."

"What do you see?"

"Nothing yet." I had never used an ancestry service before, and I didn't know how to navigate to the results. After a few seconds, I found an option for DNA relatives. The page loaded.

"There's one match," I said.

"What does that mean?"

"Shelly had a sister."

A photograph appeared, and beneath it, a name. "Shannon Pellegri," I said.

"That's her sister?"

"Born December 31st, 1961."

"That can't be right," Dr. Dupree said. "That was Shelly's birthday."

I squinted, studying results, confirming what I suspected. "Dr. Dupree, I have to go."

"What did you learn? Does she have a sister or not?"

"Yes. A twin. An identical twin."

I rushed Dr. Dupree off the phone, needing to contact Ted Wilson, my contact in the Sacramento Police Department. He and I had attended the same police academy together. We maintained a professional relationship throughout the years, and he had stayed in touch after my incident with Aaron Brooks. I wouldn't call him a friend. We weren't grabbing drinks after working every Friday or watching the game together on Sunday, but he was someone I could reach out to when needed.

As I scrolled to his number, my phone vibrated again.

Glacia's name appeared. My thumb hovered over the accept button for a moment. I had made a breakthrough in the case, though, and I had to follow up on it. Reluctantly, I ignored her call and dialed Wilson.

"Wow. You are prompt. How did you hear?" Wilson answered. "Media doesn't even know yet."

"Hear about what?" I asked, popping a knuckle.

"Well, you didn't hear it from me. Blame it on Jerry Gross. That dude can't shut up. Anyway, Jerry blabbed to you about the latest murder—third of its kind. Three murders of the same MO point to a serial killer, by definition."

"There's a serial killer in Sacramento?"

"Big time. A brutal one, too. Nasty stuff."

"I've heard nothing about that." I had been so invested in my ongoing cases, I had grown blind to the world around me. Also, until I closed the files on these cases, I would have to remain blind. "It doesn't matter right now."

"Doesn't matter. The murders are right up your alley. Vampire stuff."

My interest piqued. "Vampire stuff? Like, what? Bite marks?"

"Kind of. Not the whole fang situation, but bites to primary arteries, tearing them from the victims' bodies. We think the psycho drinks their blood, or at least collects and stores it for a rainy day."

"Three murders like that?"

"Tres, mi amigo."

I bit my upper lip, torn. I wanted to ask more questions and learn the finer details about the potential serial killer, but I already had enough on my plate, and unless the department contracted and compensated me to assist them, I had to focus on my paying clients.

"Hire me as a consultant. Otherwise, I'm blind and deaf."

"Your growing popularity has changed you. You've sold out."

"I've decided I enjoy running water."

"That's fair," Wilson said.

"Do you have a second?"

"No more, no less."

"I'm working on this case right now, and I need your input."

"You'll have to hire me as a consultant, brother, otherwise I'm blind and deaf."

"A year ago," I continued, "a man's wife died—fell off a cliff while hiking."

"He push her?"

"No." I really didn't know, but law enforcement never investigated or charged Vincent Dupree for the murder. "Recently, the ghost of his wife has returned, and she's haunting him. She shoved a gun into his mouth last night, threatened to kill him soon. Gun was in a locked safe. When he turned on the lights, no one was in his room."

"He going crazy?" Wilson didn't really ask, but accused. In his mind, I'm not sure if another option existed.

"I considered that possibility."

"But?"

"But I recently learned his late wife had a twin sister no one knew about. My question to you, at what point should I hand this case over to police? Will they take a ghost story seriously?"

"Has he harmed himself?" Wilson asked, still stuck on Dr. Dupree having lost his mind.

"No."

"Has a theft or burglary occurred? Has anyone harmed him?"

"Someone shoved a gun into his mouth."

"He legally owns the gun?"

"Yes."

Wilson clicked his tongue. "We can knock on his door and ask him about the incident from last night, or any other incidents he believed someone had trespassed in his home."

"Someone shoved a gun in his mouth and threatened his life."

"But he claims his wife's ghost performed that crime, as well as the other crimes."

I popped a knuckle. "Yes."

"Best I can do is to consider this a call from a concerned citizen. We'll head out to his place for a welfare check, ask him a few questions. If he doesn't cooperate, though, we can't really do much for him."

Based on my experience as a cop, that's pretty much what I expected Wilson to say. But I had to make sure. Each department operated from different laws and procedures, and politics and time constantly changed the way policing happened.

"Did the dead wife and her secret sister have correspondence?" Wilson asked.

I opened Shelly's messages on the ancestry site, skimming through her conversation with Shannon. After a handful of seconds, I said, "Yes."

"They met?"

"At least once."

Through their messages, they had agreed on a time and place to meet. From there, I'm sure they switched their conversation to texting. If I wanted to follow the paper trail further, I would have to ask Dr. Dupree for his wife's text receipts.

"I appreciate you looping me into this—it's always better to stay in contact than keep us in the dark," Wilson said. By us, he obviously meant law enforcement, and he subtly hinted at me not taking on a vigilante role in these investigations. "I'm sure I'll be in contact soon.

Serial killer vampire. Brutal stuff. You're the local expert on all things crazy, right?"

"I guess you can say that. Thanks again."

"Watch your six."

I opened a new tab, navigating to Facebook and typing in Shannon Pelegri. No one appeared in the search results who looked like the woman on the ancestry site. I repeated my search on a few other social media platforms, failing to find anyone of a resemblance.

"Shannon Pelegri," I said, leaning back in my chair and thinking. How did I find her?

I could wait in Dr. Dupree's house at night, hoping for the ghost to appear. However, I doubted she would show with me inside the home. Knowing that a sister existed, though, changed my entire perspective on the situation, and I thought I knew exactly how this game would play out in the end. I had the advantage now. Shannon didn't know that I had her name, her picture. In her mind, she was nothing more than her late sister's ghost, haunting the widower, carefully and methodically staging the scene to make it look like Vincent had lost his mind and blew out his brains. She wouldn't risk the gambit if I stayed over and waited for her to appear.

I made a checklist of everything I suspected.

She didn't drive to his house. If Dr. Dupree noticed a vehicle leaving from or arriving at his house, the jig would be up. Shelly's ghost would die. So, Shannon had located herself close enough to walk. Shannon also had access to enter the house freely. How? A key?

What about her motivation? Why would she want to torment, possibly kill Dr. Dupree? Because he was rich, and without a will—as he had mentioned, he never got around to writing one—his money would go to the closest of kin. He had no family. Supposedly, Shelly had no family.

Except for Shannon.

"I have the advantage," I said, speaking aloud. "She doesn't know that I know."

An idea sprouted in my mind. I feared for Dr. Dupree's life, believing I had to act quickly, otherwise...

Otherwise, I couldn't play the hero and save him. Otherwise, he would die, and I would have yet another life taken under my watch. Taken because of my ineptitude.

Digging Deeper. Thursday, April 28th, O847hrs.

With a soft-boiled plan to deal with the ghost hatched and in motion, I allotted my mental energy to the Changeling case. Maya had, unsurprisingly—she was brilliant—offered me a few legitimate leads to follow.

I stared across the office at the high reception counter shielding Fred out view from me. "Hey," I said.

"Yo."

"Can you do me a favor?"

"That's my job description."

"Call Alina, please. Check on Maya's condition. She went after it last night."

"Alina sent me some karaoke videos. Does Maya know she can't sing, like at all, and she has no business attempting Mariah Carey in the shower, let alone in public? I felt dirty watching her attempt those songs."

"Yeah, well, imagine how I felt listening to them in person."

"I'll call her."

"Make sure she heads to school, too."

Fred raised his head above the counter, sucking hard on his cheeks. "Sure thing," he said, though slowly, as if he withheld information from me.

I ignored it for the moment, scrolling to Miette's contact and calling her.

She answered before one full ring finished. "Hello."

"Miette," I said. "It's August Watson."

"Morning. How are you?"

I cracked a knuckle and rocked my head back and forth, stretching the sides of my neck. It was quite sore after lying on Maya's couch for a portion of the night. "I've been better, but I'm hanging in there. Do you have a second to answer a few questions? I'm trying to find some traction with your case, but nothing is sticking."

A few seconds passed. "Yeah, I can answer questions."

"Would you be willing to share your ex-boyfriend's phone number with me? I would like to call him and hear his side of the story. It's a long shot, but maybe we're dealing with a scorned ex-girlfriend, or a new girlfriend."

"I think he changed his number," Miette said. "Last time I tried to contact him, it went to one of those automated messages saying the number is no longer in service. I don't have any other way to reach him. He's fallen off the map. No social media activity. Emails don't go through to his address. I even, like a crazy person, drove by his apartment."

I said nothing, preferring to listen.

"I didn't see his truck. So, like an even crazier person than someone who just drives by, I went into the front office and asked if someone had seen him recently. I made up some story about having left my belongings at his place, and we broke up, and I finally had the courage to collect them."

"What did they say?"

"He missed rent a couple of weeks back. They knocked on his door. No answer. So, the landlord unlocked it, found the place empty. Apparently, he up and left without a trace or a word to anyone."

"You said his name was Justin?"

"Yeah."

"You didn't provide a last name."

"Jameson," she said, almost sounding annoyed—or maybe it was the poor reception.

"Justin Jameson. He's from Sacramento?"

"Aren't you a private investigator?" Miette asked, spitting out the question as if it tasted nasty. "Do you have to call me for the answers? You can't come across them by your own means?"

I held out my tongue for a second, biting on it... slightly confused. "I guess I can," I said. "Though that requires more resources and time, which ends up costing you more money. Should I consider that route?"

Miette sighed. "No. I'm sorry for lashing out. I've had a rough morning. I think Vanessa was in my house again last night."

"What happened?"

"Nothing... I mean, something, obviously. But nothing serious."

"What was it?"

"She left me a stuffed bear. It's stained and matted and old, ripped and sewed back together. She left it on the kitchen counter."

"Do you recognize it?"

"Yeah. I called her Honey, the stuffed bear. She went everywhere with me when I was little. I thought I had lost her."

"But you woke up this morning to the bear sitting on your kitchen counter, and you think Vanessa put her there?"

"Yes."

"How did Vanessa get your bear?"

"I don't know."

"Where was the bear the last time you saw it?"

"At my parents' house, in a box filled with a bunch of stuff from when I was a kid."

I cracked a knuckle, stood from my desk, and walked to the coffee counter, where I refilled my mug.

"Are you still there?" Miette asked.

"I'm still here," I said. "Do you think your parents know Vanessa?"

"What do you mean?"

"Maybe they know her by a different name. Maybe you know her by a different name, as does Justin. Can you think of anyone who might hold any animosity toward you?"

"No. Not off the top of my head."

"Would you mind sharing Justin's contact information with me?"

"Sure."

"What about your parents' contact information?"

A long silence ensued. I waited, unsure of her hesitancy, but I allowed her to hesitate. "Yes. I'll text it to you. Justin's number probably won't work, though."

"That's okay. It's worth a shot. One other question."

"Okay."

"Do you have siblings?"

Miette didn't hesitate to answer that question. "An older brother. Do you want his number, too?"

"Maybe." An idea churned. I entertained it. "How did he feel about your and Justin's relationship?"

"He never liked him."

"Why?"

"My brother, Zach, is... he has always been extremely protective of me. He thought Justin... he thought I could do much better than Justin, and he never shied from letting me or him know. It was quite unfair most of the time."

"Did you have boyfriends before dating Justin?"

"A few."

"How did your brother feel about them?"

"He hated them all. I guess no one can live up to my brother's expectations of who he thinks I deserve." Miette chuckled, though I thought it sounded like a noise to fill the silence. "Like I said, he's extremely protective."

"Do you think your brother could have created Vanessa?"

"What do you mean?"

"Well, maybe he created the persona of Vanessa to break up you and Justin. Do you think your brother would have created a fake account? He has access to your parents' house, where he could have snatched the bear. Does he have a way into your apartment?"

"He has a spare key," Miette said, her voice nearly vanished. "He insisted I make him one. But I don't know. Why... why circle the calendar on my birthday? What would he expose? That's what I don't get."

I shrugged. "People go to great lengths to get what they want. Maybe it was just another tactic to separate you and Justin, to make you believe in Vanessa."

"You really think so?"

I didn't know, but it sounded plausible. It was the best lead I had conjured since Miette approached me with the case. "If you don't mind sending your brother's contact information over, I can also call him and ask him a few questions. See if I can't force him into a corner."

"What if it's not him, and you're wasting your time when you should look for Vanessa?"

"I have to exhaust every possibility. Right now, he's a possibility—no matter how farfetched that might seem. Even if this line of thought is wrong, elimination is good. Elimination means progress, and that's all we can ask for in these kinds of cases. Whittling closer to the truth."

My phone dinged with another text message notification.

"I sent them," Miette said.

"I got them. Thank you."

"Mr. Watson."

"Yeah?"

"My dad is sick. He's had health problems for a while now—stress related. If you speak to him, please, be gentle."

"I will," I said.

When we ended the conversation, I placed my phone on the desk and looked across the office. The crown of Fred's bald head reflected the dim light.

"Want to go on a field trip tonight?" I asked.

"Where to?"

"Dr. Dupree's mansion to catch a ghost."

"Nope."

"Come on," I said. "I'll give you a Scooby-Snack."

"How about two?"

"I'll give you two Scooby-Snacks."

"Fine, but I also want to know who the pretty young lady was from last night. The one you danced with." He raised his eyes above the high counter, and in them, I could see his amusement.

"Patricia," I said. "A lovely lady."

"You seeing her again?"

"She shot down my advances, so probably not."

"I'm honestly shook. With your top-tier dancing, she actually had the gall to reject you?"

"We can't win them all," I said.

"But in your case, you somehow lose them all."

"I'm batting that way." I returned my attention to the computer screen, looking at the messages Miette had sent me. Justin Jameson's contact showed first. "Did you speak to Alina?"

"According to our young prodigy, Maya slept most of her night draped over the toilet. A couple hours ago, Alina helped transfer her to the bed, stocking her nightstand with feel-good pills, water, and some snacky-snacks." Fred popped his head over the counter, staring at me with wide eyes like an eager dog. "So what's happening tonight?"

"Let me make a few more calls and I'll fill you in." I tapped on Justin's contact.

As Miette had suggested, his phone went to an automated messaging system, one stating the number was currently out of service. I tried the next number on the docket. Miette's parents.

"Hello?" answered a woman.

I instantly realized I didn't know the names of Miette's parents. How had I neglected to ask for their names? My lack of sleep was catching up with me.

"Hello?"

"Hi," I said. "I'm August Watson, a private investigator for the Blue Moon Investigative Agency in Sacramento. Your daughter, Miette, hired me." I paused for a second to see how she would respond. She didn't respond, so I cleared my throat and continued. "I would like to ask you a few questions, if you don't mind."

"Is this about Justin?"

I frowned. "What about him?"

"Could we meet somewhere?" she asked, rushing through the request.

"Of course," I said, perplexed by her response. "Where at?"

"My house."

"Yeah." I jotted down her address.

"Please. Hurry."

A Bloody Surprise. Thursday, April 28th, 0904hrs.

MELISSA SNOW SAT IN her wheelchair at the breakfast nook, drinking her milk with a splash of coffee and staring at the front door, waiting for the investigator to arrive.

She lived in an average home in one of the more average residential neighborhoods in Sacramento. Gang violence didn't riddle her neighborhood, but the HOA didn't come through to suggest how high Jim had to mow his lawn or to recommend that Mary didn't hang up too many flags on her front porch. People minded their business, sticking to the boundaries within their fences.

Melissa reached out a trembling hand, picking up a napkin and dabbing her perspiring face. Despite the air conditioning, despite the table fan blowing directly at her, heat pulsed through the woman's body. Melissa hadn't felt so nervous for almost two decades—this on edge, like she might fall at the slightest touch, and she would fall and fall forever, praying for the ground but receiving no such conclusion.

Coughing sounded from the back room. Deep, guttural, phlegmy coughing that birthed droplets of blood. John, her husband, suffered late-stage esophageal cancer. It had attacked him hard, taking the booming power of his voice—John used to coach high school football, but now he couldn't draw enough breath to blow a whistle. He had once had a football player's build, too. Strong, muscular, and athletic. The cancer had stolen his vitality, shredding his body to nothing but skin wrapped around bones.

Melissa had her foot amputated from diabetes about four months before John's cancer reared its ugly head. Both of them now laid up in the house with no desire to leave, watching the world live and continue as they slowly died and ceased to exist.

A knocking occurred on the front door, loud and hammering.

Melissa flinched and gasped. In her distress, her arm flailed, knocking over her drink, spilling the contents across the nook table, soaking the unopened bills piling up. When she regained her wits, she rolled over to the front door, pulled back the shade at the side window, and glanced at her visitor.

Her heart dropped into her lap and the heat coursing through her body went cold. Melissa shivered.

"I know you're in there!"

Melissa reached for the deadbolt, breathing deeply and debating whether she should twist it. She glanced down at her stump where they had amputated her leg. From behind her, John hacked, most likely spraying a mist of blood across the sheets. Why not open the door and invite death into her home? Why remain in their purgatory, stuck somewhere between living and oblivion?

Except the private investigator had called. What if he could help? What if he could free them from the prison within these walls? Would it even matter? They had made their mistakes, and they had run from them. Melissa had only one foot now, and John was bed-ridden, barely able to roll over without falling into a coughing fit. Their mistakes had finally caught up. Why continue to hobble away? Why not turn and fight?

Twenty years ago, little Miette had vanished.

Melissa had dropped her daughter off at kindergarten that morning, but she hadn't picked her up. Rather, she had drank too much and had fallen asleep in the backyard for a few hours. That had proved the most painful sunburn of her life. Her skin bubbled and blistered as she soaked in the early afternoon to late afternoon rays, neglecting her little girl.

Zachary had woken her up.

"Where's Miette?" he had asked, at first curious—probably bored and wanting to play a game with his younger sister.

An earthquake had split Melissa's skull in half, though. The booze, combined with the sun, minus any water or food, wreaked havoc on her brain. She grunted, sitting up. Her skin exploded with pain. White light flashed behind her eyes, and she hissed a curse. She had slept on her stomach, so the burn covered her neck down to the pads of her feet. Melissa couldn't walk without a bright flash of pain cutting across her vision.

"Where's Miette?" Zachary asked again.

"I don't know," Melissa said. I don't know, like it wasn't her responsibility to know. Why would she know? What did it matter to her? She had to slide into a cold bath, cover her body with aloe vera, lay on the couch beside a fan turned to the maximum setting.

What did the whereabouts of her five-year-old daughter matter?

"Open the door!" the voice outside her house demanded.

Melissa licked her dry, colorless lips and twisted the deadbolt, unlocking the front door.

It burst open. The skinny side of the door slammed into her kneecap, wheeling her back a few feet.

"You can thank me in hell, you miserable old lady."

The gun fired. Once. Twice. Three times.

Melissa heard each report, though from a distance—as if from another world. There wasn't any pain. In fact, the opposite. All the chronic pain that riddled her physical body and mental state vanished. She was free of it all.

Melissa, ecstatic about the miracle, pushed away from her wheelchair, standing on her only remaining foot, stepping forward to thank her daughter, to hug her.

Instead, she fell face first to the ground, lying on her belly as she had laid on her belly twenty years prior, sleeping... but this time forever.

Up and Vanished. Thursday, April 28th, 0914hrs.

THE VERDIN'S LIVED ABOUT ten minutes from my office. Miette's mother had asked me to hurry, sounding rather frightened on the phone. So, in response, I had rushed out of the office, not even bothering to pour myself a fresh cup of coffee from the carafe. Some things could wait, believe it or not.

I pulled up to their house, double checking the street address with what the woman had shared with me. They matched.

As I stepped out of my car and looked over the vehicle's roof at the home, I saw the front door wide open.

Please. Hurry.

Was I too late?

Without assessing my surroundings, I sprinted to the front door, skidding to a halt as I came into the entryway.

Three yards inside the house, right in the hall, sat an empty wheelchair. Lying before it, sprawled across the ground like a rug, rested an old woman. I first noticed that she only had one foot. Then I noticed the blood. It was wet, still trickling from her body, forming a halo of death around her facedown head.

My vision tunneled, pulsing in and out. One second, the woman lay dead in her home, the next, Aaron Brooks lay dead on the asphalt. I gasped for air, breathing through a straw—fast and shallow, on the edge of panic. My legs wobbled, and I backpedaled out of the house. The fresh, warm air sucked me outside, pulled me into the yard, where I collapsed to my knees. The grass blades scratched against my bare arms as I bowed forward, resting my face on the cool ground.

Breathe, I thought. *Breathe. Get a hold of yourself and breathe.*

Slowly, the fresh air and the cool ground and my controlled breaths worked together to calm my nerves. I'm not sure how much time passed, but I regained my poise and risked raising my head, climbing to my feet, stepping toward the house once again.

With my newfound alertness and knowing what to expect when I entered the home, I reverted into police mode.

While still working in law enforcement, I had trained on active perception and alertness, completing drills that helped me assess a situation, locate the present danger, and figure out the best way to deescalate any issues without violence. The practice didn't always work—in fact, it rarely did. Too many officers feel fear, and they act on fear, same as too many perpetrators feel fear, and they, too, act on that fear. The instinct to survive is sharp and demanding.

Still, I had gone through the training, and I fell into the response. Reflexively, I reached for my hip, where I once carried the gun that stole the life of a young man. My fingers grasped mostly air and a little fabric from my clothing. I didn't have any weapons on me. I hadn't even bothered to rummage through my handy-dandy paranormal bag to grab pepper spray or a Taser.

However, I had my phone on me. I dialed Fred.

"Hey, boss."

"Call 9-1-1 and report an emergency to the address I'm at." Fred and I always shared our location for sticky situations where we would need each other's help. A break-glass-in-case-of-emergency scenario. "There's been a homicide."

"On it," Fred said, immediately hanging up the phone, asking no other questions.

Fred was annoyingly curious about my personal life, perennially hungry, and doggedly reliable. He knew when to joke. He knew when to buckle down. Maybe that was his football training—thirty seconds of catching their breath, followed by seven seconds of balls-to-the-wall action. No questions. No complaints. Work hard, play hard.

I kept my cell phone in my hand, holding it like a brick. Fishing in my pockets, I removed my car keys and held them in a fist so the sharp ends poked through the gaps in my fingers. I wouldn't win in a gunfight, but if I bumped into the killer at close range, I might have a punching chance.

I controlled my breath, creeping through the home and coming into the kitchen. I scanned the countertops for a better weapon. No knives sitting out in the open, and I didn't want to rustle through drawers and alert the murderer of my presence. However, a frying pan sat on the stovetop, crusted with the remnants of eggs. I shoved the keys back in my pocket, opting to hold my phone in case someone called, or in case I needed to call someone.

After grabbing the frying pan, I continued toward the hallway, shouldering open the first cracked door I came across. It creaked inward, revealing a dark bedroom. A human-sized lump lay in a tangle of bloody sheets.

I glanced around the room, holding my breath and listening for signs of an intruder. The house spoke to me as the air conditioning unit flipped on to keep pace with the rising temperatures outside. I flinched at the sudden, harsh noise.

Exhaling, I slowly moved further into the bedroom, peeking into the closet, dropping to my knees and checking under the bed.

Nothing. No one.

I retreated from the bedroom, moving to another room, and then another.

My phone rang in my hand, vibrating against my palm. I almost threw it against the nearest wall, but I held my composure and glanced at the screen. The number looked familiar. I recited the unknown digits aloud, tasting them on my tongue, trying to pinpoint where I had seen them before.

"Miette's mother," I whispered, clicking the accept button. "Hello."

"You won't find me there," said a distorted female voice

"Who is this?"

"Miette Verdin," the caller said. "Vanessa Brown."

I scrunched my face, cracked my neck, remaining silent and swallowing back a barrage of questions. Was this the woman who had split Miette and Justin apart, who supposedly broke into Miette's apartment and circled the date on the calendar, who had left the stuffed bear for Miette?

"She stole my life," Vanessa said. "Don't let her fool you like she has fooled everyone else."

"You killed them?"

A heavy sigh blew into the receiver. "Did Miette... the Miette you know... did she ever tell you the actual story?"

"Why did you kill them?"

"Did she tell you how they killed me?"

That confused me, so again, I said nothing, preferring for the woman on the phone to continue without my prompting. In my experience, most criminals—especially murderers—want to spill their story. They murdered for a reason, and they want to provide their excuse.

"I was five. My kindergarten class dismissed, and my mom never showed to pick me up. After waiting for two hours—an eternity for a scared little girl—I walked home. It was only a few blocks away, and I knew how to get there. My brother, Zachary, would often walk me to school in the morning or walk me home in the afternoon when Mom had to work. Dad always worked, though. He was always gone. Even when he was home, he was gone. Do you know what I mean?"

"Yeah," I said, thinking of Alina and her parents.

"Do you really know, though? Or have you only heard stories? Have you only seen movies and read books? There's a difference—experience versus perception. My parents never beat us. They weren't violent. They were just... absent. Neglectful. It was as if they cared nothing at all about Zach or me. In a weird, twisted sense, I almost envied those kids abused by their parents. At least they received attention. I would know, too. Their neglect led to me receiving plenty of abusive attention." The woman on the other end of the line snickered, a laugh bordering on disgust and dark amusement. "Anyway, I walked home that afternoon. A man intercepted me. He was charming and warm, smiling and dropping to a knee, so we spoke at eye level. He never looked down at me. I think that's a big deal, too. For adults to not look down at children."

My phone buzzed against my face. I pulled it away and read the text from Fred.

Cops on their way.

"Are you still there?"

"Yes," I said.

"He kidnapped me and held me hostage for nineteen years, five months, and twelve days. My parents eventually stopped looking for me. Do you know why?"

"No."

"They stopped looking for their five-year-old little girl because I came home eighteen months after my disappearance."

I tapped the bottom of the frying pan against my leg, enraptured by her story.

"To them, at least, Miette Verdin returned home. Their daughter was back in their home. Sure, she looked slightly different—hair color vaguely less blonde, eyes more gray than bright blue. But they reasoned those changes, didn't they? She went through the ringer. She suffered. Of course, she looks different. If those explanations grew thin, well, I was five. A kid changes so much in over a year. They grow taller. Their hair color changes. Of course, my personality would have changed during that time, too. I had gone missing—kidnapped, or so I claimed... the version of me that had returned. People obviously had questions. What had happened to me? Who had abducted me? Where was the man now? How had I escaped? Child psychologists claimed that my replacement, the Changeling, had trauma induced amnesia. My parents and my brother accepted the new me, the new Miette, into their family. Why continue searching for their missing girl when she had come home?"

I could find articles detailing the five-year-old Miette Verdin who had disappeared for eighteen months, only to return miraculously. They would all say the same thing, or so I assumed—Miette Verdin has come home to her family. Not a fraud. Not a replacement. Not a Changeling. Miette Verdin.

"You're the missing girl? You're the real Miette?"

"Me," she said, exhaling slowly. "I lived in Hell with the Devil himself for over nineteen years, while my family celebrated my birthdays with my replacement. While they made memories with the Changeling. They no longer cried for me. They no longer missed me. They no longer searched for me."

"That's why you killed them?" I asked.

"No."

"No?"

"They knew their daughter had never returned home, but they refused to acknowledge that truth. They instead accepted their new daughter, choosing to believe the lies."

"Why would they do that?"

"To squirm away from accountability. They couldn't take responsibility for my disappearance. Not only that, they couldn't accept the idea that a psychotic killer might have murdered their daughter because they had forgotten to pick me up from school. So, they welcomed the new Miette into their home, and they pretended she was me. That was it. People stopped searching. The police ended their investigation to find the missing girl. I went from Miette Verdin, the girl who vanished, to Miette Verdin, the girl who came home." A small, weak laugh—sadness disguised with humor. "They knowingly replaced me to avoid consequence."

"What about your brother? Will you kill him, too?"

Zachary Verdin, I thought. *I had to warn him about the situation.*

"I don't blame him for my parents' sins. He was only two years older than I, a child himself. Even if he suspected the Changeling, what would he have done? What could he have done?"

"Will you kill him?"

"What's your name?" Vanessa asked.

"August."

"August, Miette hired you to investigate this case, right?"

"Yes."

"Do you know why?"

"She was afraid of you."

"As she should be. It's more than just that, though. She hired you to legitimize her story and shroud mine in doubt. It's a last-ditch effort to keep the facade going."

"If it's truly a facade, as you say, what's the Changeling's real name?"

"Do changelings have real names? I don't think so. They only shift into the child whose place they stole. If she has a name, I doubt she knows it anymore."

"She would have been six or seven when she joined... your family. How does someone that young hatch that complex of a plan? It seems farfetched, almost as if you're making it up."

"I know nothing of her life or lies, other than she stole mine and adopted my truths. She will pay dearly for what she stole from me. Do you know what the best part of no longer existing is—of having that woman steal my place on this Earth? I'm nothing. No one. I'm invisible. I don't have a face. You would never know me from any other random girl in the market."

"Have you already contacted Zachary? Is he helping you? Is that how you entered Miette's apartment and planted the bear?"

"Goodbye, August." The call ended.

I hadn't moved from where I stood in the hallway since she had called me. She. Who was she? The real Miette Verdin? Vanessa? Someone else entirely?

It felt that despite her explanation, I now had more questions than before. Unfortunately, I couldn't ponder them now.

I scrolled through my messages to find Miette—the Miette who had hired me. Before I had come over to her parents' house, she had sent me three phone numbers. Her ex-boyfriend, Justin. Her mother, whose name I had neglected to ask for and the contact said Mom. And her brother, who's contact said Big Bro. Zachary.

I tapped his contact, dialing his number.

"Mr. Watson," he answered.

"Yes," I said.

"My sister said you might call me."

Which one, I thought. "Zach, correct?"

"Yeah."

I inhaled, wondering what I should reveal to him first. His parents' deaths? Would that distract him, though, prevent him from cooperating with the investigation? I needed his story to pinpoint Vanessa or Miette or whoever the girl was. Still, I couldn't withhold the terrible news from him.

"I'm a private investigator hired by your..." I trailed off, hesitating to say, sister. What else could I say, though? "Hired by Miette. My investigation led me to your parents' house to ask them a few questions. When I arrived, I found the front door open. I'm sorry." I cracked a knuckle, hoping he would understand without me having to say the words.

"Sorry about what?"

"They're both... they've been murdered."

A second of silence. "That makes no sense. I... I don't understand."

I don't understand, either. "I've notified the police. Once they arrive, I'll provide them a statement, but then I would like to meet with you."

"Wait... my parents are dead?"

"Yes."

"How?"

"Shot."

"With a gun?"

"Yes."

"Who... who shot them?"

Your long-lost sister. "I don't know exactly."

"Exactly? What's that mean? You have an idea?"

"Zach, I'm not sure if you're safe," I said. "Wherever you're at, whatever you're doing, go somewhere public. A coffee shop. When you're there, text me your location. I'll meet with you and explain everything in person. Everything I know."

"My dad had esophageal cancer. Doctors said a year, at the most, to live. My mother had severe diabetes, and the doctors predicted she might pass soon, too. I was talking to them last night, and they were joking about how competitive they were... about who would beat who to the finish line. Dark humor, but we have always defaulted to it. I guess when your family knows nothing but darkness, you either drown in it, or you create your own light source." Zach barked a sharp laugh, proving his point. "They're really dead?"

"I'm sure someone from Sacramento County will contact you later this afternoon, asking you to identify the bodies. If not you, your..." Again, I trailed off, unable to say, sister. "If they don't reach out to you, they'll ask Miette."

"Who would shoot them? Why? They were dying already, and they had nothing of value."

"Send me the location of the cafe you end up in." I hung up the phone, dropping my forehead against the hallway wall.

In the distance, police sirens cut through the neighborhood.

Daniel Quinn. Thursday, April 28th, 1155hrs.

I PROVIDED MY WITNESS testimony to the responding police officers, including a brief report on the case Miette had hired me for and what I had learned through the phone conversation with Vanessa.

Once the homicide detective arrived at the scene, he had asked me a few questions. I mostly repeated what I had already answered, and I promised I would write an email containing everything I had on the Changeling case and send it to them. I doubted my few notes would provide the detective with much, if anything at all, but I had no reason to withhold what little I had gathered. After all, my intention was never to compete with law enforcement, but to work with them to help others.

Before swinging by the office to copy my findings into an official report, though, I drove to the cafe where Zachary waited. During my debriefing with the Sacramento detective, Zachary had texted me his location. I would, with his permission, record our conversation, upload it to my computer, and attach it to the email I sent to the detective—Daniel Quinn.

As I drove to meet with Zachary, I thought of Detective Quinn. I had instantly hated the man, with his wavy and perfectly styled hair. He possessed an unattainable confidence that made me feel less than capable of blowing my nose.

The lone detective had parked beside the curb in an unmarked vehicle. He wore slacks, a button-down shirt, and a nice tie. The man walked straight to me, not bothering to greet the officers guarding the crime scene.

I stood in the driveway, leaning against the garage door. The forensic team had arrived a few minutes before the detective, and they had kicked me out of the house.

"August Watson," he said, extending his hand. "I'm Detective Daniel Quinn. Call me Danny." He had a firm shake. I wiped away the image of him practicing his introduction and handshake in the mirror, squeezing a grip strengthener. "You care if I ask you a few questions?"

"Feel free," I said, frowning.

Something about Danny off-put me, but I couldn't pinpoint it. Sure, he was arrogant—but in my experience, law enforcement officers can tilt toward arrogance, like they're above everyone and everything, including the laws they enforce. Not all, but some. Danny, for sure.

But something else about him stank, and I couldn't quite identify the stench.

Danny lifted his chin upward, staring at the blue sky and planting his palms on his hips. A superhero pose. "Tell me, August, what brought you to this home?"

"I'm a private investigator for the Blue Moon Investigative Agency. Mr. and Mrs. Verdin's daughter hired me. When I phoned Mrs. Verdin to ask her a few questions, she requested we meet in person at her home. I obliged, immediately drove here, and stumbled on the murders."

"How long from your office to here? How much time did it take you?"

"From when I hung up with her to when I parked my car..." I calculated the time. "I don't know. Maybe fifteen minutes. Maybe less."

"Killed within fifteen minutes of inviting you over to her home."

"I found it strange, too," I said.

"Ex-cop, right?"

"Yes."

"You quit."

"I did."

"Why?"

"Does this pertain to the homicide?"

"Just being friendly." Detective Quinn dropped his gaze squarely on me and flashed an award-winning smile. "Back to business?"

"Please."

"You discovered the bodies, but you had your assistant report the crime. Why?"

"I didn't want the operator to hold me hostage on the phone. I wanted to find the person responsible and subdue them. Wrap them in a pretty bow and deliver them to you."

"So thoughtful. How did you plan to do that, though?" Detective Quinn lowered his glasses and glanced at my waistline. "No weapons."

"I found a frying pan."

The man snickered. "A frying pan versus a gun. You have some balls on you, Sir. Did you find anyone?"

"I did not."

"Did you learn anything?"

I reiterated the phone call I had with Vanessa, reciting to him what I recalled at the moment.

The detective clicked his tongue. "Girl goes missing, and she stays missing for eighteen months. When she miraculously returns home, conveniently having no recollection of her time away, the family believes her story and adopts her as if nothing happened."

"To my understanding, yes."

Danny held up a finger, gesturing for me to wait. "Now, some nineteen years later, the kidnapped girl has escaped her captor. She's enacting her revenge against those responsible for her tortures?"

I shook my head and shrugged my shoulders. "That's the story I was told."

"Did she sound honest?"

"She sounded like she believed what she said."

Danny's jaw flexed. "What do you believe?"

"The evidence."

"Which states?"

"That my client fears for her life. I believe she has a legitimate reason to fear for it, too, seeing what happened to her parents."

"False parents," the detective corrected, smirking.

"Possibly."

"Well, Mr. Watson, collect your hourly rates from Ms. Verdin. Sacramento Police Department will take over from here." He turned his back to me, heading toward the front door, but abruptly stopping, glancing over his shoulder at me and grinning like he knew something I didn't. "You're not sure your client did this?"

"What do you mean?"

"Just a thought that popped into my head, Mr. Watson. Your client, Miette, right? Maybe feared whatever exposure Vanessa threatened. Knowing you were on your way to speak with her supposed mother and learn the terrible truth, she panicked. She showed up at the front door and solved the problem, cementing herself as the true-blue Miette Verdin."

An uneasy feeling nagged at me from something he had said. "The woman I spoke with on the phone, she all but admitted to the murders. Her voice wasn't the same as Miette's voice either."

"They have technology for that kind of thing, do they not? Also, all but admitted. Keep that little phrase in mind. All but. Anyway, just a thought that popped into the noggin." He tapped his skull. "Maybe it's nothing."

Then it hit me. I had never shared Miette or Vanessa's name throughout the entire conversation. I had stuck to daughter, my client, or Ms. Verdin. I had never used their first names, though. "Detective Quinn."

"Danny."

"How did you know their names?"

His shoulders stiffened, and he faced forward again, staring at the open front door. "It's my job to know. We'll be in touch."

I pulled into the cafe's parking lot, cutting the engine. That entire encounter with the detective chilled me, and it deserved another round of thought—later, though. Now, I had to meet with Zachary.

Filling in the Blanks. Thursday, April 28th, 1156hrs.

ONLY ONE MAN IN his mid-twenties sat alone in the cafe. He was skinny and short, and he had orange hair and a patchy orange beard and freckles across his face. If I had to pick Miette's brother out of a lineup, I would have chosen Zachary last, and I don't even know what the other men would look like.

I approached him, dragging a chair across the tile and sitting. He looked at me with swollen eyes, mouth slightly ajar.

"Mr. Verdin," I said, resting my hands on the round table for two.

"Mr. Watson." He had a whiny voice—not quite high-pitched, but no bass within it, almost something like Daffy Duck.

"Again, my deepest condolences."

Zachary sniffled and pawed at his face, wiping away drying tears. "We weren't ever close, my parents and I. Recently, once they received their year-long outlooks on life, I tried my best to build a decent relationship with them. After Miette went missing, though, they let go completely. They gave up. Became shells. Ghosts."

"That's why I needed to meet with you," I said.

"I know," Zachary said.

"What can you tell me about your sister?"

Zach swallowed, dropping his head and speaking to his lap. "My mom and dad never truly believed she returned. They both knew they had forever lost their baby, but they pretended the girl who returned was Miette for their sakes, for my sake, for the community's sake. They pretended because it was easier than accepting they had lost their daughter." He made a strange sucking sound and sighed, looking at me. "The mind is a powerful thing, and it can rationalize about anything to help numb the suffering of life." Fresh tears sprouted in his eyes. He didn't bother to prevent them from falling. "I convinced myself, too. But I knew otherwise. Still, I had gained a sister, and I accepted that truth—to be the big brother I had previously failed to be. To protect her this time around. The imposter provided us all with a chance to redeem our past mistakes."

"The imposter?"

"That's what she was... is, I guess."

"Do you still speak to her?"

"Of course."

"Have you had contact with…" I paused, licking the back of my teeth.

"With Miette," Zachary said, finishing my sentence. "With my actual sister?"

"Have you?"

"You need to understand the entire story. Miette was five when she went missing. My parents weren't the most present before her disappearance, but they vanished when she vanished."

"What do you mean?" I asked.

"My father dove into his work, spending every waking minute on his job. If he found himself with free time, he went to a bar and lost himself there. My mom slept all day, every day. She slept, and she drank. I don't know, maybe she dabbled with some hard drugs, too. I was seven, though. I can't say for sure. But that's the point. They still had a seven-year-old kid, one they abandoned to fend for himself. When Miette returned, or when the little girl arrived who claimed to be Miette, we all believed what we needed to believe."

"Did they look alike?"

"Not really. They had different hair and eye colors—but only slightly different, so you could convince yourself otherwise. They had different builds and personalities, too. Again, easy enough to rationalize. She had gone missing for nearly two years. I hated being alone, and her presence offered me someone to love, to love me back." Zachary swallowed a lump of emotions and shook his head, staring at the tabletop.

I held my tongue and allowed him his moment to recover.

When he settled himself, he said, "I was nine when she came home. I'm thirty now. Nineteen, almost twenty years I spent with the imposter Miette, who I picked as my sister." His face twisted and crunched together. "The other girl... as you implied, my actual sister... I only had five years with her. I never grieved with her. I never shared my fears and my accomplishments with her. We didn't experience life together. Does that sound terrible? Does that make me a terrible person?"

How did I answer that question? It made him, and his parents, selfish, I thought. They abandoned their blood for a replacement, for the thin belief she had returned when they all knew she hadn't, so they could feel better about themselves. It honestly made me sick. They allowed that little girl to remain missing and tortured, so they didn't have to suffer.

In the end, I ignored his question. "To eliminate confusion, we'll continue to refer to the woman claiming to be your sister as Vanessa. Have you spoken with Vanessa?"

"Yes."

"She claimed to be Miette, your actual sister?"

"Yes."

"Do you believe her?"

"What does it matter?"

"Do you believe her?"

"Miette is my sister, not Vanessa."

"Do you believe Vanessa is the little girl that went missing nineteen years ago?"

Zachary licked his thin lips. He hesitated to admit to himself what he knew—that he and his family had all made an extremely poor decision, and they probably deserved whatever fate Vanessa had in store for them.

"Yes," he whispered.

I leaned back, digging into my pocket for a stick of gum and popping it into my mouth. "I would like to speak to her. Do you have a way for me to contact Vanessa?"

Zachary raised his attention, fixing a hard glare directly at me. He set his jaw and narrowed his eyes, balling his hands into fists. "You can't talk to her. You can't help her. Miette hired you to protect her from that stalker, to expose that woman. That's your job. Do you understand me? Don't get any noble ideas about what's right and wrong in this situation. You don't know us. You don't know our family. Stick to what you know and do your job."

"Mr. Verdin," I said, not flinching to his vague threats, "you bring up a new line of conversation. The Sacramento Police Department has asked me to step away from this case, as it now falls in their jurisdiction because of the double homicide. The lead detective entertains the idea that Miette murdered your parents to frame Vanessa." My heart stopped beating in my chest and my breath hitched. For a flash of a second, a puzzle piece clicked in my mind—but the pieces were upside down. I couldn't see the picture or quite grasp what I stumbled upon. It was like having a common word stuck on the tip of my tongue, there in my mind, but nearly invisible.

"Miette didn't kill them."

"Maybe not, but you're going to have to choose a side. Your prodigal sister, or the one who stole her place." I stood. "Or you can help them both. Give me Vanessa's contact information."

I returned to my car, sitting in the front seat and catching my breath before pulling onto the road and into traffic.

Over the past week, I had solved three cases, putting my life in danger on two of them. I now worked three more, hoping to save the lives of those clients. Who would have thought paranormal investigation would prove so dangerous? It didn't help that I hadn't slept in over twenty hours during that span of time, most of which had occurred the night with Glacia. I needed a weekend, or at least a day, to decompress.

Could my clients afford that, though?

"Could they afford me dying on them?" I asked aloud.

In response to my question, my phone rang through the bluetooth. Maya.

"Hey," I said.

Maya groaned, mumbling as she spoke, "Don't talk so loud."

"Sorry!" I shouted.

"What's wrong with you?"

"Are you just getting up?"

"I woke up earlier on the bathroom floor. Woke up two hours later in my bed. When I tried to eat something, I threw it all up. Stumbled into the living room, passed out on the couch. Just woke up for the third time."

"I miss hangovers the most. How do you feel?" I asked, knowing the answer. I had spent a fair share of mornings in a similar state.

"Like I funneled sand down my throat, then I slammed a hammer into my face repeatedly until I knocked myself out, and that's how I fell asleep. That's how I feel."

I cracked a genuine grin. Maya, despite her often obnoxious behavior, always knew how to tug the corners of my lips upward. "That's because you drink nothing but cheap, artificial alcohol, and you mix it with juice and soda."

"But it tastes so delicious."

"It doesn't."

"It does."

"Shot of tequila. Jack and Coke. Coors."

Maya gagged. "Stop it."

"Stop what?"

"You're going to make me vomit."

"I thought it tastes so delicious?"

"At the moment of consumption, it does. Not the day after. My mouth tastes like a skunk sprayed it, then shoved a dry dog turd down my throat."

"That analogy doesn't make you sick, but me saying vodka does?"

"Ugh. Stop. Please, stop. Why did we even celebrate last night?"

"Because you turned in your article."

"I know, but... who cares? Why didn't we save the celebration until I got the job?"

"What if you didn't get it?"

"You think so?"

"Not at all, but there's always a possibility."

"Well, we could have gone out for consolation drinks."

"It was your idea to celebrate."

"I often have bad ideas," Maya said. "That's why I keep you around. You prevent me from killing myself. Except for last night. Speaking of last night and killing, I had the news on earlier. I accidentally laid on the remote control when I stumbled onto the couch, and it turned on the television. Did you hear about our newest serial killer? They're calling him the Vampire of Sacramento, or something stupid like that."

"I heard. Ted Wilson told me."

"Mm. Now he's a juicy slab of man-meat."

I didn't know how to respond to that, so I said nothing.

"Anyway," Maya said, "did you notice the victim?"

"Wilson never said."

Maya held kept quiet for a moment. My heart rate spiked. Why would I have noticed the victim? Did I know them?

"Who's the victim?" I asked.

"Patricia."

"Who?" But I knew as soon as I asked. Patricia, but my friends call me Patty. She wiggled and jiggled, dancing around me, making me feel alive for the first time in years.

"The lady you danced with last night."

I stared out my windshield at nothing at all, falling into my thoughts and memories, thinking of Patty dancing, drinking, sitting at the bar and chatting me up.

"I think I'm going back to sleep," Maya said. "Call me later, okay?"

The line went dead. I drove back to the office thinking about vampires and changelings, and how happiness comes and goes like the dark, violent waves that crash against the shore.

A Number to Call. Thursday, April 28th, 1331hrs.

I ARRIVED AT THE office and debriefed Fred on the double homicide and my chat with Zachary Verdin, along with the numbing news of Patricia being the vampire's latest victim.

"You okay?" Fred asked.

I nodded. "I don't know."

"We investigating that case now that it's personal?"

Still nodding, I said, "No."

"You're providing some very mixed signals."

"We have to stay focused on helping the people counting on us. If Sacramento Police Department or the Sheriff wants to approach me, we'll spend our time looking into the vampire. Until then..." I plopped into my chair and woke my computer screen.

"Well, can you tell me what's happening tonight with Dr. Dupree? Daphne was asking if she should be worried."

I shared my plan with Fred. He acted skeptical for the sake of giving me a hard time, but if he really held any concerns, the big man would have shared them or outright refused to attend the stakeout.

After settling on a time to meet later that evening, he went back to the paperwork, and I focused my attention on the Changeling case once again.

I jotted notes on a yellow legal pad. Longhand writing had always proven more effective to unlocking doors and pathways in my mind. I had no established system. Whatever popped into my head, I wrote it down. If I deemed it important, I circled it or put a star beside it. I drew lines, connecting different ideas.

- *Miette Verdin: Changeling: came into the Verdin family eighteen months after 'Vanessa' went missing, claiming to be the original Verdin girl. Family accepted her as their daughter and sister, and they never looked back, despite inconsistencies in appearance and behavior. For almost twenty years, she remained a part of the Verdin family. No questions asked. No doubts spoken, though probably harbored.*

- *Vanessa Brown: The Real Miette Verdin: mom forgot to pick her up from school, so the five-year-old girl walked home alone.*

Kidnapped. By who? (I circled that part—by who?) Twenty years later, she escaped from custody and returned to her home. Did she contact her parents? I think so. She contacted her brother. Did her parents shrug her off, as Zachary had, choosing the Changeling over their daughter? Maybe. Is that why she shifted her attention to the Changeling? Is that why she tormented her?

- *Of the two Miettes, who murdered the parents? *I put stars on either side of that question, knowing I needed the answer.**

- *Zachary Verdin: Brother: admitted he chose the Changeling over his actual missing sister because he hated being alone. After nearly twenty years, though, he and the Changeling were now as close as actual brother and sister, and he had grown extremely protective of her.*

- *Did Zachary murder his parents to protect the Changeling? (I circled that question, too.)*

- *~~What about Justin?~~ I crossed that out.*

I didn't think the ex-boyfriend played much of a role beyond Vanessa breaking him up with the Changeling to hurt Miette. Justin was a stepping stone—a taste for Miette—to the greater pain Vanessa would cause.

I had little investigative options remaining, with both parents now dead and Zachary protecting his ego and the Changeling. Still, I had one route, thanks to the brother. He had come through in one area.

I dialed the number he had shared with me.

It rang four times. I nearly pulled the cell phone away from my ear and hung up, not planning to leave a voicemail.

"Mr. Watson," said a female voice—not the distorted one I had spoken with earlier.

I cracked a knuckle. "Ms. Verdin, I would like to meet." I used the name she believed belonged to her on purpose, hoping to build a semblance of rapport between us. "Now," I said hurriedly, before she could refuse my offer or end the call, "I don't have any proof that you committed those murders. Without proof, I can't have you arrested. We can meet anywhere you want. But I think it's best that we meet and talk face to face about what happened to you."

"What about the Changeling? What about your client? Does she know about this conversation?"

"No," I said, whispering the word. The Changeling also didn't know, at least not from me, that the police had kicked me off this case. How would she respond when she learned I had met with 'Vanessa?'

"Why do you want to meet with me?"

I cracked another knuckle. "I need to know the truth."

"What truth? I'm Miette Verdin. The other one, she's an imposter. That's the truth."

"It's moved beyond that, Miette. Two people have died." I avoided using the word innocent to describe her parents, because to Miette, her parents were anything but innocent. "This case is no longer about identifying who you are. It's about finding a murderer."

"If I murdered them, then what?"

"You know that answer."

"Then you'll be my new captor, the one who puts me behind bars."

"Can we meet?"

A moment of silence. I thought, for a second, that she had abandoned the call.

She whispered, "Her real name is Vanessa Snow. The Changeling's name." Then the call ended.

I wrote Vanessa Snow on my notepad, and I stared at the name for a long time, wondering how I wished to approach the conclusion of this case.

The office door clicked open and Alina waltzed into the room, heading directly for her temporary chair near my bookshelf. She dropped her backpack on the ground, kicked up her feet on the end table, and said, "What's up, ladies?"

I glanced at the clock. A little before 1400hrs.

"Shouldn't you be in school?"

"School, my robot friend, is for fools."

"Alina, we have a work permit."

"For what reason? You don't pay me. I volunteer my time here. This should be community service."

"Why are you here?"

"Teacher had some emergency and had to head home early. School couldn't secure a substitute teacher, so they assigned my class to a study hall. Why sit in study hall when I could volunteer my time in the community?" Alina clapped her hands together. "So, what's the word, bird? Any breaks in the cases?"

"You talk to Maya recently?" I asked.

"Not since I woke her up this morning to make sure she would wake up, you know? That girl, despite her petite size, can put down some drinks."

"She nearly drank me under the table a year back," Fred chimed in. "I never stumbled around so badly. Playing corn hole, too. She hustled me. Daphne still hasn't forgiven me for my embarrassing display."

"Oh, yeah. That's a bad call," Alina said. "Maya can corn hole with the best of them. Speaking of legitimate corn holers, what did you think of that video I sent you last night?"

Fred burst out laughing, lifting his head above the high counter. "Which one? Of white boy dancing or tone deaf singing?"

Alina nodded at me, grinning.

"You know," Fred said, "I offered to teach him how to dance recently, but he refused my offer."

"You wanted to dance with me," I said. "Like arm around my waist."

Fred glanced at Alina, who stared at him, and they both shrugged.

"I don't see what the big deal is," Fred said.

"He's insecure about his masculinity," Alina said. "It's probably because he doesn't have a girlfriend."

Fred pointed at the girl. "Never corn holes. I see what you're saying."

"Fred! She's sixteen," I said. "What's wrong with you? Alina, next time you have a study hall, maybe practice the word that's in the actual title and study. Do you never have homework or tests?"

"I do… but August, we're talking high school here, not medical school—though Maya reversed the two, pouring her soul into high school and dropping out of medical school." Alina waved away the comment. "Doesn't matter. Tests are easy. Homework is easy. The hardest thing about high school is being at high school."

I massaged my temples. "Fred and I have a plan to close the Dupree investigation tonight."

"You solved it?"

"I think so, thanks to your ancestry suggestion."

"Like I said, community service. I'm saving the world one life at a time. Can I come?"

"No."

"Why?"

"You showed up too early today," I said. "It'll exhaust your legal work hours, as signed by your teacher and parents on the permit."

"You're the most annoying human alive."

I folded a stick of gum into my mouth. "If you're here early, you're going to work."

"I solved my case already."

"There's two more that we haven't solved. Vanessa Snow. She was a little girl who went missing somewhere around the age of five to seven. I don't know from where or how. Case would be unsolved, as she's still missing twenty years later. Probably presumed dead."

"That's all I get?" Alina asked.

"What else do you need? I gave you a name."

Alina pursed her lips and sloshed them back and forth. "How about lunch?"

"Yes!" Fred said, popping his head over the counter again. "Lunch. What she said."

I was hungry, too, so I volunteered to escape the stuffy office and collect lunch for everyone.

I returned forty minutes later and divvied out the food. We continued to work as we ate—Fred doing whatever Fred does and Alina digging into the Changeling. While she worked that case, I scrolled through Claire Balzan's social media accounts to earn a better grasp on the woman.

- *Claire Balzan. Married to Simon Balzan. Five years. Video evidence surfaced of her having an affair with her therapist, Robert Woods. Simon left. Video evidence of Claire stealing drugs from the hospital she's employed at. She was once addicted to Adderall. (I circled that.) Loses her job. Simon transfers all their money out of their joint account. Where? To what account? (Circled that.) Dr. Woods discovered Simon's body on the shore of Sacramento River, along his jogging path. Video evidence of Claire murdering Dr. Woods. Motive: Kills Simon because he left her, stole her money, didn't believe her claim of innocence. Revenge, maybe? Kills Dr. Woods. Did he know she killed Simon? Did he suspect something? Did she kill him because he released the video to Simon?*

I tapped my pencil on the notepad, thinking. I couldn't interview Simon or Dr. Woods. So, who were the names connected to them? Who could I speak with?

- Simon's parents and siblings. Simon's friends and exes. How did they feel about Claire?

- Dr. Woods' staff—Trisha Berry found his body. What did she know? Dr. Woods' family and friends. Did they know about the affair?

- Did Claire lie about her innocence? Did a doppelgänger kill her husband and therapist? If so, who? Why? How? Video evidence showed Claire having an affair, stealing drugs, murdering Dr. Woods. DNA evidence pinned Claire to the scenes of the murders. Motive existed. She had no alibi. Who? Why? How?

I traced over those last three questions, darkening the letters and thinking about impossible scenarios where Claire was actually innocent.

"Got it," Alina said, breaking my trance. "I mother trucking got it!"

I glanced at her, dropping my pen and leaning back in the chair. "What?"

"Her."

"Who?"

"Vanessa Snow."

I leaned forward, cracking a knuckle. "What did you find?"

"Six years old when she went missing from Modesto. About a year after her disappearance, her parents moved out of state, to Idaho, where, to the best of my knowledge, they remain."

"Why?" But I knew that answer.

Unfortunately, the more I learned about the world, the darker it became. I didn't like that perspective. I would rather believe in the paranormal than know that humans were the actual monsters lurking in the dark.

"Why did they move?" Alina asked. "Probably to escape the memories of losing their daughter."

"Do you have a phone number?"

"I have one, yes." Alina grinned over her laptop. "Would you like it?"

"Yes."

The girl shared it with me, and I dialed it into my phone.

"Ronald, dad. Karen, mom," I said, reading Alina's notes on Vanessa Snow's parents' names.

I tapped the green button and called the number.

This Missing Girl. Thursday, April 28th, 1449hrs.

The phone rang twice before a weathered voice—rusted and beaten—answered.

"Hello?"

"Hi," I said, enunciating and speaking as calmly as possible. If Ronald Snow, Vanessa Snow's father, had answered, I didn't want to confuse him or scare him into hanging up. I had one shot at this conversation—at getting it right. "My name is August Watson. I'm a private investigator based in Sacramento, California. I'm calling to speak with Ronald or Karen Snow."

An unhealthy pause. If not for the muffled radio in the background, I might have thought I screwed it up, and he hung up on me.

"What is this about?" he asked.

"Vanessa," I said.

A longer silence. I obviously couldn't see the old man, but I imagined him sitting and smoking cheap cigarettes on a chair in a messy, hot room, beer cans littered about. He sat and stared out a grimy window, battling with his past demons, hoping not to cry on the phone with a stranger.

"Who?" he said after a handful of seconds.

"I'm not affiliated with law enforcement. You're not under investigation. You have no pending legal trouble. I have a few questions to ask you, and you'll never hear from me again."

Though I couldn't smell the man, I imagined him stinking of body odor and stale cigarettes in that hot room. When his silence stretched to a certain point, I assumed control of the conversation and asked my first question.

"Am I speaking with Ronald Snow?"

"Yeah."

"You're married, or you once were married to Karen Snow?"

"She passed a few years back. Cancer."

"I'm sorry for your loss."

"Me, too."

"Did you two have a daughter named Vanessa?"

One. Two. Three. Four. Five. I counted in my head to pass the seconds he remained quiet.

"We did."

"What happened to Vanessa?"

One. Two. Three. Fo—

"She went... she went missing twenty years ago."

"Mr. Snow, I'll reiterate that I'm not affiliated or contracted with or by any police department. I am under no obligations to report whatever you share with me." I licked my teeth and cracked a knuckle. "Your daughter, Vanessa, hired me. She's alive, and she's possibly in trouble. I'm trying to help her the best I can. Can you help me do that?"

Another stretch of silence, filled only by the indistinguishable music playing in the background.

"What happened to Vanessa?" I asked.

He sighed heavily—the exhale of defeat. "We loved her, Sir. We really loved her more than the world itself. Don't think us terrible people or poor parents. We did what we thought was best for her."

"I believe you did, Mr. Snow. Can you tell me, though? Can you tell me what happened?"

"We were young, Karen and I. Only kids ourselves. Heck, babies, even. Fifteen and sixteen. Karen's parents were the religious kind. They demanded their daughter move to one of them houses that accepted pregnant women out of wedlock. They said Karen was to give up the baby at birth. My wife refused, though. I had little in the way of parents myself. Dad in jail. Mom always working to support me and my six other siblings. So Karen and I ran off together to raise our baby."

I glanced at Alina, who had just turned sixteen, and I imagined her with a baby of her own, living alone, fighting to support her fledgling family. Sure, with enough backing, the girl could raise a child... but without the help, what then?

"I struggled to find a job that supported us," Ron said, falling into a speaking groove. "I had no choice but to resort to crime to make money and feed my family. The law caught me, though. Like my daddy, I spent a lot of time behind bars. Too much time. Karen couldn't work and raise a baby, not when we didn't have family around to help. She and Vanessa were homeless while I was in jail. They slept in shelters or on the streets. Nessa—that's what we called her—got sick at some point. Really sick. Fever. Vomiting. The whole thing. I stood behind bars. Karen had no money. She didn't know what to do, how to provide for or protect our girl. We debated giving her up to foster care—but I'm sure you've heard the horror stories. We couldn't take that gamble with our princess. One day, though, Karen read the paper, and she saw the missing girl. Fifteen months had passed since she had vanished. That little girl, after that much time, she wasn't coming home. But maybe, we thought, maybe she could. Vanessa looked enough like that girl that maybe those poor folks would accept her as their daughter."

There it was. The Changeling taking the place of the actual child.

"Vanessa went along with it?" I asked. "How did you convince a six-year-old girl to do that?"

"For three months we… we brainwashed her. I guess that's the best way to put it. We stopped calling her Vanessa or Nessa. Instead, we called her Miette. She eventually responded to it. We told her we weren't her parents, but they were. John and Melissa Verdin. We showed her pictures of them. We told her she would move in with them soon enough. Move in with her parents. After three months, we dropped her off in front of their house, and we drove away."

For a second, I didn't have a thought in my head. His confession completely baffled me—the idea of parents training their child to morph into another kid.

"What if she blew it?" I asked. "What if she insisted you were her parents, that her name was really Vanessa Snow?"

"It was a risk we could take. She actually believed those were her parents and her name was Miette Verdin. We had done a good job of that. We also had faith that grieving parents desperate to have their little girl back would do about anything to have her back, even if that little girl wasn't their little girl. At eighteen months missing, they knew as well as we knew their Miette had vanished forever."

I wanted to ask a personal question, one to feed my curiosity. How did a parent willingly give up their child to another family… a stranger family? Instead, I forced myself to remain professional.

"One more question, if you don't mind."

"I'm tired, so make it quick."

"Did you keep track of her? Did you watch your little girl grow up from afar?"

One. Two. Three. Four. Five. Six.

"We wanted to, but we couldn't. If I saw her, I was apt to kidnap her and bring her back home, back into a miserable existence. My wife and I never found our footing in this world. We grew old long before our time, always working hard jobs, desperate jobs, criminal jobs. We couldn't, under any circumstances, allow Vanessa to glimpse that world. That's why we moved to Idaho."

I did not know if his actions and decisions were noble or cowardly. But I knew he had convinced himself to believe they made the correct decision on Vanessa's behalf.

"Thank you for your time," I said.

"Detective."

"Investigator."

"Is she... is she okay?"

I thought of the double homicide. I thought of the real Miette reentering the scene. Should I tell the old man who had abandoned his daughter the truth, though? That Vanessa was on the verge of losing everything. Honestly, I'm not sure what the man deserved. When in doubt, though, I never strayed from the truth.

"No, Mr. Snow, she's not okay." I ended the call right there.

Over the past two years, I hadn't so much as craved an alcoholic beverage. Right there and right then, after hanging up the phone, I wanted nothing more than to forget about everything going on in my career and life—to drink until only numbness remained.

Reflection. Thursday, April 28th, 1824hrs.

Despite the chaos of revelations swirling around the cases, I convinced myself dinner with Sarah Herling remained a good idea. Worst-case scenario, we would discuss work, hopefully making further progress with Claire Balzan's investigation. Best-case scenario, we avoided any discussion relating to work, and we had a relaxing, stress-free dinner.

I leaned on the brick wall beside the front door leading into Frank Fat's—the restaurant below my office. There, I waited for Sarah to arrive.

The stakeout at Dupree's mansion loomed heavy in my mind, only a few hours away now. More complicated and nearly as pressing, I scrambled to think of how to approach the Changeling situation.

Since Quinn's recommendation, I had identified Vanessa Brown as the real Miette Verdin. I could hand that information over to my client—Miette Verdin, who I had identified as Vanessa Snow. I think to save confusion on all ends, I'm going to refer to Vanessa Snow (my original client) as the Changeling, and I'll refer to Vanessa Brown by her god-given name, Miette. Anyway, if I handed the new information over to the Changeling, I could step away from the case and tie up my involvement. However—and there's always, it seems, a massive 'however' hanging on the horizon, flashing in neon—what about Miette Verdin? So many people had turned their backs on her in favor of the Changeling.

Could I do the same?

That question, I guess, depended on one simple answer. Who killed the Verdin parents? Three viable suspects popped into my mind.

Zachary Verdin was the least likely, in my humble opinion, but the word 'likely' remained in that statement. The Changeling had warned me he was protective and would do most anything to keep her safe. I saw glimpses of that trait during our meeting. I also saw the regret of his continual actions and decisions to forget about his blood sister. That's why he had shared her phone number with me. Deep down, he wanted to protect them both. Maybe he believed he could do that by killing his parents and silencing the true story from releasing into the world. Least likely, but still likely.

Vanessa Snow, the Changeling, perched on the middle tier of likely suspects. After learning everything I had learned about her life, I struggled to understand why she had hired me. Why dig up that forgotten ground? Why expose those buried skeletons? I had a few suspicions, but nothing substantiated. Though, I figured the answers would parallel with why she killed her adopted parents—to protect her false identity and the life she had built. It all seemed... wonky, though.

Miette Verdin, the real Miette Verdin, had the strongest motivation to kill everyone involved. What did she have to lose? Her family had abandoned her two decades ago, choosing a stranger over their little girl. That stranger had fit too perfectly into her life, as if Miette Verdin was replaceable. Why not escape her captor (if that's what happened? I still had no insight into that part of the story.)? Why not come back and avenge her memory by killing all those who had given up hope?

Zachary Verdin. Vanessa Snow. Miette Verdin. Whodunnit?

"August, hey," Sarah said, standing two feet from me.

She had approached without me noticing. The defense attorney wore a navy blue suit, with a white button-down blouse beneath the blazer, and low high heels. She had her hair loose, falling around her shoulders. In her hand, she carried a leather briefcase.

"How's it going?" I asked.

"It's going. Sat down with Claire again today. We had a solid conversation. But I'll tell you when we're seated. I need a cocktail. You don't mind, do you?"

I shook my head. "Not at all."

"I heard you're sober, and I would hate to, you know, accidentally tempt you out of that situation."

"Last night, my friend Maya went overboard with the alcohol. This morning, she reminded me why I stay away from the stuff." I smiled with my lips. "You look nice."

"Not a date, Investigator Watson."

"Shall we go inside?" I opened the door for her, like a true gentleman, and we stepped into the red-walled, gold-trimmed, low-lit restaurant.

Work Dinner. Thursday, April 28th, 1829hrs.

At 1830hrs, a boastful amount of people populated the restaurant. The greeter found us a table without having us wait, though.

I sat, pushing my few notes to the side of the table and opening the menu. I wasn't too hungry, having eaten a late lunch, but I had a long night and promised Fred I would order him takeout as compensation for joining me later.

Sarah didn't glance at the menu. She opened her briefcase and removed a folder, setting it on the table and opening it. "Before we get into anything, I want to draw a line. This isn't a date. It's a work dinner. I won't go home with you, and I won't have you come over to my house. I won't give you my personal cell phone number. And I won't kiss or hug you when we leave."

I rolled my shoulders, moving the tension from them. Her upfront declaration had gone a long way in easing my mind.

On a date, or a suspected date, I was a blabbering wreck, never knowing if I should make small talk or explore deeper conversations. Never knowing when I should settle to hug someone or lean in for a kiss. Never knowing when to invite someone back to my place.

I hated, almost more than anything, making people uncomfortable—which, honestly, usually led to uncomfortable situations.

"That's perfect," I said. "That actually takes a lot of pressure off me. Thank you." I set the menu down. "So, what happened in your meeting with Claire?"

Sarah smiled, glowing behind the candlelight.

"Howdy, fine folks." A waiter appeared. He wore poorly fitting clothes, everything too baggy on his plump body. "My name is Jake the Snake, but you can call me Drew, like Andrew. Never Andy. I'm not a cowboy doll, with a snake in my boot. Though I am Jake the Snake, often in the boots of my enemies."

"Don't you mean Woody?" Sarah asked. "Andy was the kid who owned Woody."

"Do you have a lot of enemies?" I asked.

"No enemies that I know of, unless you're my enemy." He looked directly at Sarah. "No one has ever corrected me before. Is that something my enemy would do?"

"I'm not sure," Sarah said.

"There's this twelve-year-old kid I play online games with. He lives in New York or something. I never met him, but I imagine he lives on the east coast. He often comments on my mother, and how he's my daddy. I tell him that makes zero biological or temporal sense. How could he be my daddy if he's, at the least, a decade younger than me? I mean, sure, maybe in a certain situation, he could marry my mom and be my stepdad. He's twelve, though, at most. I don't think my mom dates twelve-year-old boys. Heck, that's not even legal in most places. I tell him that, too. I say you're wrong. Read a book."

"Have you asked your mom about this kid?" Sarah asked.

"I don't dare. What if she is dating him behind my dad's back? What if they get a divorce because of it? What if MILFhunter42069 marries my mom and then becomes my new dad?"

I cleared my throat. "I would like a water, please. I believe the lady would enjoy a cocktail." I gestured at Sarah.

She rested her chin on her fist and bit her lip.

"Oh, uh, um... I don't actually work here," the man dressed like a waiter said.

"You don't say?" I asked, scratching my neck. "You had me fooled."

"My mom works here, actually."

"The mom in question?" I asked.

"Her, yes. I tag along sometimes and help."

"You're doing a bang-up job."

"Thank you."

"Is your mom a waitress?" Sarah asked.

"A chef," he said. "The manager, his name is Frank, but he doesn't own the restaurant. That's funny, though. Frank manages Frank Fat's."

"Hilarious." I faked a chuckle.

"Yeah. I told that to MILFhunter42069, but he said it was dumb. I told him he was dumb. My mom says I play too many video games, and it squashes my brain. I also told that to MILFhunter42069. He said he squashes my mom's brain. I'm not sure what that means, though."

"Andrew!" A stern yet small woman hiked across the restaurant. "Go back into the staff room. Now."

Jake the Snake turned to us and smirked, sharing a shy wave. "So nice to meet you two."

"Tell MILFhunter42069 that you hope he contracts herpes from a toilet seat, because that's the only chance he has of getting an STD," Sarah said.

"Wow," Andrew or Jake the Snake, but definitely never Andy, said, widening his eyes and covering his mouth to suppress an embarrassed laugh. He trotted off, muttering the insult to himself.

I glanced at Sarah. "The kid's twelve, at the oldest. You hope he contracts herpes?"

She shrugged and snickered.

"I'm sorry about that," the woman with lips so thin they barely existed said. She dug into her apron, drawing a receipt pad and a pen. "That's Meredith's son, Andrew. He's supposed to stay in the staff room, but occasionally he escapes and socializes with customers. I'll comp you both a drink. What would you like?"

I looked at Sarah, nodded for her to order. "And an old fashion with rye. No cherries."

"And for you, Sir," the woman asked, turning to me.

"Same."

Sarah narrowed her eyes, staring at me with disappointment.

"My name is Becky, and I'll be your waitress for the night. I'll be back with those drinks."

"Thank you," I said.

"An old fashion?" Sarah asked. "I thought me drinking wouldn't tempt you into drinking? I'm going to have a panic attack. I almost feel as guilty as that time I found out my boyfriend had a wife. I can't feel my heart."

"Stop being dramatic," I said. "I ordered it for you. What was I going to do, spend my comped drink on water?"

Sarah chuckled, smiling at me. It was a very contagious smile.

"That a true story, though?" I asked.

"What?"

"The boyfriend having a wife thing."

"Big time."

"That sucks."

"Big time." She tapped the table with her index finger. "Want to work, though, or discuss my sexual history? I'm open for either."

"I'm open to discuss work. What did Claire say?"

"Nothing conclusive, but we have a string to pull on. She took your homework seriously, and we dove into all her time-stamped records—emails, receipts, text messages, phone calls. If she went somewhere, we pulled all available security cameras for the time-stamps. Gio worked his ass off to collect a lot of this information. Some of it we'll have to subpoena, and some of it we won't have access to. But in the short time we've had to look, we've found... we've found enough to build an argument. Maybe not a good one, but still an argument. That's a fighter's chance. My dad always said, if you're in a ring, even if you're fighting Muhammad Ali, it only takes a well-landed punch to bring him down."

"The anticipation is killing me," I said.

"I know. I see it in your eyes."

"You're a menace. What did you find?"

"A few discrepancies in the timeline. The video of her having an affair with Robert Woods was taken at 1421hrs. The video data and a clock in the background confirm that time. Well, Claire, on that day at 1423hrs, purchased Starbucks. The transaction shows on her credit card history and Starbucks app. The nearest Starbucks to Robert Woods' house is five minutes away."

"I'll play devil's advocate here," I said.

"Perfect."

"Someone hacked into her account, or someone has her login credentials. They purchased the drink without Claire ever knowing."

"I had the same thought." Sarah tapped her head. "Except Gio combed through Claire and Simon's home and Claire's vehicle. Guess what he found stuffed in a cupholder?"

"A receipt."

"A printed receipt of that exact purchase with a timestamp. 1423hrs on the same day as the video." Sarah smirked. "I don't know about you, but I've watched that sex tape way too much. Maybe Dr. Woods' is seconds from fireworks, but I don't think so. Pretend he is, though, for the sake of a healthy argument. He accidentally shoots off the grand finale a little early and rolls over, not caring for Claire's firework show. Well, she still has to clean up, dress, find her belongings. She has to walk to her car, start it. She has to drive five minutes to Starbucks, wait in line, order her drink, make the purchase."

"Which happened at 1423hrs."

"And the video happened at 1421hrs. You think she did all that dressing and driving, ordering her drink and receiving a printed receipt in two minutes?" Sarah shook her head slowly back and forth. "Not a chance. What do you say about that, devil's advocate?"

I cracked a few knuckles and considered the evidence.

After a few seconds of not coming up with a retort, Sarah continued speaking. "I present to you exhibit two." With her elbow planted on the table, she raised two fingers.

"Proceed."

"On the day in question, we have video surveillance taken from the defendant's place of employment, Sutter Hospital, in Sacramento. In this clip, we see the defendant riffling through a drug cabinet and stealing a bottle of pills. An entire bottle, ladies and gentlemen. Not discreetly, especially considering the hospital takes inventory of all prescription medicine. Also, there are other medicine cabinets in the hospital, ones without a camera pointed directly at them. It's my conclusion the person shown in the video wanted to get caught."

"What if she did?" I asked. "Addicts do crazy, unpredictable things. They think differently, right? What if she wanted to get caught without having to come forward about her addiction, instead preferring for someone else to approach her?"

"Great question," Sarah said, flipping through her notes. "On the date in question, the defendant didn't work. She had the day off. Two consecutive days off, actually. With her husband having recently left her, believing she had performed extramarital sins with another man, the defendant didn't want to spend those two days alone."

From my periphery, I noticed Becky return with our cocktails, along with two waters. After handing them out, she took our order and tended another table.

Sarah sipped the old fashion and rolled her eyes back into her head. "So good."

"I preferred it with tequila."

"An old fashion with tequila?"

"Yup."

"Never even thought of such a thing."

"Instead of sugar, use agave. It's incredible."

"Noted," Sarah said.

"Claire didn't want to be alone on her two days off," I said.

"Not willing to spend the weekend alone and drown in self-pity and confusion over her life falling into shambles, our defendant hopped in her car and drove to Monterey, where her cousin lives. They grew up together and were more like sisters than best friends."

"Has anyone contacted this cousin?"

"Gio had a conversation with her. She checks out from what he says. She also corroborated this following part, so listen carefully."

"I'm Dumbo," I said, pulling on my ear.

Sarah giggled, but didn't take the bait to insult me. "We have, on the day in question, at exactly 0921hrs, a video of our defendant stealing drugs from the hospital. At 0851hrs, I will present to you exhibit three. Another receipt, this one from a gas station, accounted for on her credit card transaction history and also found printed in her vehicle." Sarah covered her mouth with the blade of her hand, as if telling me a secret. "I told her to stop printing receipts and save the world. She said it's an old habit her father burdened on her. Either way, her habit has helped her tremendously."

"What gas station? Where at?" I asked.

"Fairfield," Sarah said, leaning back in her chair. "Exactly thirty minutes before stealing drugs from the hospital, we have her location in Fairfield, which is fifty minutes away from Sacramento. Not only that, the gas station complied with our request and provided us with security footage. At exactly 0851hrs, there's Claire, filling up her tank with unleaded gas."

"Maybe she drove to Fairfield to create a false trail, sped back to Sutter, and stole the drugs," I said, not really believing that. It would have required a traffic miracle for that to happen.

"Maybe. It's a forty-eight minute drive, according to Google Maps. No traffic. No cops."

"Okay."

"She speeds. Even going a hundred, she's arriving in twenty-five minutes. She has to park. She has to run into the hospital. She has to climb stairs or ascend the elevator to the third floor. She has to head to the room where she stole the drugs. It's possible, but it's farfetched, especially considering this next exhibit."

"Claire's cousin?"

"Katlyn Aarseth. Claire's cousin. She lives in an apartment complex with security cameras. She also has a security camera on her front door. Not only that, each guest has to sign in with the security guard at the gate. Not only that, there's a text from Claire to Katelyn at approximately 1130hrs, which sings harmony with all the cameras around the premises, saying, 'I'm here.'" Sarah slapped the table with both palms. The patrons nearest us glanced in our direction.

"Monterey is what… a three-hour drive from Sacramento?" I asked.

"Three and a half hours. As nearly impossible as it is to drive from Fairfield to Sacramento in exactly thirty minutes, it's more impossible to drive from Fairfield to Sacramento in thirty minutes, then all the way to Monterey in only three hours. It didn't happen."

I drank my water and set it back down. "I'm going to need something stronger than this."

"Soda?"

"Coffee."

"What do you think, though?"

"I'm thinking about the murders. So you disprove the infidelity and the theft. Do you have an alibi for the murders? That's what matters here. Can you explain away the DNA found at the crime scene?"

"If I discredit the first two videos, I can cast doubt in the jury's mind that the murder video is also not her. All I need is a reasonable doubt. That's all."

"You've gathered evidence pinning her in different locations than the videos prove. Do you have that for the murder video?"

"No. She has no alibi for that."

"If she didn't kill her husband and Dr. Woods, who did?"

"We don't know."

"Ideas?"

The victorious expression Sarah had worn seconds prior dissipated, and she slumped in her seat and nursed her cocktail. "None."

"I'm sorry to kill the mood," I said, half-chuckling to lighten things.

"I mean, no, you didn't. In the back of my mind, I know we need to disprove the murders. We've only been at this a day, though. I'm surprised how much evidence Gio has collected in that short amount of time. If we can keep this pace, we can get to Sacramento from Fairfield in thirty minutes, you know? We'll do the impossible and disprove that she murdered anyone."

"I'm going to contact Simon's parents and siblings tomorrow, as well as his friends and exes," I said. "I want a better sense of his and Claire's marriage, and how the family viewed them. Not only that, I want to get an idea if they had burned any bridges, or if anyone hated Claire enough to destroy her life like this. We need a better sense, outside of Claire's perspective, of who the Balzan's were."

"Yeah," Sarah said. "That's a good point. Gio and I will keep tracking her credit card history and pulling as much video footage as we can to contradict the incriminating evidence."

"We can meet again on Monday, same place and same time?"

"I'll try the tequila old fashion."

"You won't regret it."

We mostly avoided talking about the Claire Balzan case the rest of the evening, and we had a pleasant time. Sarah was witty and hilarious and charming. If I didn't know any better, or if I were a casual observer, I would say our work dinner had naturally evolved into an actual date.

In the Dark.
Friday, April 28th, 0231hrs.

VINCENT DUPREE'S PROPERTY SAT on a square twenty-acre lot, the property covered with olive trees. He had neighbors to his east and west and north, with a country road running past his driveway on the south side of the property.

Fred and I pulled onto a dead-end street off the road north of Dr. Dupree's property, parking on the wide shoulder beneath an oak tree. The location was a little more than a mile away from the mansion. We hiked along railroad tracks, which led to a creek cutting through his neighbor's cornfield, following that to Dr. Dupree's olive orchard.

I paced between the two nearest trees, unsettled and slightly nervous about our plan. Fred sat against a trunk and tossed some trail mix into his mouth as he peered at the open sky glimmering with an explosion of stars.

"You don't really have this view in the city," Fred said behind a mouthful of raisins and peanuts. "All these stars. Do you think people get used to it?"

"What do you mean?"

"Like, do you think Dr. Dupree walks outside at night and just, I don't know, doesn't look up?"

"I'm sure."

"How can he not look up? That's like the most stunning woman in the world following you around, naked. Sure, everyone who comes to visit will ogle, but do you grow tired of her? Do you stop enjoying the view?" He threw another handful of trail mix into his mouth, shaking his head.

I glanced at the sky, then back at my phone's dim screen. My stomach twisted into tight knots—ones which seemed impossible to untie.

Dr. Dupree promised he would call me at 0230hrs on the dot, about the time the other appearances had occurred. Three minutes had slipped away from our arrangement. Where was he? Why hadn't he called? Did something happen?

I glanced through the row of olive trees separating us from the mansion's backyard. Dr. Dupree's living room window had glowed a dull yellow all night—the soft illumination from a table lamp, I assumed. If I tried hard enough, I could determine, or so I imagined, Dr. Dupree's slight frame reclining back in his chair, watching television or reading a book in that low light. When I shifted my attention to the window, though, the orange-yellow had burned away, replaced by a white-blue hue. Only the television lit the living room now.

I glanced at my watch. 0234hrs.

"Fred, something isn't right."

"Yeah, it's these damn raisins they pollute the trail mix with. Just add more M&M's. I mean, who prefers the raisins? Serial killers, that's who. The Vampire of Sacramento. I bet he wishes the trail mix had more raisins and less M&M's."

"Something is wrong with Dr. Dupree."

"What?"

That sinking feeling landed hard at the bottom of my stomach. I couldn't wait around for Dr. Dupree to hold up his end of the bargain. He could have drifted to sleep, losing track of time, and forgoing our plan. I had to act.

"It's go time," I said, bursting forth from the orchard and sprinting across the dark-drenched yard to Dupree's sliding-glass door.

The Taste of Death. Friday, April 28th, 0234hrs.

VINCENT DUPREE HAD DOZED off on his recliner after polishing off two entire bottles of wine. For him, wine hardly ever went to his head, but it made him sleepy enough. Sleep he needed, too. He hadn't slept for over four hours in over four months. He had lost weight from never eating—weight he barely could afford. His mind moved through sludge, when it moved at all.

The wine helped him sleep, though, as did the old movies. After his third glass and the first act, Vincent hardly had the strength to hold his eyes open. He definitely didn't have the energy to stumble through his house and climb into his bed, as he and August had planned.

Speaking of the plan, Vincent had to stay awake to call the private investigator.

Earlier that night, August Watson had called him, claiming he had an idea to catch the ghost. Vincent had scoffed, not believing it possible—but also, maybe, not wanting to believe it possible. He had asked for clarification, but August said he had to remain discreet about the matter.

"Do one thing for me, though, okay?" August had asked.

"Anything," Vincent had said. By then, he had finished his first glass of wine and worked on his second.

"Call me at 0230hrs. Earlier if you feel yourself falling to sleep. Can you do that?"

"Yup."

"I'm going to accept your call, but we will not talk. You're going to set your phone on your nightstand, and if anything happens, you'll call out for me so I can hear you through the shared line. Do you understand?"

"Easy enough," Vincent had said.

Except, his easy enough had proven impossible. He polished off his third bottle of wine, halfway finished an old movie, and had hardly slept for a quarter of a year. It all caught up to Vincent, knocking him out cold. Knocked him out an hour before 0200hrs had rolled around.

The empty wine bottles stood on the coffee table and the grind of the movies' second act played on low volume, as the doctor sawed logs. His snores echoed through the emptiness and the vast halls of his mansion. He drooled as he snored, the saliva absorbing into this shirt. His wine glass, empty in his hand, had tipped over and now rested on his lap.

"Fasten your seatbelts," Bette Davis said on the television. "It's going to be a bumpy night."

Vincent's snoring abruptly ceased, and his eyes shot wide open.

The familiar taste of the gun's barrel fit into his mouth—his teeth chattered against the steel.

"Tonight's the night, Vinnie," Shelly said. "Tonight you die."

Vincent shook his head, feeling the end of the gun's barrel grind against his cheeks and scrape against his molars.

"The saddest part of all, Vinnie, no one will know the truth. They won't know what really happened here. They will all see a sad man who saw ghosts. In fact, he feared his wife had returned from the dead to murder him. The pathetic old man hired a paranormal investigator. Desperate, crazed, and mad. That's what they will say about you. The well-renowned, successful dentist lost his wife and lost his mind. He couldn't live without her, so he killed himself to reunite with her."

Tears streamed down Vincent's face, some of them from terror and some from excited anticipation. He continued to drool, the saliva no longer drooling but pouring from his mouth. He screamed, but the gun muffled his voice.

"Before you commit suicide, would you like to know a secret?" The ghost of his wife leaned in and whispered in his ear. "I'm her twin sister. Her biological twin sister. All that is yours will flow downriver, finding itself in my possession. So, thank you, Vinnie. Thank you so much for your donation. Now, it's time you and Shelly find each other again. May you two spend all of eternity together in marital bliss."

The ghost snickered, pushing the gun impossibly further into his throat.

Vincent Dupree closed his eyes. He saw Shelly in his mind—he could almost smell her and taste her lips on his.

He exhaled, calming himself. Why not rejoin her in death? Would that really be so bad? In his head, he shouted, "I'm coming, Shelly! I'm on my way."

Ghost Busted.
Friday, April 28th, 1207hrs.

During our conversation earlier that night, I had convinced Dr. Dupree to leave the sliding-glass door leading from the back patio into his master bedroom unlocked. Hopefully, he hadn't neglected that duty, as he had forgotten to call.

I reached the sliding-glass door, wrapping my hand around the handle, and pulling. To my relief, Dr. Dupree had remembered to unlock the door. It slid open without a noise.

Dr. Dupree, as I already knew, didn't sleep in his bedroom, though. The sheets lay taut across the mattress, and the throw pillows stood before those he slept on. *What single man makes their bed with throw pillows*, I thought fleetingly as I rushed to the hallway.

The ghost of Shelly Dupree stood over Dr. Dupree, holding a gun deep in his mouth. She must have noticed me from her periphery, for she whipped her head to the side and stared as I emerged from the dark hallway into the room lit by the television's glow.

Luckily, my sudden emergence didn't startle her into pulling the trigger and uncapping the top of Dr. Dupree's skull. She startled, though, ripping the gun out of Dr. Dupree's mouth with a wet rattling sound, pointing the weapon at me.

That was a successful start to a rescue mission—taking the heat away from the potential victim.

I smirked with pride. My plan had worked, to an extent. If only Dr. Dupree had followed through on his end, staying awake and calling me, I probably could have intervened sooner.

I raised both hands above my head, showing the ghost my empty palms. "I'm not armed. I'm not dangerous." I dared not glance over my shoulder and alert the ghost to Fred's presence. A fourth person might define a party, and I did not want this gathering to pop off.

I did, however, briefly wonder why Fred hadn't followed me into the house... or had he? *Where had he gone?*

"Who are you?" the ghost asked, not bothering to disguise her voice and sound spooky. It was a sharp question from someone annoyed more than anything.

"I'm August Watson. A private investigator. Dr. Dupree hired my services to rid his house of his wife's ghost. That's you, I presume?" I didn't move—not to step closer to her, not to scratch my heinie.

She had the gun, the hostage, the positioning. My plan had shifted to playing it slow and remaining calm.

We regarded each other for a few tense seconds. The woman wore a sheer white outfit, which covered her entire body. Under other circumstances, the outfit might have fallen on the sexier side of the bedroom spectrum. Not in this circumstance. She had paled her face with makeup and dyed her hair white, styling it on end as to impersonate someone experiencing severe electrocution. I'm not sure how, but the effect worked. In the glow of the blue television light, with the surrounding darkness to play tricks across the imagination, she resembled functionally what some might consider a ghost.

"Shannon," I said after a moment, pushing my luck. "That's your name, right? Shannon Pellegri."

"I'm Shelly Dupree, Vincent Dupree's dead wife, and I have returned to avenge my death." I'm not sure what Shannon Pellegri did for a career, but I would have bet Dr. Dupree's life she didn't act. Her delivery landed flat, and she pursed her lips, as if realizing her rehearsed line had convinced no one.

"Shannon, you're here to claim his fortune. I mean, how exciting to find a long-lost twin sister, right? How exhilarating to learn she married an extremely successful dentist? I wonder, did you follow them on their hike? Did you push her off the ledge?"

Shannon's hands trembled as they held the gun, and her eyes widened with shock. "No. I would never."

"I didn't really believe you did. I thought it, though," I said, remaining rooted in place. No reason to scare the woman into pulling the trigger. "I'm often called a cynic, so those thoughts naturally crossed my mind—that you murdered your long-lost twin sister."

"I didn't. I wouldn't."

"I know. I'm actively working on my outlook on life. I'm trying to see the world in a more positive light. It's tough, though. It takes practice and patience to always find the positives." I sighed, risking a shuffle step closer to her. "For the sake of a friendly conversation, let's pretend I never notice the positives. I'm a cynic, remember? As a cynic, don't you find it fortuitous that your recently discovered twin sister stepped off a cliff and fell to her death?"

"Fortuitous?" Shannon asked, scoffing.

"I mean, Shelly had no other family. Of course, there's Vincent... but he doesn't have any family either. It's only him standing in the way of all that money you would inherit. That's the dream, right? The rich uncle nobody has spoken of or to in fifty years finally kicks the bucket and his vast fortune funnels directly into your bank account."

"I will shoot you."

"I don't think you will," I said.

"I will." Her hands trembled as she tightly gripped the gun, stretching it nearer to me.

I turned my back to her, really testing her threat. I went on tiptoes and glanced into the kitchen, searching for a coffee pot. Dr. Dupree had a Nespresso. That would work.

I returned my full attention to Shannon. "If you were to shoot, you would have shot Dr. Dupree two minutes ago, before I arrived. You had it all thought out, though, and you were following the plan."

"You know nothing."

"Shelly and you were identical twins, right? After her unfortunate accident, you appeared in the house and slowly introduced yourself to Dr. Dupree. Noises in the night. Notes left out for him. References to information only he and his lovely wife would know... which you learned through her journals, I assume. We found one, but none of the others. How many did she have?"

Still no answer.

So, I continued my best Sherlock Holmes impression, and laid out the mystery as I had figured it.

"You eventually presented yourself to him, in your lovely costume, of course." I broke off a side smirk and gestured at her outfit. "Identical in appearance to Shelly, you fooled the poor, desperate man. Your slow burn antics, the notes and the noises and clues—you hooked him and reeled him into believing Shelly's ghost actually haunted him. Not only that, but you waited patiently for him to seek help, to express his fears to another living soul, to create a record of his paranoia and supposed mental instability. You planned for it to look like a suicide, didn't you?"

Shannon's jaw clenched, but the gun wavered as she lost strength and will.

"Why not stage the suicide tonight?" I glanced at the coffee table, noticing the two empty bottles of wine. "Dr. Dupree drank too much, right? He had entertained the idea before—at least in the minds of others, of those he had confessed his ghostly experiences to. Drunk, funny thoughts tickle a person's brain. You had the gun in his mouth, pointed in a direction so it would appear like a natural suicide. I must admit, your attention to details and your patience... well done. Now, lower the gun. You won't fire it."

"You don't know that."

"I know as well as you know. You wouldn't have listened to me ramble and share your story for that long if you planned to shoot us. See, Shannon, I know you're intelligent, and you're running through the scenarios and the options right now, and you don't see any light at the end of the tunnel if you shoot me or Dr. Dupree. However, there's a faint glimmer if you drop the weapon. Run toward that beacon of hope."

"Why?" Dr. Dupree asked, his voice cracking.

His recliner, where he sat, faced the television. I stood behind the recliner, unable to see anything of him beyond his socked feet. When he spoke, though, his voice seemed near to shattering, and I thought he might break into sobs at any second.

Shannon turned her face from me, looking at Vincent. As she did, she lowered her gun further. The barrel now pointed at my crotch, and I half-wished she leveled it back to my face.

For a second, I entertained the idea of crossing the ten feet between us and wrestling the weapon from her grip without discharging it, but something tugged at me and begged me to stand down. When I served in law enforcement, I learned to decipher those who would pull a trigger and those who wouldn't. Of course, we all make mistakes. Even the greatest in their respective field of expertise stumbles.

Everyone within the criminal justice system defended my murder of Aaron Brooks, calling it a justified shooting. The kid had pulled a weapon, pointed it directly at me. I had responded with equal force, eliminating the perceived threat before he could kill me. The problem was, I had acted out of anger and fear. Anger at ancillary circumstances from the night before. A few hours before I punched into my shift, someone had shot an officer in Sacramento, killing the man, and that single act had filled every officer I knew with a primal, vengeful rage.

When Aaron Brooks pulled his weapon, I feared I might die—my anger had me itching for a reason to pull the trigger.

With Shannon lowering the weapon, she had all but surrendered herself. Why exacerbate the situation by rushing her, by imposing violence after her peaceful act?

Maybe my cynicism was lessening, after all.

"Why what?" Shannon asked.

"Why go through so much?" Dr. Dupree asked. "Why not introduce yourself to me? Why not ask me for money?"

"I didn't..." Shannon trailed away, falling silent for a while. "You didn't know me."

"You're my wife," Dr. Dupree said, folding his legs, lifting the recline of his chair. He scooted forward, standing to his feet. Gently, the small man reached out and wrapped his fingers around the hand gun, pulling it away from Shannon.

She allowed him to take it from her, to set it on the table beside the empty wine bottles. Dr. Dupree faced the woman dressed as a ghost. They stood near the same height, weighed about the same, too.

"I would have given you anything you asked for," he said.

I frowned, jutting my chin forward, confused by this turn of events.

Dr. Dupree held the hands of Shannon, staring directly into her eyes. "You're alive?"

"Yes," she said, whispering.

"You're my Shelly?"

"I can be, if you want me to."

"More than anything. I would pay all the money in the world to have my wife back. To hold her again. To kiss her." He angled forward and pecked Shannon on the side of her lips.

Her mouth parted. "You mean that?"

"With all my heart. Everything I own belongs to you, as long as I can have you. My Shelly. My Boo-bear."

I cleared my throat to snag their attention. In hindsight, I probably could have backed away and left with no one noticing, but I did not know how to respond to what was happening in front of me. I exhaled, drumming my lips.

"Vincent," I said, "I barely know you, and maybe I'm overstepping here, but I feel I can offer some insight into this situation."

"Please, speak your mind."

"That woman psychologically terrorized you for months. She planned to murder you and stage the murder, so it looked like you lost your mind and committed suicide, hoping that maybe—and I don't even think anyone knows if this would actually happen—your fortune would transfer to her. You caught all that, right?"

"I'm up to speed."

"She meticulously planned your murder. She shoved a gun into your mouth."

"Thank you, Mr. Watson, for your services. I will write a glowing review about the job you did. You not only saved me from my dead wife, but you resurrected her, bringing her back to me."

"Please don't write that in a review," I said, thinking of all the grieving spouses who would read that and inquire about my necromantic services.

"Write your invoice, and I'll pay it," Dr. Dupree said. "Pick any number. It doesn't matter."

Shannon frowned, facing me and shaking her head. "You can pick the number you two agreed upon. Vinnie will add a generous tip as well."

I cracked a knuckle and remembered Fred. Where the heck was that guy, anyway?

With the threat diminished, I glanced over my shoulder and called back for him.

The big man appeared around the corner, lazing into the room and eating a granola bar. "Hi," he said, waving at the room. "Congratulations on finding each other. Love is such a rare and fleeting emotion. My advice to you two, savor this moment. Remember this forever. There will be a time when you'll want to kill each other."

"Literally three minutes ago," I said. "She wanted to kill him literally three minutes ago."

"Love, like all emotions, fades away with time," Fred continued. "So, work every day at finding reasons to love your person. Their laugh or smile. Their warmth. Their kindness. Their sexy-ass body. Whatever the reason, always find the greatness in others... especially in those you love."

Was I drunk? Had I finished that bottle of wine? Was it laced with some hallucinogens? Was I dreaming? If none of those answers equated to a yes, what in the h-e-double hockey sticks was happening?

"I've always wished to speak at a wedding," Fred said, "or offer dating advice to my future kid, or to my best friend. Unfortunately, my best friend," he stared daggers at me, "won't ever get married because he's a blubbering imbecile around women." He sighed, fixing a mask of contentment over his face. "Daphne and I have such a magical relationship. I wanted to impart some of my wisdom to the younger generation of lovers."

"Dr. Dupree and Shannon are both twice your age," I said. "But none of that matters. Vincent, I have to report Shannon's crimes to the police. She broke into your home. She vandalized your property. She not only threatened you, but she shoved a gun into your mouth. That's attempted murder."

"I'll deny it all," Dr. Dupree said without removing his eyes from Shannon. "I will deny everything you say."

I bit hard on a knuckle, completely shellshocked about the situation. "Okay," I said, defeated. I had solved the case, but somehow I felt like I had lost. "Fred, we're out of here."

"Wait!" Dr. Dupree shouted, finally ripping his attention away from Shannon and regarding me. "Thank you. I don't know what will come of this, of us, but I would like to resume my marriage with Shelly. If that happens, Fred, would you officiate?"

Fred took two steps back and dropped his granola bar to the ground, placing his hands on his chest. I had never seen him relinquish food for anything. "You mean that?"

"We do," Shannon said, snuggling her face against Vinnie's bony shoulder. "We'd love for you to officiate."

"Yes. A thousand times, yes. Yes. Yes. Yes!" Fred said, raising a hand to me for a high-five.

"No," I said.

"Mr. Watson," Dr. Dupree said.

"No," I said.

"Would you be my best man?"

"No."

"Please."

"That won't happen."

"I don't have brothers or a father. You know this. You know I don't have a family. I hardly have any friends."

It wasn't a stretch of the imagination to wonder why the old doctor had little to no friends.

"No," I said.

"Free dental care for life."

"What?" I asked, tilting my head.

"Free dental care for life. My personal guarantee." Dr. Dupree placed a hand over his heart, as if pledging an oath.

"Dr. Dupree—"

"Vinnie, please. No more Dr. Dupree. We're friends now."

"Vinnie..." I hesitated, glancing up at the ceiling.

Who was I to convince this man that Shannon—who had attempted to murder him—wasn't his wife? Why steal his happiness? Why allot myself so much power to ruin another person's life? He had hired me to save him from the ghost, and I had done that. Why not be happy with a job completed?

"Yeah?" Vinnie asked.

"I'll do it."

He and Shannon hugged.

Fred went for another high-five, and I obliged. I even, amidst all their hollering and laughing, cracked a slight smile.

Why not? Life was crazy. Enjoy that crazy.

Waking Up.
Friday, April 28th,
0844hrs.

I SLEPT POORLY. SURPRISE, surprise. I never went to my apartment and collapsed in my bed, but I headed straight to the office after dropping Fred off at his house. I fell asleep at my desk around 0500hrs, reading Wikipedia articles on changelings.

My phone woke me.

I pawed at my desktop, searching blindly for the buzzing and blaring device to hit snooze. Except, somehow, through my grogginess, I recognized the sudden and obtrusive noise as my ringtone. Also, I remembered it was Friday, a business day.

Without rubbing the sleep from my eyes and checking the caller, I answered the phone. "Hello," I mumbled, my voice still thick with sleep. Also, I had failed to brush my teeth before dozing off last night, and speaking forced me to realize the unfortunate—my mouth tasted like raw sewage.

"August," said a raspy, jolly voice. Oddly familiar, as if from a distant memory.

I pulled the phone from my ear and checked the Caller ID. Lloyd Henderson, my parents' pastor of the past twenty years. Last week, I had reached out to him for help.

A grown man had lost his mother in a freak accident. They had a very Norma-Norman Bates relationship, except maybe more dysfunctional. With the mother deceased, Randall Fincher did not know how to survive on his own, and I feared he might hurt himself or others. So, I had contacted Lloyd Henderson to find Randall support, believing the church would drop everything to help those in need.

Fortunately, Lloyd had made that sacrifice.

"August, you there?"

"Mr. Henderson," I said. "Good morning. Is everything okay?"

"Everything is… it's good. Randall has agreed to see a psychiatrist. She's a member of the church, and she volunteers once a week to speak with people in the congregation. After a few sessions, she will refer them out. Anyway, Randall agreed to meet with her."

"That's good," I said, grimacing at the taste of my voice. "Not to sound rude, but… why are you telling me this?"

"Volunteers have also gone to the house and cleaned it. They found his Confession room."

It wasn't a room at all, but a coffin holding his father's remains. Randall's mother, Muriel, had forced her son into the coffin, closing the lid, and keeping him there for days at a time. The entire display was one of the more horrific things I had ever witnessed.

I cracked my neck, waking up my spine, waiting for Lloyd to continue reasoning why he had called me about Randall Fincher.

He cleared his throat. "Anyway, I'm calling on behalf of Randall. You did a good thing for him. An amazing thing. If you don't know this already, or if you haven't heard it recently, you're doing good work. You're helping people who can't help themselves. That's all that matters in the end. Helping other people. Thank you."

My initial annoyance leaked away. I sucked on my lips, taking a second to appreciate Lloyd Henderson's words.

"Thank you," I said.

"Of course you're under no obligation, but Randall has mentioned he would like to see you and thank you for helping him. He'll remain in my care for the foreseeable future, so if you decide to meet with him, you can contact me."

"Okay," I said.

"Okay, then. Get back at it."

"Yeah. Thanks again."

I ended the call and exhaled, staring out the window overlooking the neighboring building. After a minute, I stood, walked over to the coffee, and started a pot. As it brewed, I went into the bathroom, grabbed my travel toothbrush off the counter, and brushed my teeth.

As I finished splashing water over my face, my phone rang again. I hurried back to my desk. Sarah Herling.

"Good morning," I said.

"You sleep in the office?"

"How did you know?"

"I slept here, too." A light chuckle cut through the receiver.

I shuffled to the beeping coffee machine and poured myself a cup. "Make any progress?"

"Just digging through phone records and credit card transactions, looking for discrepancies in the timeline. I found nothing to contradict the murders, though. We're still stuck there."

Someone knocked on my door. I walked over and opened it.

Sarah stood in the hallway, wearing the same outfit she had worn for our work dinner. She wriggled her fingers at me, waving.

"Good morning," I said, still speaking into the phone.

She hung up and entered my office, glancing around. "Just you this morning?"

"Alina has school," I said, doubting my words. Something was off with that girl's schedule, and I needed to figure it out. "Fred and I had a late night solving another case. Didn't get home until around 0400hrs. He needs at least six hours of sleep to function like a normal human, eight hours to communicate like one. So I'll wait until eleven before badgering him. There's not much going on today, anyway."

I mentally ran through my schedule. Meet with Claire Balzan. Go on a date with Cambria Parker (thanks, Mom).

"Did you schedule me a time to speak with Claire?" I asked.

"That's why I called... and walked over here." Sarah grinned. "Also, I needed to get out of my office and clear my head. Everything started melting together. I had to change my scenery."

"I get that."

"Eleven. Does that work? I know you have to call Fred around that time, but you think you could push the call back... give him an hour of extra sleep?"

I scratched my neck, sipped my steaming coffee. "That works for me."

"Perfect."

"Have you contacted Simon's family or friends?" I asked.

"Haven't made a single phone call since our dinner last night. I didn't want to impose on anyone while they slept. I plan to make some calls now, though."

"Need any help?"

"Gio and I have it covered. You just meet with Claire. See if you can learn anything new from her. That's it." Sarah smiled.

"Alright," I said.

"Alright then. See you around." She found her way to the door, crossed the hallway, and looked back at me when she stepped into her office. "Take it easy."

"I don't know what that means."

The morning skipped by like a rock bouncing across a still body of water—one event to the next, filled with exhaustion-induced amnesia between them.

I met with Claire at the assigned time. Stress and life in jail had caught up to her. She appeared skinnier than she had a couple days ago, and older. The guard had allowed Claire to sit in our private room with handcuffs, though. Claire scratched at her face when it itched, and she constantly twisted her wrists in circles. Unfortunately, apart from her declining state and ability to use her hands without restraint, I gleaned nothing relevant or new from her.

After our visitation, I went back to my office and existed in a haze of fatigue.

Dating Advice.
Friday, April 28th, 1752hrs.

ALINA OFFERED ME POINTERS on how to dress for my date with Cambria—the date I had zero interest in attending, but did so for the amusement of my mother.

I wore boots, tight-fitting jeans, and a chic T-shirt. I had shaved, but not to the skin. A shadow of stubble remained. I had also messed up my hair, which apparently, according to Alina, was my best look. Purposefully and stylistically messy hair. It made no sense to me, but I knew next to nothing of fashion, so I heeded her advice.

Alina and Maya sat at my kitchen table in my apartment. My place, since Alina's departure, had remained sanitary, much to everyone's surprise and delight. I'm proud to admit I continued with the upkeep, though only a couple of days had passed. Still, I had washed and put away my dishes, folded the laundry, and made my bed.

After showering, grooming, and dressing, I stepped out of the bathroom, ready for my date.

"How do I look?" I asked, spreading out my arms.

"Like a younger, but far less attractive, version of Jensen Ackles," Maya said.

"Oh my gosh, yes. Exactly like that," Alina chimed in.

"Thank you," I said, rolling my eyes, completely unaware of who they meant—though I made a mental note to Google the name later.

"I mean 'far less attractive' in the nicest possible way," Maya said.

"Oh yeah, for sure. It definitely sounded polite."

"There's something about him, though," Alina said, staring at the ceiling. "About Jensen Ackles."

"It's called raw sexual attraction," Maya said. "He just oozes carnal pleasure, like he knows exactly what to do with a woman. I think that's what makes him so sexy. Also, probably why August is a less attractive version of that." Maya glanced at me and scowled. "No sexual magnetism there. Like nothing at all."

"You still mean all this in the nicest possible way?" I asked.

Maya poked out her tongue.

I hurried the two women out of my apartment and thanked them for their help in preparing me for the date. Once they had vanished, I hopped into my car and headed toward Cambria's place.

As I drove, I reflected on the day.

Nothing much had happened in the way of progress with my two remaining cases. Simon Balzan's parents lived out of town, but I spoke to them over the phone after meeting with Claire. They both adored their son's wife, and they couldn't believe she would ever have an affair, let alone murder him.

Simon and Claire Balzan had a "fairytale marriage," Simon's mom had said. "They adored each other like two teenagers brand-new to love."

I had asked about anyone who might wish them harm.

Neither of the parents had a reliable answer.

"Everyone loved them. Even when you wanted to hate them, you loved them," Simon's dad had said. "I want to hate Claire right now, for what she did, but I love her still today." He had remained silent during the rest of the call.

"Do you believe Claire murdered him?" I had asked.

"It's impossible to believe, but they have her on camera."

I had also spoken to Simon's friends and his brother. They had colored within the same lines as his parents. Amazing people. Loved each other wildly. Hard to believe Claire could do such a horrendous thing.

As for the Changeling case, even less had happened. No one contacted me, and I didn't reach out to anyone. Detective Quinn had asked me to step away, and I effectively had... for the moment. Sometimes the best way to solve a case is to wait a couple of days and re-evaluate the evidence, to see the story in a new light. I would place the Changeling case in a drawer until Monday, unless, of course, something new reared its head at me and demanded my attention.

I more or less had a weekend with nothing but one shift at the used bookstore with Maya... and my date with Cambria.

Maybe I would actually relax this weekend, take a nap, watch a movie, drive down to Galt where my parents lived and visit with them, my sister and her husband, and my brother before he returned to college in San Diego. Maybe I would surprise my mom at church on Sunday.

I sparked a small grin as I imagined the look on her face when she saw me unexpectedly walk into her church. Heck, if my date with Cambria went well, she and I could walk hand-in-hand into the church and give my mom a heart attack on the spot.

As if my thoughts tugged on her subconscious's ear, my phone rang in the cupholder. I didn't even waste my time glancing at the caller ID to know she called.

"Hi," I answered.

"It's after six. You better be on your way to pick her up."

"I'm one minute to arrival," I said, turning onto Cambria's street.

"Do you look nice? Send me a picture of what you're wearing. Did you shave? Put on cologne? Gussy, please tell me you showered."

"Yes, yes, yes, and yes. All of it."

"You dressed okay? You've never known how to put yourself together."

"I invited Maya and her niece over to offer pointers. They dressed me."

"Good. That's good. Are you nervous? I'm so nervous."

"Why are you nervous?"

"What if she doesn't like you?"

"Why wouldn't she like me?"

An extended pause. She refused to answer the question.

"Well, Mom, I'm not interested in her. I told you that last Sunday, and I told you that a couple days ago, and I'm telling you that now."

"With that attitude, she's definitely not going to like you. Remember, Gussy, open the door for her, pay for dinner, and listen to her when she speaks. It wouldn't hurt to smile, either. You have such a lovely smile, but you never show it."

"You always told me if I'm good at something, never do it for free."

"Well, you can smile for free. Did you brush your teeth?"

"Yes." I pulled up to the address matching the navigation on my phone. "I'm here."

"Okay. Okay. We got this. Just breathe."

"I'll be fine. Bye, Mom."

I exhaled and stared at Cambria's front door, flipping through my mind for a viable excuse to stand her up without it reflecting poorly on my mother.

I couldn't conjure a single legitimate excuse to leave. So, I stepped out of the car and headed toward her front door.

Dinner Date.
Friday, April 28th, 1807hrs.

I rang Cambria's doorbell and waited, exhaling the knot of nerves sitting in my stomach. I felt like my turn to speak in front of the class, and I had forgotten to write a speech.

What would I say to Cambria? What would we talk about? Our last meeting had mostly been her tongue moving aggressively inside of my mouth, while I stood still, lips slightly parted, allowing the unwelcome intrusion.

For a split second, I considered for the umpteenth time spinning around and hurrying back to my car, driving to the first town where I ran out of gas. From there, I would change my identity and begin a new life, one where I never had to face my mother for bailing on the date she had orchestrated.

As the fantasy hopscotched through my imagination, the front door opened.

Cambria Parker stood in the door frame like a painting framed in a picture. She had short, blonde hair—a choppy bob cut I would later learn was the correct term. She wore ripped blue jeans, a tucked-in white T-shirt, and high-heel sandals.

My voice stuck in my throat, and I coughed on it.

"Hi," she said, stitching a shy smile across her face. I remembered her from church last weekend as assertive, as far from shy as humanly possible.

I cleared my throat, grunting like a caveman.

"I almost didn't open the door," Cambria said. "Honestly, I don't really want to go on this date, but I love your mom to death. So, I agreed. Her precious heart would break if I stood up her sweet baby boy."

I smacked my lips a few times, figuring out how to use my mouth again.

"I told her I would send her a picture of us at the restaurant," Cambria said.

I cleared my throat again.

"Are you okay?"

"Yeah," I said, finding my word footing. "You surprised me. You look... really great."

She smiled again, glancing at the cement porch and not meeting my eyes. "Thank you."

We stood on her front patio for a full three seconds, though it felt like an entire lifetime, in awkward silence.

I scratched my neck and cracked a knuckle. "Well, what do you think? Should we head out and grab a drink?"

"I thought you didn't drink. I mean, that's what your mom told me."

"I don't drink alcohol, but I drink coffee. In my experience, I have found both alcohol and coffee perfect conversation beverages."

"Before we head out," Cambria said, "can I apologize for what happened at church on Sunday?"

"There's no need," I said.

"There is." She clicked her tongue. "Here's the thing... your mom can be quite persistent, and I can be quite a pushover. It's a people-pleasing trait I have and can't help but default to. Anyway, when I'm pushed to do something that I really don't want to do but can't say no to, I become petty or passive aggressive because I also don't enjoy conflict."

"I thought you were a very agreeable person," I said.

She chuckled. "Yeah, well, my goal was to come on so strong and desperate, I either scared you away, or someone caught us in the act while in the church, told your mom, and she hated the idea of me with you and dropped the issue. It was dumb and immature, and I'm sorry if I made you uncomfortable."

"Well, joke was on you—here I am, picking you up for a date after our amazing make-out session."

Cambria frowned. "Please don't remind me of that."

"I've thought it about every night since then."

"Stop it. I will slam this door in your face."

"The way you touched me, the way you kissed me… incredible. Unforgettable."

Cambria giggled, shaking her head. "Expect nothing like that tonight."

I extended my arm for her to loop hers into, and we walked down the driveway. "So, what do you think?" I asked. "Should this be the worst date ever? You and I are so incompatible that we sat in terrible silence the entire meal? I would normally play the bad-guy role in this situation and allow you to blame me for a horrendous date… but my mom. I would hate for my mom to think I messed this up." We arrived at my car, and I opened the passenger door for her. "I would hate for her to think you messed it up. So, if you're not interested—" I shut the door and circled the hood, opening the driver's door.

"And you're not interested," she said. "We tell her the truth. When we first met at church, we didn't click. We overlooked that incident, though, and we went on a date. It failed in a glorious, blazing inferno. We gave it a shot, though."

"Exactly," I said. "She can't be mad at either of us, then."

I turned on the radio, which was set to an Americana/Folk station that most people I knew despised. We listened to the music as we drove to the restaurant. Cambria sang along to a few of the songs, claiming how much she loved them.

Uh oh.

The hostess at the restaurant asked if we had a reservation. I said we had a table for two under Watson. She scrolled through her tablet, finding our name, then she led us to an outdoor table.

In late April, the weather was mostly warm, but a cool breeze riddled the evening. Cambria shouldered on her jacket, and I, as predicted, promptly ordered a hot coffee. Cambria ordered hot sake. The hostess obliged, but noted she would send over the waiter, who would take any other orders we had.

"It's nice here," Cambria said, glancing around.

I agreed.

A water fountain stood in the center of the back-patio seating area, playing a relaxing melody. The breeze rustled through the thick trees growing around us. It was nice—peaceful and isolated, as if we had walked through a portal out of Sacramento and into our own private night beneath the rising moon.

"Since we're on a terrible date," I said, "you don't mind if I ask straightforward questions?"

"Shoot."

"Why do you go to church?"

Cambria cocked her head. "What do you mean?"

"What do you get from the services, the community, the idea of God? What does it do for you?"

"You don't believe in God?" she asked.

"I don't know what I believe. I think I would like to, but it's hard for me to… justify God's absence in this world, I guess."

"Thy kingdom come, Thy will be done, on Earth as it is in Heaven," Cambria said. "Do you know that?"

"The Lord's Prayer."

Cambria smirked, her face shadowed by the dimming light and the shade of the overhanging trees. "I'm not an expert, but I've gone through my doubts and soul-searching, and I've come up with answers that suit me." She exhaled. "You really want to do this?"

"Hit me," I said.

"On Earth as it is in Heaven. God sent His son to this world to set an example of how we should live, and to save us, right?"

"Sure."

"I think by sending His son and providing us with that example of love, He showed us how we should love others. How we should live within this world." Cambria glanced at the sky, staring at the first glimmering stars. "It's hard to put into words."

"Try," I said.

"We are God's church, and the Holy Spirit dwells in us... or however you want to phrase it. We are extensions of Heaven. It's our job as Christians to bring Heaven to Earth. That's how we surrender and serve. We can't just have faith and sit around and judge and condemn others. We have to have faith that God will provide as we go out and do His work. His work meaning bringing Heaven to Earth—or loving people. That's it. His work, Heaven, it's all just love. Unconditional love. Everyone and always. Most Christians miss that message, I think. They follow rules and think that by following rules, they're saved. I don't buy into that logic—it's lazy and irresponsible. Jesus broke the rules when he lived on Earth, but He always loved and accepted everyone. He brought Heaven to Earth. To answer your initial question, how do I justify God's absence... He lives through us. His absence is a lack of human dedication to His calling and purpose. Our service to Him, doing His will, brings the kingdom of Heaven to the world."

The waiter appeared with our drinks. "Are you ready to order, or do you need a minute?"

"We need a lot of minutes," Cambria said, smiling at him. "I haven't read a single word on the menu."

"Take your time, please." The waiter bowed his head and walked away.

Cambria returned her attention to me. "Maybe I'm wrong. But I would rather be wrong for loving others than be right for judging those who don't agree with me."

"What about the supernatural?"

"What do you mean?"

"Ghosts. Spirits. The afterlife. Do you believe that exists?"

"Yes."

"Yes?"

"The Bibles says as much. At least I interpret it that way."

"And you believe we can communicate with those spirits?"

Cambria narrowed her eyes. "Yes, but I don't believe just because we can do something we should. Why do you ask? Do you plan on finding a medium and speaking to the dead?"

"If I believed in that nonsense, I might."

"Who would you want to contact?"

"It doesn't matter," I said.

"It does." Cambria shrugged and leaned back in her chair. "We're doing this to amuse your mother, right? It's an isolated incident. Why hold back?"

"Okay." Tears pressed against my eyes, stinging them. I ground my jaw for a second, fighting the surge of emotions. "Okay."

"Okay."

"I once killed someone."

Cambria, to my shock, leaned forward and reached across the table, grabbing my hand in both of hers. She didn't look scared or nervous, but determined. Maybe it was her 'love everyone always' mantra. But she held me and looked at me, like really looked at me.

"I shot a kid—nineteen years old. That's why I do what I do. I doggedly seek evidence proving the paranormal exists, because if it does, I might find Aaron and speak to him. If it does, I can apologize for what I did." I planted my tongue on the roof of my mouth and blinked my eyes rapidly, wading through the tide of regret flooding over me. "Most people have a different reaction when I admit my crime." I sniffled and grinned. "You already heard about it, huh?"

"Your mom told me," Cambria said.

"Figures."

"Have you spoken to Aaron's parents?"

My heart stopped beating. "What?"

"I don't know, but maybe you will never speak to Aaron's spirit. However, you can speak to the part of him that remains in this world—his blood."

"I can't do it," I said, thinking of my fist hovering near the Brook's front door. "What would I say to them? Apologizing won't bring their son back. I would never want to explain why I did what I did, like some cheap excuse to get me off the hook. I should never be off the hook."

Cambria squeezed my hand. "I can't tell you what to say or what to do, because I don't know. But we're here right now, right? We both wanted to avoid this night, to skip out on the other person? I don't know about you, but I'm having a pleasant evening. It's better than sitting on the couch and re-watching *Grey's Anatomy.*"

I chuckled.

"Confronting Aaron's parents might be a disaster, like this date could have been. It might be awkward and filled with uncomfortable emotions. It could also prove revitalizing and life changing for both of you. You and I agreed to meet here for your mother's sake—because we both love her in our own way. Maybe you and Aaron's parents can meet for his sake."

Cambria held my hand, so I couldn't pop a knuckle, but I needed to pop something. I cracked my neck. "You're not what I expected."

"What did you expect, then?"

"Well, considering how Sunday went, I expected a little more aggressiveness from you. Honestly, I thought you would blabber on about nothing of importance, run up my tab with drinks—"

"I still might do that."

"Then try to shag me at the end of the night."

"That's so bad?"

"I don't know. It just seems..." I trailed off, thinking of Glacia. "It seems frivolous—shallow, I guess. Before the incident, Aaron, I feel like I purely lived to get laid. Upon reflection, that was an empty life, and the incident exacerbated that emptiness. I had no one or nothing afterward, and those who stuck around, I always kept at length. Why would I allow them to share my pain? They didn't deserve that. In short, I was an emotional wreck, and only recently have I clawed myself free of that self-loathing hole. So, yeah... I think sex, for the sake of sex, is unhealthy for me. It reiterates the loneliness and the cheapness of life I wish to move forward from."

Cambria released her hands from mine and sat back in her chair. "You're not what I expected, either."

I laughed through my nose.

A silence settled over us, but not awkwardly tense—comfortable and calming.

We picked up our menus and scanned the selection. The waiter reappeared, and we placed our order. The food arrived shortly thereafter, and Cambria and I ate, sharing four sushi rolls. We spoke, though our conversation had devolved into first-date small talk.

She worked as a hair stylist in an upscale salon. She used to show horses, and she currently owned two of them, which she boarded out in Wilton.

I told her about my venture with the paranormal investigation, and she found it intriguing. She had heard about the voodoo doll murders and the living gargoyles, and she asked if I would take on the Sacramento Vampire.

I said nothing for a moment, thinking of Patricia and the life she had shared with me, that she had reminded me of. I licked my lips and shook my head. "Only with a contract. I'm busy enough as it is." I pointed at Cambria's short hair. "Do you cut your own hair?"

Cambria ran her fingers through it, messing the texture up a little. "No. Not a chance. I have someone at the salon who I trust enough. I usually grow it long, chop it, and donate it to a charity. That's why it's so short right now. I chopped it two weeks ago."

"It looks great," I said.

"I told you, I trust the lady who cuts it."

Placing my chopsticks across an empty plate, I sat back in the chair and huffed, feeling stuffed to the brim.

"Actually," Cambria said, "the lady who accepts the hair I donate shared a story with me. You might appreciate it, considering your line of work. Her niece, who's like six or something, asked, 'If someone who received donated hair committed a crime, and they left the hair at the crime scene, would the person who donated the hair get arrested?'"

I dropped my head, staring at the table—at the empty plates, bloodied with leftover sauce.

"Would they?" Cambria asked. "I really don't know. It's scary to think about, though."

My mind and thoughts had tripped, fallen from the present date to the doppelgänger case. Hair left at the murder scene. DNA evidence connecting Claire to the crime.

"Holy enchilada," I said. "What if she really is innocent? What if we can prove it?"

"What?" Cambria asked.

"What if?" I asked.

"What if what?"

"What if you donated hair, and the recipient committed a crime and left DNA evidence all over the scene?"

"That's a brilliant question, one already asked by a little girl, and one I secretly hoped you would answer." Cambria snickered, though nervously.

"I have to go," I said, pushing back my chair and standing. "My mom paid for dinner already. Run up her tab all you wish. She's rich."

"Wait, what? You're leaving?"

"Thank you so much for tonight. I had a wonderful time."

"Where are you going?"

"To work," I said.

"To work?"

"I'll call you later and explain, but I have to go."

Before Cambria could argue, I walked back into the restaurant, navigating around the tables and out the front door to my car. I paused, realizing I had driven her and she would need a ride back home. Silently, I cursed to myself and hurried back to the patio.

"Hi," I said. "We need to get you home."

"I'll call an Uber," Cambria said. "Go on."

"You're sure?"

"I'm sure." She smiled. "Do your thing. Go save the day."

I hesitated. "Would you possibly consider a second date?"

Cambria pursed her lips and tapped her chin. "Only under two conditions."

"Okay."

"One, you tell me why you had to rush away tonight."

"Deal."

"Two, you tell me how Aaron's parents responded to your apology."

"I can't—"

"Bye, August."

I sighed. "Goodbye."

Death Threats.
Friday, April 28th, 2023hrs.

I drove directly to the office, calling Sarah Herling on the way. My heart hammered in my chest—a combination of my pleasant date with Cambria and the revelation I thought I had learned. The donated hair.

"August," Sarah answered.

"Do you have a second to talk?"

"Yeah. Is everything okay?"

I must have sounded frenetic. I felt frenetic. "I think I learned something."

"What?"

"The DNA discovered at the crime scenes, it was hair stands, right?"

"Yeah."

"Did Claire ever donate her hair?"

"What do you mean?"

"Did she ever donate her hair to a charity?"

"I don't know."

"Bare with me, then. What if she donated? What if whoever received her donated hair used it as a wig, strategically leaving behind DNA evidence to frame her for the murders?"

Sarah remained quiet for a second, clicking her tongue to fill the dead space. "Not possible."

My stomach hollowed out. "What do you mean? It has to be possible."

"Hair found at crime scenes usually has the root still intact. You need the root to make a conclusive DNA match. If the hair came from a wig, that means someone had cut it, and cut hair doesn't have the root. Also, charities like Locks of Love usually take three different donations to form a single wig. If someone fabricated evidence against Sarah, they would have no way of determining which hair belonged to her and which hair belonged to the other donators. Also, forensics would have noted any of that in their report, but they didn't. I just pulled up the pictures of the strands they identified as Sarah's, and there's a root attached to each one. The hair came from her head, not from a wig."

I had sped through Sacramento, racing back to my office, but I slowed the vehicle after Sarah debunked my theory rather easily. I probably should have phoned her while at the restaurant, rather than abandoning Cambria. I really had enjoyed our time together—a fact my mother wouldn't have to learn unless something serious came of it. We would cross that bridge if it ever arrived, though. Still, I had flown from the restaurant, probably erasing any chance at a second date.

"August," Sarah said. "You there?"

"Here."

"It's a good thought, but not credible to our situation."

"Someone framed Claire," I said.

"I think so, too. But who, and why?"

I shook my head, unable to answer those questions.

My entire life, I had followed evidence. I had allowed the evidence to speak truth into my decisions and actions. During a murder investigation, I never pigeon-holed a suspect based on whether they seemed the most likely. Instead, I allowed the evidence to lead me to the actual killer. Facts ruled my life. Except for now. Why couldn't I find contentment in the overwhelming evidence that Claire was guilty of murder? Why did I believe her claim of innocence?

Sarah and I ended the call, and I climbed the stairs to my office, dragging my feet.

Once at my desk, I powered on my computer and checked my emails. I had a few unread messages, mostly discount opportunities from websites Fred had signed up for using the company email.

One subject line stood out, though. It shared my address and my parents' address.

Curious, I opened the email.

August Watson,

Stop investigating. I know where you live. I know where everyone you love lives. I hope you enjoyed your date tonight as well. Speaking of, I also know where Cambria Parker lives. Sarah Herling. Glacia Vasquez. I know your sister is pregnant. I know your brother is home from college. I know Alina moved in with Maya.

I know everything.

So, stop your investigation immediately. You know which case I mean, too.

Death is only a sweet release that the tortured and tormented beg for.

Yours truly.

I read the email at least fifteen times, always stopping and reading three times over the part where the sender mentioned my sister's pregnancy.

How did they know? Only my sister, her husband, and I knew. Rachel hadn't shared that news with anyone beyond me, not even our parents.

I also reread the last little quip on each read through.

"Death is only a sweet release that the tortured and tormented beg for," I read aloud. The meaning was clear enough. Whoever had emailed meant to torture someone I loved until they begged for death, unless I ceased all investigative practices... to which case, though?

I only had two ongoing cases.

Except with the Changeling case, Detective Quinn had asked me to back off and leave the work for the big boys. If the sender knew every other detail about my life, I'm sure they knew that little factoid as well.

That left only one case. The doppelgänger.

Had Claire Balzan's doppelgänger sent the message?

Time clicked away. The evening slipped into night, late night. Midnight.

I worked through my notes, reevaluating everything I had on the doppelgänger case. It all pointed to Claire committing both murders, stealing drugs, and having an affair on her husband—other than the inconsistent timestamps on the drug theft and infidelity. How had she recorded those videos and bought Starbucks or filled up with gas on her way to Monterey?

It was impossible, unless she hadn't recorded those videos.

I glanced at the clock—1207hrs. Awesome. Another night with no sleep.

I should have called Sarah hours ago, asked her if she received a threatening email.

Could I call her this late? Probably, but I didn't dare. The unprofessionalism of it screamed at me to stop and wait until morning—which was a Saturday morning. Could I call her then, on a weekend? Usually not, but I thought the circumstances warranted a mid-morning phone call.

Massaging my temples, I stood and paced the office, not sure what to do next. Sleep wasn't an option, not after the message. As I went back and forth, my phone rang.

I grabbed it from my pocket. A Miette Verdin—the original Miette Verdin, not the Changeling—called.

"Hello," I answered

Slow breathing on the other end.

"Miette, what's going on?"

"I'm meeting my brother, Zachary... in person."

"Now? Do you think that's a good idea?"

"It will be the first time I have seen him face-to-face in almost twenty years."

"Why now? Why not tomorrow morning, somewhere safe and in broad daylight?"

"I'm really nervous." Her voice trembled as she spoke. "I didn't know who else to call. I'm sorry it's so late."

"I'm awake. Where are you meeting him?"

"He said he met with you."

"Yeah. Yesterday."

"He said you could help me, and that's why he gave you my phone number."

"I can help you."

"He feels guilty about the past, and he wanted to help me. He said we needed to meet again, but Vanessa Snow couldn't know about it. Do you trust him?"

I held my tongue, unsure of how to answer.

"Does he want to help me, or does he want to help her? No, never mind. Don't answer that. I don't want to know the truth. I want to believe that Zach wants to help me."

"Where are you meeting him?" I asked, breathless, squeezing the edge of my desk tightly.

"Why?"

"Someone should know."

"Do you think he'll hurt me?"

I didn't know. I had struggled to read Zach's intentions, to deduce whose side he stood on, but I didn't like the idea of a secret meeting happening after midnight.

"Do you think he'll hurt you?" I asked.

Miette allowed her breathing to fill the void for a few seconds. "Yes."

"Why?"

"I never wanted to kill them. Not my parents, not Zach, and not Vanessa. I only wanted them to admit their mistake to me and to the world."

"Did you murder your parents?" I asked, holding my breath.

When I had asked two days ago, she had dodged answering the question every single time. Now, she hesitated, but I imagined her nodding her head in confirmation from the driver's seat of a dark vehicle.

"No," she said.

"No?"

"I didn't murder them."

"Who did?" I asked.

"One of them."

"One of who? Vanessa or Zach?"

"Yes."

"Now you think they'll hurt you so Vanessa can continue living her lie?"

"Yes." A soft whisper that barely crossed the phone line.

"Why are we meeting with him, then?" I asked.

"In case I'm wrong. I lived through those twenty years because of hope. I guess I still hope he will accept me as his sister. That's why I'm meeting him."

"Where?"

"Land Park. Will you watch the performance?"

Before I could answer, Miette disconnected the line.

I knew exactly where she meant, though. There was an outdoor stadium at Land Park in Sacramento, an old-fashioned amphitheater for high school drama students to perform Shakespeare plays outside, or for musicians to play live music on warm evenings.

Snatching the keys off my desk, I rushed to my car and drove toward the park.

It was a ten-minute drive, but I would push to make it in five. I wasn't sure if Miette's life was in jeopardy, which meant I didn't have a reason to call the police. If I had to bet, though, I would bet everything she faced grave danger.

Crashing the Party. Saturday, April 29th, 0036hrs.

I TURNED OFF THE Honda's headlights as I pulled into Funderland, an amusement park for children located across the street from the Sacramento Zoo. Funderland's parking lot overlooked the William A. Carroll amphitheater at Land Park.

The lot was empty, apart from one other vehicle inhabiting the area—a Toyota sedan. I pointed my vehicle away from it, parking on the opposite side, nearer to the children's amusement park than the stage.

I opened the door, stepped out, and gently closed it behind, careful not to make a sudden noise in the dead of night. If something was amiss or if someone was in danger, I didn't want to alert Zachary or the Changeling to my presence.

Though the Changeling had hired me to investigate Vanessa Brown, and though she had yet to pay me for my services, I couldn't stand by and allow harm to come to the real Miette Verdin.

I crept across the parking lot, avoiding the circles of light created by the poles, sticking to the shadows, hiding behind fences and trees.

I peered down the steep hill toward the small amphitheater. Only the moonlight cast a glow over the stage, drenching it in a dreamy, pale luminescence.

On the stone benches sat a single audience member. A silhouette in the night. A phantom. A ghost.

On the stage, highlighted by the stars, stood Zachary. His lank body and slumped shoulders and bright-red hair gave him away. He spoke loud enough for any potential person sitting in attendance to hear his monologue, though.

"I was seven. You have to understand that. What else could I have done? You returned after eighteen months—nearly a quarter of my life then. I had such a small perspective on everything. And though you seemed different in some ways, Mom and Dad told me it was okay. They said that's normal. You had endured so much, and you had changed from those experiences. Who was I to argue with them? They knew. They were my mom and my dad. They knew. So, I did what any seven-year-old would do. I trusted my parents. Was I wrong about that? Yes. And I live with that mistake every single day of my life."

The audience member sitting stage-side on the bench responded, grunting and groaning, her voice muffled. I assumed that was Miette, and her inability to speak forced me to wonder if they gagged her.

As I snuck forward, risking a better vantage, a blur caught my attention from the corner of my eye. I barely registered the movement, and I had no time to turn and identify it.

A brilliant force bludgeoned my skull. My legs wobbled. I lost my balance and dropped. The world pulsed in and out of focus. Something stiff and scratching tightened around my wrists. Something dry clogged my mouth, followed by a stretch of tape.

Everything went completely dark.

When the world returned—along with an exploding headache—I slouched on the stage against the single mortared wall on the back edge.

The Changeling stood beside me, looming over me like an unfathomable monster. She was looking down at me, right at me, just watching and waiting, I guess, for me to open my eyes.

"Mr. Watson," she said, grimacing, as if standing over me pained her. "I'm sorry you found yourself here tonight. The good news, you will learn the entire story behind the Changeling case. You will not die curious." She tilted her head and smirked. "You really are a determined and resourceful investigator."

I went to respond with a sincere thank you, but my gag prevented me from speaking.

The Changeling had also bound my legs to a chair, my arms behind the backrest. None of the initial natural beauty she had exemplified from our first meeting shined that night. Whatever radiant energy she had exuded, whatever beaming attractiveness she had shed paled beneath the moonlight. Her weariness swelled beneath her heavy eyes, and her haggardness mussed her hair into a tangle. If I had to guess, I would estimate she hadn't slept since murdering her adopted parents.

Behind her, directly across from me, sat a gaunt, skeletal woman, also restrained in a folding chair. She had bright-orange hair, pale skin, and an emaciated appearance—her cheeks sank into her face, her eyes sat in hollow depressions, and her skin hung off her bones like sheets on a wire. The real Miette Verdin, in adulthood, looked nothing like her replacement, apart from a physical sadness they both wore on their sleeves like cufflinks.

Zachary stood behind the Changeling, between Vanessa Snow and Miette Verdin. He stared at his biological sister, though—at Miette Verdin. I couldn't see his face, only his posture. One arm barred across his chest, holding the biceps of the other, shoulders slumped, head directed downward.

The Changeling, Vanessa, about-faced and shuffled over to Miette—running her toes off the stone stage with each slow step. When she came within a few feet of the girl, she squatted. "I studied you for months—everything the media reported about your life, my parents burned that information into my brain. They stopped calling me Vanessa, Nessy, or Nessa. Instead, they referred to me as Miette. Miette. Miette. That was who I was. You. They turned me into you.

When they were confident in my identity crisis, they dropped me off at your front door."

Miette never moved. She stared at her lap and absorbed the story.

"Your parents and your brother welcomed me into their home, believing despite the differences that their daughter had returned. They loved me as their own, and they provided me with a family far more stable than my last. I stopped pretending after so many weeks, adopting your persona for real. Vanessa Snow died, and Miette Verdin lived again." She reached out and tapped Miette on the cheek. "Now we have a problem, don't we? Two Miette Verdin's can't live at once. There can only exist one of us... and that's me." Vanessa reached into her back waistband, concealed by a baggy shirt, and she drew a gun. She pressed the barrel against the bottom of Miette's chin, lifting the woman's shriveled face with it.

Miette showed no emotion. I might have guessed that she relaxed on the sofa with a glass of wine and watched a boring movie, mostly paying attention to her phone.

The Changeling continued to speak. "You killed your parents after escaping your captor and returning home. After learning they abandoned you, that they replaced you with me, after experiencing so much trauma and abuse, you snapped. You shot them dead. You contacted your brother, planning to kill him, too. Though he lived, you shot him." The Changeling adjusted the gun's aim to Zachary, and she pulled the trigger.

A white burst exploded, followed by the deafening report.

Zach yelled and dropped to the ground, clutching his leg beneath his knee, bleeding onto the stage.

"You failed to kill him. A colossal mistake, though. As you took aim at me, ready to reclaim your supposed life as Miette Verdin, Zach pushed away his pain and his fear. He saved me—he saved his actual sister. I grew up with him. I told him all my secrets, and he shared his with me. I went to him for advice. We were best friends. Not you two. Us. He knows that. He doesn't know you. So, he saved me, putting down the woman who tried to steal my life from me. Before any of that, though—"

The Changeling turned to me. She extended the gun forward, leveling at my chest.

"Investigator Watson appeared. He learned the truth of everything, for he is a dogged and persistent investigator. You murdered your biological parents. He witnessed you shoot Zachary. In a display of bravery, he reacted. So did you. You shot him."

The bullet hit me like a train, slamming into my shoulder and skidding the chair I sat in back a foot. I shouted in pain, but the rag muffled my voice.

The Changeling painted a delightful picture for us, detailing the exact story she and Zach would share with the police. Miette Verdin, or rather Vanessa Brown, created the carnage. Zachary and Miette, the Changeling, had responded in self-defense, killing the crazed imposter.

It was a lazy plan. I wished I could point out the flaws of the Changeling's logic to stall her, but the rag impeded any chance of speaking. Forensics investigated all deaths, though, and they would probably run DNA analysis on Miette Verdin's body, if the Changeling killed her. Results would undeniably reveal her as the biological daughter to Melissa and John Verdin, exposing the Changeling as a fraud.

Her plan made certain sense to me, though.

The Changeling had approached me. She had asked me to look into the woman named Vanessa Brown, who tormented her, who broke into her home, who threatened to expose her. All that was true. Yet, the Changeling, knowing she was a fraud, had approached me. Why? Because she had an unwavering confidence. She had performed in the role for almost twenty years, and no one would find her out. No one would discover the truth of the story. It's like when serial killers become sloppy before their eventual arrests—their sense of invulnerability permits sloppiness and arrogance. They have outwitted, outsmarted everyone for so long, they believe they can get away with it forever.

The Changeling returned the gun to beneath Miette's sharp chin. With her other hand, she ripped the tape from the woman's face and fished out the rag in her mouth.

"I'm not a complete monster," the Changeling said. "Do you have any last words you would like to share?"

Miette stared at her brother.

He clutched his leg and hissed in pain.

"I was five when that man abducted me," Miette said, never taking her eyes from Zach. "He never shared his full name with me, but he asked for me to call him Norman. Like Norman Bates. I don't know if he enjoyed likening himself to the character, or if that was his actual name."

The Changeling yawned. "Hurry it up."

I strained my ears, listening for the sounds of eventual sirens. Two gunshots had sounded in a public park. Someone had to have heard and notified the police. That was our only chance at surviving this ordeal. I heard nothing, though—nothing but the breeze and the distant traffic.

Miette swallowed and licked her lips. "Zach, do you remember the day we went hiking with Mom and Dad? You and I wandered off and got lost. I cried. Remember that? It was only a few weeks before Norman took me, so maybe you don't—but I do. Whenever Norman, well... I would close my eyes and think of us lost, of me afraid and crying, and I would think of you hugging me. You whispered in my ear that day. 'I will protect you. I will get you back to Mom and Dad. To safety.' You repeated it like ten times. And I believed you then. I believed you during my time in hell. I still believe you."

The Changeling cocked her head. I couldn't see her face, but I can't imagine it was anything sweeter than Norman's face. "That was an inspiring story. Thank you for sharing. Belief is such a powerful thing to have, isn't it? Without it, would we be here tonight? I doubt that—or should I say, I believe you wouldn't. Now, Zach has a romantic heart and a tendency to make grand promises. He swore to me, when I first arrived at your house so many years ago, to stand by my side no matter what. To always have my back. To never leave me. For twenty years, he has kept that promise."

A desperate scream cut through the dead night. Zach had discreetly positioned himself into a three-point stance, and he launched at the Changeling, slamming into her with his shoulder.

They both rolled, fighting for control. Zach was a small man—five-foot-seven and maybe a hundred-fifteen pounds when fully dressed and soaking wet. The Changeling had to have matched that size with ease, if not surpassed it.

In their wrestle, the gun registered.

Boom! Boom! Boom!

Three explosive reports.

Miette yelped. "Zach!"

I flinched with each shot.

Boom!

A fourth, and a final report, coinciding with a cascading arc of blood and brain matter coming from Vanessa Snow's head. The Changeling went limp, her full weight falling on Zachary.

From my position, it didn't seem like he had much energy to squeeze himself free. He wriggled, though, grunting and groaning, yelling like a bodybuilder maxing out his deadlift. Zach slipped loose, crawling away from Vanessa and falling into Miette's lap. He wrapped his arm around his sister's waist and sobbed.

After a few seconds, his wits must have returned. Zach loosened Miette from her binds. She stood on wobbly legs, embracing her brother.

"I'm sorry," he said. "I'm so sorry. I'm so, so sorry. Please forgive me. Please."

Miette shushed him. "It's okay," she said, her forgiveness intermixing with his apologies. They both cried, holding each other.

I sat in the chair, restrained, gagged, and shot, dropping my head back and staring at the night sky. The darkness closed in, overwhelming my vision from every direction until I knew nothing more.

Home Visit. Saturday, April 29th, 0838hrs.

Sarah Herling stood before Trisha Berry's apartment door, hesitating before knocking. She had been reading over previous interviews she, Gio, and the police had had with anyone connected to Claire Balzan, Simon Balzan, and Robert Woods.

While flipping through the reports, a picture of Claire had caught her eye. She couldn't remember ever seeing that photograph of her client, so she stopped on that page for a closer look. The woman in the image mirrored Claire in nearly every sense, except... something was different. Slightly off.

Sarah scanned the page, quickly finding the inconsistency. It wasn't a picture of Claire Balzan at all, but of Trisha Berry, Robert Woods' secretary. Sarah flipped through more documents, finding a picture of Claire, comparing the two women side-by-side.

Trisha had bigger eyes, like Disney princess eyes—wide and round. When looking at her face, Sarah couldn't help but look into those eyes. Claire, though, had droopier eyes—ones that carried the weight of all her worries. They also didn't have the same hair color, though that was simple enough to fix.

Leaning back in her chair, Sarah recalled her interview with Trisha. The woman had checked off every box, never raising any red flags. Also, during that initial interview, Sarah hadn't noticed the resemblance. Was it just that picture, then? A trick of the light? The style of editing?

"Or was it purposeful?" Sarah asked aloud, reading the piece of paper for Trisha's cell phone number. When she found it, she typed it into her phone.

"Hello?" Trisha asked.

"I'm sorry to bother you on a Saturday morning. My name is Sarah Herling, and I'm the defense attorney Claire Balzan hired. Do you know her?"

"I do. The police arrested her for murdering Dr. Woods. I'm sorry, but I'm confused. We've... you and I have already spoken. Did something else happen?"

"No. No, Claire maintains her innocence, though, and I am her defense attorney." Sarah smiled, though no one knew it but her. "We spoke a few days ago, but I was hoping we could speak again. I wanted to ask a few more questions."

"Okay."

"Do you care if we meet?"

"In-person?" Trisha asked.

"In-person."

"Sure."

"I can drive to your apartment, if you don't mind. Save you a trip."

"Yeah, okay. That works."

In a flurry of excitement, Sarah had driven straight to Trisha's place, rehearsing what questions she would ask to trick her into possibly confessing to the murders. She had forgotten to notify anyone of where she rushed off to.

Now, she stood before Trisha's door, hesitating to knock, realizing no one knew her location. Before Sarah could fish her phone from her pocket and make a simple call or send a message to Gio, the front door swung open.

Trisha stood in the doorframe. She had chopped her hair much shorter than the style she wore in the photograph, and she had dyed it a raven black. Still, despite the drastic change, Trisha and Claire Balzan could have passed as twins.

"Sarah," Trisha said. "Come in. Please. I made coffee."

"Thank you," Sarah said, stepping into the apartment and glancing around.

Nothing abnormal or incriminating popped out. Trisha had decorated her place in a minimalistic, color-barren manner. It was clean and organized.

"Do you care if I use your restroom?" Sarah asked, glancing down a hallway.

"Sure. First door." Trisha disappeared into the kitchen. "Would you like coffee?"

"Yes, please." Sarah padded through the bathroom door, turning on the light.

The bathroom didn't boast the same cleanliness as the living room had. A small gathering of laundry piled against the wall. The mirror had smears and water stains across it. Brushes and combs and makeup lay scattered across the countertop... along with a kit to dye hair stacked in the trashcan. After a few minutes of inspection, Sarah flushed the toilet and ran the faucet, pretending to wash her hands, then she returned to the living room and joined Trisha on the couch.

"I didn't know if you enjoyed cream or sugar in your coffee," Trisha said, smiling.

"Usually both. But don't worry about it. I enjoy it black, too."

"No. No." Trisha stood, collecting Sarah's mug with her left hand and carrying it into the kitchen. "I'll be right back."

As Trisha disappeared, Sarah removed her phone and clicked on the voice recording application. She rolled her shoulders and exhaled, praying to a god she didn't believe in to watch over her. As if in response, her phone rang. August Watson.

"Good morning," she said. "Working on the weekend, I see."

"Is Claire left-handed?" he asked, speaking faster than usual.

"Excuse me?"

"Is Claire Balzan left-handed?"

"I don't know." Sarah closed her eyes to picture Claire in the visitation room, signing a sheet of paper. Had she used her left or right hand? Sarah had paid little attention.

"I don't think she is," August said.

"What do you know?"

From the kitchen, Trisha called out. "You okay in there?"

"August, hold on." Sarah raised her voice, responding to Trisha. "It's August. He's a detective working the case with me. I think he knows something about Claire... something that might help her." She lowered her voice, speaking to August again. "Sorry. I'm with Trisha Berry, Dr. Woods' assistant."

"Share your location with me," he whispered.

"What?"

"Share your location, then leave immediately. You're in danger."

"You're scaring me."

"Sarah!" he shouted. "Sarah, leave!" A second elapsed. "Call Alina now."

"What?" Sarah asked. "August, what's—"

Sarah gasped as Trisha emerged from the kitchen carrying a gun in her left hand. With her right, she gestured for Sarah to hang up the call. Without hesitation, she obeyed.

Hospital Visit. Saturday, April 29th, 0838hrs.

I AWOKE TO THE harsh sound of a chair scraping across tile. The noise grated against my skull, dragging barbed wire along the surface of my brain. Though my eyes were closed, I squeezed them tighter, hoping I could suffocate the pain in my head.

Except the grating sensation wasn't close to the worst part.

An ache in my shoulder radiated into my chest and down my arm—like molten metal hardening. I couldn't move my limb, and breathing was more difficult than usual. I squeezed my eyes tighter, picturing myself asleep again, lost in the oblivion of darkness.

Foreign fingers crawled up my fingers, and a warm palm rested over the back of my hand.

Please don't be my mom. Please don't be my mom, I thought.

A terrible thought, I know. But I had deduced that I lay in a hospital bed, recovering from a gunshot wound. My mother would cry and worry and blame me for acting recklessly. I would then have to talk her off the ledge, comfort her, appease her worries, and I didn't have the energy. So, I wished she had yet to hear the news about my condition, or at least hadn't arrived at the hospital.

Despite my thought, I doubted she held my hand. It was much too large and all-encompassing.

My father, then?

Please don't be my father, I thought. With him came my mother.

I braved opening my eyes, blinking against the uncomfortable white brightness within the room.

Fred angled over me, holding my hand. He wore a concerned grin—one of those soft-eyed, lip smirks someone flashes when they're relieved, exhaling through their nostrils any tension they held.

"Hey, Sunshine," he said, his voice low.

I yanked my left hand away from his. My good hand. Something about left-handedness tickled my memory. "What—" A coughing fit cut me off.

He shushed me, placing a bent straw periscoping out from a cup to my lips.

I hated myself for drinking water like a child, especially water offered by Fred, but I had little choice in the matter. If I refused, I might hack up a lung.

"Thank you," I croaked.

"How you feeling?"

"Like someone shot me in the shoulder."

"Can't relate."

"How long was I out?"

Fred glanced at his clock. "I received a call around one this morning. It's nine. So, eight hours." He grinned ear to ear.

"Who would have thought eight hours would feel so exhausting?" I asked. "I feel more lively after three hours of sleep."

"I think the massive hole in your shoulder played a role in your poor sleep quality," Fred said, continuing to smile.

"Probably." I adjusted my position, but collapsed back into place. An exploding pain shot through my arm and down my side. I grimaced, biting my lip, slowly exhaling through my nose. "Stop smiling like that."

"Like what?"

"It's creepy."

"What is?" He refused to budge on the exposure of his teeth.

"Why are you smiling?"

"I received a phone call."

I closed my eyes again, wishing more than ever to fall into a dreamless sleep, possibly to never wake again.

"I'm your go-to emergency contact?" Fred asked.

"Yes."

"I'm flattered."

"It was you or Maya, and I trusted you a little more with my life."

"Not your Kim?"

"You mean, my mom? And no. Not my mom or my dad or my sister. When I find myself here, in a hospital bed, I would prefer someone other than a first-responder inform them of my condition." I opened eyes again. "Speaking of, did you inform them?"

Fred slowly shook his head. "Not yet. I waited for you to wake up."

I sighed. "How long have you been here?"

"Since a little after one this morning."

"Who called you?"

"Miette Verdin. The real Miette Verdin. She called from inside your car, or so she said, while driving you to the emergency room. Apparently, you passed out from blood loss."

"Where is she now?"

"The waiting room. Not entirely for you."

I stared at the white ceiling and thought of Zach getting shot in the leg. "Who else knows?"

"No one. I figured you would spill those stinky beans."

"Always leaving me with the dirty work," I said.

"You know me. I can't stand getting dirty."

"Did Miette share anything else with you, like what happened to Zach?"

"I didn't ask, she didn't say."

"Could you call her in here, but... don't leave. I trust her, but if that proves mistaken, I would like you sitting in my corner—literally, too. Call her in here and sit quietly in the corner."

Fred disappeared, leaving me alone.

A minute later, he and Miette returned. Fred found a corner to stand in. Miette sat in the chair beside my bed. In the morning light, under the buzzing fluorescents, her pale, gaunt skin seemed more extreme and emphasized—a fresh corpse, still warm, though barely, risen from her grave and walking among the living.

For a while, we regarded each other with mutual respect, or so I think. Maybe I had regarded her with a lot more respect, though. The woman before me had overcome twenty years of hell to face her family, who had replaced her, and to take on the woman who had walked in her shoes. I doubt I could have done that.

I didn't enjoy facing my family as it was, and they had done nothing but stand beside me and chase after me during my time in hell. If they had abandoned me, though... I don't think I ever would have sought them out. I would have carried that hate and sense of betrayal forever, allowing it to devour me little by little until nothing remained but emptiness.

I closed my eyes, opening them again after a second.

"Thank you," Miette said, blinking fast.

"What happened to Zach?"

"He waited with her... with Vanessa. He called the police and waited for them to show up. He's here, in another room, but I haven't heard from him yet."

I wanted to ask her how she had escaped her prison, how she had escaped her captor, but it didn't matter. Her story would break, and soon the entire world would ask her that question on repeat, along with a million other questions, forcing her to relive those moments of feeling alone and lost.

Miette must have read the conflicting emotions typed across my face. She must have heard my thoughts. I didn't have to ask her.

She willingly shared her story.

"I'll speak to the police," Miette said. "I'll tell them everything that happened. I'll answer all their questions, no matter how long it takes, only to bury it all. I won't ever speak to the media. I won't ever write a book about my experience. I will bury the nightmare with the police. End of story."

I nodded, wanting to crack my knuckle, but not wanting to move my arm and endure the shooting pain. Such trivial pain in comparison.

"You deserve to know the truth," Miette said. "You took a bullet for me." She glanced at Fred.

"You can trust him," I said.

"I know."

"One of my best friends is a journalist. She'll want to know everything I know. Can I share with her if she swears not to publish anything?"

"Only what you know before this moment."

I nodded. "That's fair."

Miette turned her head and stared at my feet. "We always had dinner together. He was an incredible cook. I don't know what Norman did during the day, like as a career, but he could have made it as a talented chef. That night, we had burgers and sweet potato fries. Simple, but delicious. He updated me on the world, the national, and the local news. He updated me on my family—which I found more torturous than relieving, knowing they continued life so blissfully unaware. During our last dinner, Norman suddenly grabbed his chest. He was overweight... obese. His entire body went rigid, and his eyes widened like something from a cartoon. That's it. I watched and waited for him to die. When he fell to the ground, I pilfered his keys and walked to his front door. Twenty years after kidnapping me, he died in that basement, and I walked free." The girl pinched my sheet, pulling free a strand of hair. "Gross. Did they not wash your sheets?"

I shivered, thinking of who had laid in this bed before me. Had they died? "Probably fell off of a nurse or doctor," I said, more to convince myself of that idea. As the statement bubbled from my lips, I froze like a solid block of ice.

Probably fell off a nurse or doctor. It had fallen from someone's scalp (gross), and Miette had pinched it between her index finger and thumb, prying it off my sheets. Did it have a root ball attached to the end?

"Probably," Miette said, sliding it off her fingers and dropping it to the ground before I could ask to examine the stray hair. "I stood in Norman's front doorway, though. The gateway to freedom. I couldn't walk through it. Twenty years, and the world had changed so much. Norman had shared all that change with me, of course. But it's one thing to hear about it, another to experience it. It overwhelmed me. On the one hand, I couldn't remain in his home. What if he hadn't died? What if he trudged up those stairs like some monster from a horror movie? I had to leave, but I couldn't. I physically couldn't move. I was too scared to step forward, too scared to step backward." Miette hesitated for a moment.

I took that time to reflect on my life—too scared to step forward, too scared to step back. That sounded familiar. I thought of Aaron Brooks' parents, and how I had never surrendered myself to them. Too scared to step forward, too scared to step back.

"Anyway, standing there frozen, I thought of Norman's job. It was a Thursday, so the next morning would be a Friday. If he didn't show up to work, they would send someone by to check on him, right?" Miette chuckled. "I mean, I don't know. He had abducted me at five. Everything I know of the world comes from movies and books, and Norman, of course. But I thought that was logical, especially if he didn't call in sick. His place of employment would send someone over to check on him. What if that someone arrived and saw me standing in the doorway? I didn't have the strength to share my story with anyone, and someone would ask me who I was, why was I there, what happened to Norman. I couldn't answer those questions..."

Miette's voice faded into a distant hum. My stomach and chest went into zero gravity, and my innards floated within my body.

How had I not seen it before?

The hair strand. Missing work. The airtight alibis. The affair. It all snapped into place.

"Fred," I said, cutting off Miette with a sharp, forceful tone.

"Yeah?"

"I need to go."

"What? Like pee? I'm not helping you with that. We can call a nurse, though."

"I figured it out."

"Figured what out?"

"The doppelgänger case. I figured it out."

Fred narrowed his eyes. "They won't let you leave."

"I have to leave. I don't care if you break me out of here or you convince a doctor to discharge me. We need to go now."

"I'll distract the charge nurse," Miette said, jumping for the chair. "I'll distract the nurse, and you two sneak by."

"Thank you," I said, reaching out with my good arm and grabbing her hand. "You're not alone. You'll never be alone again. If you need anything, even someone to talk to you, you can call me. Never hesitate to reach out."

Miette sucked in her lips and nodded. "Thank you." She turned away and exited the room.

"Let's go," I said.

Fred sighed, but unhooked me from the equipment and helped me dress.

He and I walked out of the room, moving casually to not attract attention.

"Miette handed me your keys when I showed up earlier," Fred said. "She told me where she parked, too."

"Okay. Lead the way, then."

"When we're in your car, where are we going?"

I didn't respond, allowing my mind to wander. I thought of the email I had received, threatening the safety of everyone I knew if I continued to investigate the doppelgänger case.

Fred led us into the parking garage, meandered around a little, then found my car. We loaded in (Fred in the driver's seat, me in the passenger seat), and I removed my phone from my front pocket, scrolling to the video of Claire Balzan murdering Robert Woods. In the video, she stabbed the man repeatedly, holding the weapon in her...

"Left hand," I said.

"What?"

"She's left-handed."

"Okay. Why does that matter?"

I dialed Sarah Herling's number.

"Good morning," she said. "Working on the weekend, I see."

I didn't have the poise to apologize for calling on a Saturday morning. My heart beat too hard. "Is Claire left-handed?"

"Excuse me?"

"Is Claire Balzan left-handed?"

"I don't know."

"I don't think she is," I said, thinking of her hands being free yesterday. She had scratched her face with her right hand. She had tucked her hair behind her ear with her right hand. She had impatiently tapped the table with her right hand.

"What do you know?" Sarah asked.

A distant voice said something to Sarah from her side of the call.

"August, hold on." Sarah responded to her company, her voice muffled. I assumed she had covered the receiver with her hand. Still, I deciphered most of what she said. "It's August. He's a detective working the case with me. I think he knows something about Claire… something that might help her." She came back online, her voice clear again. "Sorry. I'm with Trisha Berry, Dr. Woods' assistant."

My breath caught. My entire body flexed, and my balls shriveled up inside of my stomach.

"Share your location with me," I whispered.

"What?"

"Share your location, then leave immediately. You're in danger."

"You're scaring me."

"Sarah!" I shouted, losing patience as fear overwhelmed me. "Sarah, leave!" I tapped Fred's leg and mouthed for him to call Alina.

"I can't read lips," he said.

"Call Alina now."

"What?" Sarah asked. "August, what's—" She gasped.

The line went dead.

The Doppelgänger. Saturday, April 29th, 1011hrs.

"HELLO?" ALINA ANSWERED, SOUNDING groggy. Fred had clicked his phone to speaker so I could listen and speak without him having to mediate.

"Did I wake you?" Fred asked.

"Not the time," I said, cutting into their conversation. I stared at my phone, waiting for Sarah to share her location, though I doubted the pin would ever drop. "Alina."

"Yeah?"

"Can you find an address for me?"

"I can do anything, but only after a cup of coffee. I have had no coffee this morning, and Maya had me up all night. She drank herself into oblivion again, losing her guts in the toilet—well, not quite in the toilet. She missed, splashing her dinner all over the wall and floor. Guess who had to clean it?"

"Trisha Berry," I said, not worried about Maya's poor decision making at the moment.

"Who? No. I don't know who that is, but I had to clean it. Me. Alina Mylene Moore."

"That's Robert Woods' assistant at his psychiatric practice. Trisha Berry. She's the one who discovered his body."

"Oh yeah. Okay. What about her?"

"I need her address. Her home address."

Over the speakerphone, I heard Alina's fingers tapping against the keyboard.

A minute passed.

Two.

"Hurry," I said, incapable of exercising any more patience.

"Calm down. I have it right here."

"Send it to me."

"It's an apartment complex."

"I don't care." My phone buzzed in my hand. Alina had shared Trisha's address. I synced the directions to my car's navigation screen. "Next left," I said to Fred.

"I can see it."

"What's going on?" Alina asked. "You two having fun without me?"

"I cracked the doppelgänger case. And the Changeling case."

"What? I thought you went on a date last night. It went that bad, huh? Was it the jeans? I told Maya they were too tight with that shirt you wear. You have to always go one baggy and one tight, never two baggy or two tight. Why did you listen to her?"

"I need you to contact everyone close to Trisha. Her parents. Her siblings. Her best friends. Everyone. Determine her exact location. If we arrive at her apartment and she's not there, we need to know where to go. Someone has to know where she is."

"Okay," Alina said.

"If all goes well, we'll meet up for lunch afterward."

"That's breakfast for me," she said.

"Perfect. Find a brunch spot that serves breakfast late into the afternoon."

"On it."

"After you locate Trisha."

"On that first."

Fred glanced at me with a worried expression after hanging up the phone.

"What?" I asked.

"You know the girl doesn't go to school, right?"

I swallowed, too worried about getting to Trisha before she could hurt Sarah to care about Alina's attendance. Still, I nodded, having figured something was off.

"She forged the work permit," Fred said. "She forged her parents' signatures, the teacher's signature, and any other signature needed to be on there. After you signed it, she crumpled it up and threw it in the trash—literally five feet away from you."

"What?"

"I noticed it, asked her about it later," Fred said. "I told her if she came clean, I wouldn't tattle on her to you. So, if she asks, you figured it out on your own."

"Okay."

"The school records attendance, right?"

"Sure."

"Well, if a student doesn't show up by a certain time, the clerk marks the student as absent, which triggers an automated call to their legal guardians. After so many absences, it becomes a legal matter. I think Alina hopes the school will harass her mother's phone, or somehow find her mother, and her mother will worry about her daughter's absences, come back home, and well, come back home. That's my guess, at least."

"Take a left there," I said.

Fred turned, barely touching the brakes. "The office offers more stability than that girl has ever known. You provide her with a sense of permanence. She might make fun of you, but she respects you, and I'm sure she expects you to know she's been skipping school. Don't lose her respect by not following up with that. You need to sit down with her and have a serious conversation before she finds herself in real trouble. And August."

"Yeah."

"Don't fire her. Don't threaten to fire her. I grew up in a similar situation to her. You take this away, you're taking away something she considers reliable and secure. You will throw her world into a chaos. Work with her, not against her."

I thought of Alina getting upset about moving out of my apartment and into Maya's place. She had admitted to never knowing stability, and she hated change because of that.

We finished the drive in silence.

I juggled too many worries, and I could barely keep them all in the air, especially with Sarah's safety constantly pestering me. What had happened to her? Had Trisha attacked her? Killed her?

Fred pulled into the apartment complex's lot, illegally parking along the curb near the administrative office.

I rushed from the car, bumping my bad shoulder on the frame. An explosion of red, wavering pain staggered me, and a wave of heat pushed sweat from my forehead and down my spine. I waded through the nausea and continued to the electronic side gate.

The complex locked it, and I didn't have a code.

Fred, a former professional athlete, made himself useful, hopping the eight-foot high fence with grace, landing on the other side and opening the gate.

I bustled through and followed the signs that directed us to Trisha's apartment number.

"What if she's not there?" Fred asked, chasing after me.

"Hopefully Alina comes through," I said, barely able to squeeze my voice through my tightening throat.

"What's the plan? We going to knock on her door and hope she lets us in?"

I stopped walking, realizing Fred had a point. We needed a way inside.

I glanced around, looking for an idea. I saw it as a short, stocky man with a backwards hat and sunglasses.

"Wait here," I said, taking off to the young man. I took a deep breath, doing my best to calm my nerves before saying, "Hi."

"Hey." He looked confused at my greeting.

"Can you do you me a favor?"

The young man frowned, ticking his head back and forth. "Depends."

"Last night, I slept with the woman who lives in apartment 234."

"Trisha?"

"Yeah."

"Nice, bro." He held out a fist for me to bump.

I obliged, buying time and scrambling for my story. "She found that I'm married, though."

"Dude, seriously?" He sounded disappointed.

"Separated, but still married."

"Still, man. Not cool."

"You're right. Not cool. I left my wallet in her apartment, though. Like you said, not cool, and I probably deserve for her to max out my credit cards, but can you help me out here? Please. If she sees me, she might kill me. But if you ask, maybe she'll give it to you."

"I don't know. Seems shady."

"I'll give you all the cash I have in there. It's like two hundred bucks."
Not a lie, either.

"Just to knock on her door and ask for your wallet?"

"Yes."

The man nodded, sucking on his upper lip. "Why not?"

"Thank you. Thank you so much."

"Dude, it's what bros are for."

The unnamed frat boy led me directly to Trisha's door. He motioned
for me to stand off to the side, out of view of the peephole, a habit
I always practiced anyway after my time with law enforcement. I had
heard too many stories of an officer knocking on a door and getting
showered in buckshot. In the academy, the teachers showed us how to
knock and step to the side—unless there was a window, of course.

Without a front window, I stepped to the side, nearly in the planters.

The young man knocked and waited. He knocked again and waited.
When Trisha failed to open the door after a minute, the young man
turned to me and shrugged.

"She was just in there five minutes ago," I said, glancing over my
shoulder.

Fred had followed us from a distance, finding a seat on a bench and monitoring us while eating something from a plastic bag.

"Can you try one more time?"

"You sure, man?"

"If she doesn't answer, there's no cash for you."

The young man sighed. "Sure. Why not, then? What will it hurt?" He knocked again.

The heavy door burst open, swinging outward hard, smashing the young man in his square face. A sickening crack split the quiet morning. Blood poured from his face. He grabbed his nose and moaned, cursing in a muffled voice like speaking underwater.

I reacted quick as I could, springing forward and shoving the college kid out of the way.

Another crack split the quiet morning. A firing gun snapping like a bullwhip. If the bullet struck me, I didn't register the pain. If it had connected with the young man helping me out, I hadn't noticed him respond.

My attention solely belonged to Trisha.

I bulled through the open doorway just as she fired again. The bullet whistled past my ear. My bad shoulder crashed into her outstretched arm, knocking the gun free. The pain cast a billion stars across my blurry vision. A sharp, sudden puncturing fire cleared my head. Clear as crystal, I saw a knife handle jutting from my hip; the blade lodged deep into my flesh—possibly in my bone.

Trisha had scrambled to her feet and ran to the fallen gun, leaning over to pick it up. She raised it with her left hand, pointed it squarely at my face. I should have applied for a job as a silhouette target based on the amount of people aiming weapons at me in the past week.

The woman resembled Claire Balzan more than Shannon Pellegri had resembled her late identical twin, Shelly Dupree. Trisha and Claire shared the same facial features, head shape, and physical build. The parallels between the two women were disconcerting.

Before she could fire, though, something small and rectangular flashed across the room and smacked her square in the temple.

The gun fired, but she had pulled her aim. Debris rained down on my head from the ceiling.

A half-second later, Fred fully showcased why the NFL had drafted him in the first round, and why he spent seven years as one of the best linebackers in the sport. He wasn't only big, like B-I-G big, but he was fast and unbelievably strong. He could tackle another professional athlete running directly at him with a full head of steam.

What he did to Trisha... well, it was incredible she lived through the impact. I would have bet she had a greater chance at surviving a head-on collision with a train. It wasn't a textbook tackle, though. That's my only critique.

In the NFL, they train the defensive players how to tackle properly to avoid harming the other players.

Well, Fred had retired from the league a few years back, and he must have become rusty during that time. The tackle was vicious, meant to produce great bodily harm.

Trisha's body hit the tile floor with a crunching impact.

Fred climbed atop her, pinning her to the ground with his behemoth size. He reached forward, grabbed the gun, and slid it out of reach. With an accomplished grin, he looked at me.

"A little sloppy," I said, grunting from the inferno of pain building in my hip. "You're out of practice."

"Nah. Sometimes you need a nasty, penalized hit to wake up your team and scare the other players. Do you think it worked?"

Trisha didn't move. For all I knew, Fred had accidentally killed her, which wouldn't have been ideal.

I groaned, touching my leg where the knife jutted from. On a positive note, it muted the pain in my shoulder. So, silver linings and all that, right? I gritted my teeth and fought through the excruciating, nearly debilitating pain, dragging myself to the front door to check on the frat kid.

He sat in the grass off to the side of Trisha's entry, still holding his face, staring at the sky. Luckily, the bleeding had slowed.

"Hey," I said. "How's it going?"

"I think she broke my nose. She definitely snapped a tooth in half. Your two-hundred bucks better stretch far enough to cover dental bills."

Luckily, I had free dental care for life. Maybe Dr. Dupree's promise would extend to the young man with a chipped tooth.

"Since you're able to talk well enough," I said, "call the police."

I dragged myself back into the house, moving like a zombie that missed one arm and one leg—in an awkward slither, almost. I inhaled through my teeth and forced myself to stand. My left leg was about as mobile and flexible as a stone statue, but I had more pressing issues than worrying about my discomfort.

I hobbled through the house, searching for Sarah, hoping beyond hope Trisha had kept her alive as a bargaining chip.

"Sarah," I called through the dark hallway, pushing a door open.

It revealed a bathroom. I moved to the next closed door, twisting the handle, opening to a bedroom. Leaning against the doorframe, I called for Sarah again, waiting for a response.

I heard a thump coming from another closed door within the room—presumably the closet door. I limped over, opening that door.

A bundled Sarah, bound in yards of plastic wrap, probably from the kitchen drawer, and gagged with an old sock, lay on the floor amongst shoes and dirty laundry. She stared up at me with wide, relieved eyes.

I glanced at the knife stabbed into my hip, pointing it out to her. "A better man than me would pry this from his leg and cut you free." I smirked. "But unless you want me to vomit all over you then pass out, I don't think that's going to happen."

The Whole Truth. Sunday, April 30th, 1223hrs.

THE DOCTORS HAD INOCULATED me with a generous supply of painkillers. The medicine worked its magic, making me a little loopy in the head, but also numb and without the dull or throbbing aches from gunshot and stab wounds.

A monitor standing beside my bed beeped incessantly. The last time the nurse checked on me, I had meant to ask her if she could turn the sound off, but I had forgotten after her barrage of questioning about how I felt. Answering had exhausted me more than I believed possible. I hadn't the slightest clue how to work the machine either, and I didn't care to break anything.

My remaining stay within the hospital hinged on a doctor assessing my condition, checking off certain boxes, and discharging me back into the wild, dangerous world of ghosts and changelings and doppelgängers.

As I lay in the bed, woozy and high, listening to the heart monitor beep, beep, beep, the door clicked open.

Footsteps crossed through Stan's portion of our shared room. Stan was an old man who coughed like he had no lungs, wheezy and rough. In our sparse stints of conversation, he seemed like a nice enough fellow, apart from his misogynistic and slightly racist perspectives on the world. Whenever he hacked words through his throat, the old man never failed to mention the 'Good Old Days.' Whatever that meant.

The flowered curtain separating our two spaces slid open.

Detective Daniel Quinn entered my room, sliding the curtain shut behind him. He wore pressed jeans, a long-sleeved shirt with the cuffs rolled up to his elbows, and loafers without socks. I cringed at the idea of wearing any kind of footwear, apart from sandals, without socks. Maybe my feet sweated more than average, though.

"Nice shoes," I said, unable to push away from the no-socks style.

"Discount bin."

"I don't believe you."

"Wise." Detective Quinn lingered near the closed curtain. "May I come in?"

I had a feeling he would entertain his notion of intruding, with or without my permission. "Please," I said.

Detective Quinn walked around my bed, sitting in the chair beside the window which overlooked the parking lot. He pried a notebook from his back pocket before crossing his legs, and he pulled a pen from the spiral wire holding the papers together, tapping the instrument against the notepad.

"How you feeling?" he asked, like a therapist inquiring about their patient's latest mental collapse.

"More or less like someone shot me in the shoulder and stabbed me in the hip with a hunting knife." I raised my hands, holding them six inches apart to portray the length of the blade Trisha had used against me.

"You'll enjoy knowing that Sacramento Police arrested Trisha Berry last night," Detective Quinn said.

"I enjoy that very much."

"She's currently in a holding cell at the county jail."

"What about Sarah?" I asked, remembering her bruised face and restrained body and terrified eyes.

Detective Quinn licked his teeth, pushing out his lips with his tongue. "A detective currently sits in a dreary room with Fredrick Norville Rogers." Fred's full name—horrendous, I know, and I've let him know occasionally. "Christian Pierce rests somewhere within the white-washed walls of this hospital."

"Who?"

"The kid with the broken nose."

I nodded, remembering the squat frat boy who had knocked on Trisha's door for me. "What about Sarah?"

Detective Quinn glanced at his spiral notepad and popped his lips. "Sarah Herling is in a hospital bed, much like you and Christian. She suffered superficial injuries, but it's wise to run a complete screening in cases such as these."

"You've spoken with her?"

"Not yet." Detective Quinn uncrossed his legs and leaned forward, staking the points of his elbows into his thighs. "I wanted to hear the story from you first."

"Have you not heard the story from Trisha?"

The detective cocked his head and furrowed his brow. "I did, but I trust your voice, Mr. Watson. You are much like me, part of the brotherhood of law enforcement."

"I quit."

"We both know well enough that once family, always family." He grinned, but nothing like a soft and warming grin. It made me more uncomfortable than I had felt in the past week, and I had felt uncomfortable often. "Now, please, tell your story from the beginning. What evidence led you to learn Trisha Berry murdered Simon Balzan and Robert Woods?"

"I feel like the mystery gang explaining the case at the end of a *Scooby-Doo* episode." That was supposed to remain a thought in my head, but the abundance of drugs had allowed it to form off my tongue. I sighed, rolling my eyes upward to stare at the ceiling and collect my thoughts.

After a few seconds, I shared everything with the detective. That after speaking with Claire Balzan, I believed her innocent. To further my hunch, she had time-stamped alibis, proving the affair video and the Adderall theft security footage couldn't have been Claire.

"But that wasn't enough, was it?" Detective Quinn asked. "The video evidence provided a convincing argument against those alibis."

I remained silent for a few seconds, regarding the detective with speculation. I couldn't hurdle the no-socks outfit. What department allowed their detectives not to wear socks?

"Did she have an alibi for the murders?" he asked.

"No," I said, my voice soft. "We also had to swim against the DNA evidence. Hair strands with the root balls still attached. Sarah and I accepted the impossible—proving Claire's innocence by disproving the video and the DNA evidence."

"Most would've settled for a plea deal."

"She was innocent. I meant to prove that."

"Did you?"

"I don't know." I sucked on my cheeks for a second, reflecting on the information I had deduced. The drugs swirled my thoughts, though, making it difficult to follow logic for too long. "If Trisha confesses, I guess Claire walks free. If Trisha maintains her innocence, Claire will head to trial, and there's no telling what the jury will decide."

"What evidence would Sarah Herling present to prove Claire's innocence?" Detective Quinn leaned back in his chair, allowing his notepad to rest in his lap, and he crossed his arms over his chest. "I'm only curious to know why you believe Trisha Berry should sit in jail right now."

"Well, for starters, she kidnapped Sarah Herling, took a few shots at the Christian kid, and she stabbed me."

The Detective smirked. "Well played."

"To entertain your curiosity, though…" I trailed off. "Why do you care, anyway?"

"I'm a detective. It's my job to care."

"You were investigating the Miette Verdin case?"

"I was."

"When the cops arrested Claire Balzan, they had their suspect. Open and shut case. No detective work needed. Video evidence. DNA evidence. Motive."

Detective Quinn raised his chin, looking down his nose at me.

"Did someone mention to you that Trisha Berry possibly murdered Claire Balzan's husband and therapist?" No socks. Who allowed no socks? I didn't know, but I didn't think many departments allowed such a casual dress code while on duty. "You're here on your time, aren't you? Why?"

Detective Quinn blinked, and his entire facial demeanor shifted from curious to cold. "Let's play a simple game. You tell me what I want to know, and I'll share with you what you want to know. The old, 'I show you mine if you show me yours.' What do you say?"

My fingers slipped to the edge of my bed and grabbed the chord attached to the call button. I walked it up to my palm.

Daniel Quinn's gaze dropped, noting my ploy. "There's no need to call anyone to come in here. I won't hurt you. I only want to know why you confronted Trisha Berry. That's it. That one simple nugget of information. What led you to her? I'm a curious detective asking a capable investigator for a sneak-peek into the brilliance of his mind."

I relaxed, but slightly. Something about the detective from the first time we crossed paths made me uncomfortable—now more than ever that we sat alone in a hospital room, with me drugged, shot, stabbed, and less than able to defend myself.

Speaking carefully while watching every movement the man made, readying myself to defend against any threat, I said, "I try to always allow the evidence to guide me before honing in on a single suspect. The evidence stacked strongly against Claire Balzan. But when I spoke with her, I couldn't help but believe her claims of innocence. So, I assisted

Sarah Herling in the case. I barely paid it any mind at first, knowing everything pointed to Claire as the murderer. Until I watched the murder video for about the dozenth time. I didn't know what exactly, but something felt... off. Unnatural. I went back and watched the other two videos—of her stealing drugs and of her infidelity. After speaking with Claire, after meeting her, something about those videos felt wrong."

"Like it wasn't her?"

"Like it wasn't her," I said. "Then the alibis fell into our laps. Claire had strong alibis for the theft and the affair, but not the murders. Still, those alibis convinced me of her innocence. Not only that, but the videos themselves almost felt staged."

"What do you mean?"

"Have you watched them?"

"Yes."

"You didn't think they felt... I don't know, wrong?" I asked. "The woman on camera intentionally stepped into view to get recorded."

"You can't prove that."

I shrugged, sending a mild current of pain through my shoulder. "There were other drug cabinets in the hospital, ones not guarded by a security camera. The woman posing as Claire chose that one, though."

"Maybe she didn't know about the other cabinets."

"Claire would have, though," I said. "She works at the hospital. Pretend she didn't know, though, for the sake of conversation."

"For conversation," Daniel Quinn said.

"Robert Woods had cameras placed throughout his house, but only at entry points—exterior doors. Half of his home remained blind. No cameras. His bedroom, where they recorded the affair, was one such room. Why go through the trouble of murdering someone in place where you knew the cameras are? Same with the theft. She knew a camera was in that room."

Quinn popped his lips. "To get seen."

I pointed at him, using my good arm. "My exact thought. To get seen. But... but not to get caught. The person recorded wanted to frame Claire, so no doubt existed in anyone's mind that she murdered Robert Woods and Simon Balzan."

"According to you, someone—Trisha Berry—framed Claire Balzan? Why?"

"You'll have to ask Trisha that question."

"What do you think?"

"The person on video used her left hand to key open the medicine cabinet and collect her pills. Sure, anyone could do that and not be left-hand dominant. However, in the murder video, she stabbed Robert Woods with her left hand. Trisha Berry is left-handed."

"Claire Balzan?"

I hesitated, unsure but almost certain she was right-handed.

"Interesting," Quinn said, scratching his neck.

"Trisha reported Robert Woods' death a few days after his murder. I find that strange."

"Do you? Why?"

"Dr. Woods had missed a couple of days of work before Trisha went to check on him. Maybe she called him that first day, or maybe she messaged him. You'll have to confirm with her phone records. Either way, he never called her back. And she was A-okay with sitting at her reception desk, fielding calls and canceling appointments without a legitimate reason from Dr. Woods. I bet if you contacted those clients who she canceled on, they will say she gave them an excuse. Something like, 'Dr. Woods is out sick today.' Guarantee it."

"What about the DNA evidence? How do you explain the hair found at the homicides?"

"Claire Balzan was a client of Dr. Woods." I thought of the strand of hair Miette had found on my hospital bed. "Trisha, after Claire's appointment concluded, could have pilfered any loose strands of hair she noticed in Dr. Woods' office. She could have planned this for months or years, methodically collecting the evidence, creating the perfect resemblance—have you seen her?"

"Who? Trisha?"

"Her and Claire resemble each other like sisters. With the correct application of make-up and hair-dye, they're indistinguishable."

"Why go through it all? What's Trisha's motive? That's what a jury will want to hear."

I shook my head, unsure about that question. "You'll have to ask her."

"I already did." Quinn cleared his throat and stood. "Trisha loved Simon Balzan. Despite what Claire believed, her and Simon had a far from perfect marriage. He and Trisha had an affair with each other, unbeknownst to Claire."

I blinked rapidly, working against the drugs to absorb the information.

"When Simon refused to leave Claire for Trisha, though, the woman's heart and mind broke, and she blamed it all on Claire with a seething hate. With a little nudging in the right direction, she learned how she might destroy Claire's life. Ruin her marriage, her career, her finances, and her freedom."

I cocked my head, hoping the shift in cranial direction would help my speed of processing. "With a little nudging?"

Daniel Quinn slowly approached the bed, looming over me. "Same as Miette Verdin."

"What?"

"She required a little support when she escaped Norman. She needed someone to provide her directions to her parents' house, to provide her with information about the woman who stole her life and how to steal it back." Quinn smirked—he had a devilishly handsome smile. "When Vanessa Snow and Claire Balzan needed a hero to turn to, someone who could save them from their evil twins, well, why do you think they both approached you?"

"What are you saying?"

The man leaned over my bed, bending to my ear and whispering. "We are brothers, but we're not brothers of the badge. You, much like me, no longer serve that brotherhood. I stopped policing years ago. But where you applied your skill set to investigating the paranormal, I applied my skill set to... using the paranormal to get what I want."

I don't know if the drugs had muddled my mind, but I couldn't comprehend what Quinn said. "What?"

"The Living Gargoyle case caught my attention. I followed you as you investigated the Voodoo doll murders and simultaneously cleared familial ghosts from an inherited home and solved the hallucinogenic Bigfoot dilemma. So, I decided I had found someone worthy to play cat and mouse with. But I had to test you, just to make sure. The Changeling and the Doppelgänger. I'm most impressed and wildly excited about our future."

"Our future?"

"August, we're the next Batman and Joker. Clarice and Hannibal. Holmes and Moriarty." Daniel Quinn kissed my temple and stood straight, exhaling. "I've been wanting to tell you that since we first met. I have so many adventures planned for us."

"Why wouldn't I just report you to the police?"

He chuckled through his nose. "I'm not actually a detective, and my name is not really Daniel Quinn, but everything else I have said is true. Now, get your rest. You'll need it. I'm planning our next adventure, and it's going to be a doozy."

Before I had the chance to catch up with what Daniel Quinn had admitted, the man walked around my bed, pulled open the curtain, and disappeared.

Tying Knots. Sunday, April 30th, 1556hrs.

FRED PICKED ME UP after the doctor cleared me, though on the condition that I promised to take it easy and rest. I obliged, knowing that anything exceeding three hours of sleep counted as taking it easy and resting in my book.

Maya had snagged a table for seven at a local brewpub about a mile from the hospital. I padded into the establishment, slightly leaning on Fred for support. It smelled like beer and fried food, which, all things considered, wasn't the worst scent ever.

In the back corner of the pub, Alina and Maya sat on the booth's bench. Sarah Herling, Zachary Verdin, and Miette Verdin sat in individual chairs on the other side of the table. A lone chair remained vacant at the head.

Fred climbed into the booth beside Maya. I plopped into the empty chair with a grimace and a grunt, regarding the table. Twelve eyes stared directly at me, anticipatory of something I couldn't predict. Hopefully, they didn't care for a speech.

"Hi," I said, not enjoying the undivided attention.

Sarah, who the hospital had discharged after running a few tests, appeared vibrant as usual. She had a swollen, blackened eye, a split lip, and bruising around her neck, but nothing that dulled her appearance. She smiled at me, catching my gaze.

"You doing okay?" I asked.

"Super-duper," she said, "considering the kidnapping and slight beating."

"Why did you head over there, anyway?" Alina asked, curious as usual.

Sarah shook her head, scoffing. "I was stuck in the investigation. I had the alibis to form a defense for Claire, but nothing else. With her on video, those alibis felt paper thin, too. So, there I was, up late, burning the midnight oil, rereading reports."

"Sounds familiar," Fred said, nudging my arm with his elbow. Luckily, not my bad arm.

"Trisha's picture appeared, stopping me cold," Sarah said. "I'm not sure how I missed it before, but I mistook her at first for Claire. They look eerily familiar. So, I went back over my prior interview with Trisha, realizing I had only spoken to her once after Claire hired me.

During that conversation, Trisha had answered all my questions with flying colors. I scratched off her name from my suspect pool… at least until I saw that photograph from the corner of my eye."

"They look that much alike?" Alina asked. "How did you not connect that before?"

"Well," Sarah said, "they have different hair and eye colors. Also, their personalities are wildly different. In person, a personality can mask physical appearance a lot. On camera, though, not so much. Trisha wore colored contacts and dyed her hair to match Claire's appearance. I only noticed the similarities because I saw the picture from the corner of my eye."

"It's like seeing a face in a mess of dots," Fred said. "A brainteaser. You know what I'm talking about? They have a bunch of random shapes or dots spread across a page, and if you look at it long enough or at the right angle, a face appears."

"Exactly," Sarah said, pointing at Fred. "Just like that. I saw Trish's picture from the right angle and Claire's face appeared. Anyway, a buzzing rang in my ear. I couldn't silence the noise."

"Like spidey sense," Alina said.

"Yup. Like spidey sense," Sarah said. "So, knowing something was off, I replayed the recording of Trisha's and my interview. She kept asking me if Claire really did it, if she murdered Simon and Bobby. She asked how we know for sure that she did? Did they find her hair? Did security cameras catch her in the act? I thought nothing of those oddly specific questions then. Even listening to the recording again, they struck me as strange, but not incriminating." Sarah drank some water, glancing at me. "You called me about the donated hair."

My mind immediately switched to Cambria. I had abandoned her on our date Friday night, and I had failed to call and apologize or reschedule another dinner. Almost two full days had passed. Would she agree to another date after my behavior? Probably not. That sucked. I had enjoyed her company, and I wanted to spend more time with her.

A twinge of guilt twisted my chest as I thought romantically about Cambria, and I glanced at Maya. She stared back at me, sharing a finger-waggle wave. I waved back.

"Anyway, I called Trisha," Sarah said. "I asked if I could follow up our last interview with a few questions about Robert Woods and his relationship with Claire Balzan. She agreed. I went over to her apartment, sat on her couch, removed my cell phone to record the conversation while she grabbed me a cup of coffee. That's when you called." Sarah nodded at me. "When Trisha returned, she had a gun, not coffee. Woke me up about the same, though." She chuckled at herself.

"You think she meant to kill you?" Alina asked, leaning forward.

"Eventually, yes, but not in her home. She was too smart to leave a bloody crime scene where she lived. Instead, she restrained me with an entire roll of Saran wrap, beat me a little to prove a point, then threw me in her closet to figure out what to do next. That's when August and Fred showed up."

I chewed on my cheeks, wondering if I should share Detective Quinn's visit with the group. I decided not to. Not then, at least. Instead, I asked, "What about Claire? Will she go to trial?"

"No," Sarah said, smiling proudly. "Trisha confessed everything to me once I was properly bound and beaten. People love to share their accomplishments with others, to prove how intelligent they are. Criminals, though, they often can't. They have to swallow their pride, and the taste grows sour. So, when a safe opportunity appears, they run their mouth. Trisha never thought you would arrive and rescue me, so she spilled the entire story, smiling like a clown the entire time." Sarah mirrored what Trisha's smile must have looked like, proud of herself. "I had my phone's voice recorder activated."

"Badass," Maya said. "That's a girl after my own heart. You ever consider a career in journalism?"

Sarah glanced at Maya and shook her head. "I enjoy law. Speaking of, if the recording doesn't get admitted into evidence for a trial, we need actual evidence proving Trisha committed the murders and framed Claire. That's easier now, though, since we have probable cause to search through her records."

"And?" I asked.

"Detectives found evidence of Simon and Trisha having an affair. Apparently, Trisha loved him, begged for him to leave Claire, but he refused. So, she slept with her Dr. Woods disguised as Claire, sending the video to Simon to make him jealous—whether of his wife or of his mistress, I don't know. He ended up texting Trisha that day, meeting with her. Claire never saw or spoke to him again, so there's a legitimate chance Trisha murdered him that night. Trisha needed to cover her tracks, though, so she donned the doppelgänger costume to look like Claire. She also needed to create a motive for Claire without casting shade on herself. So, Trisha ruined Claire's career, transferred all her money out of her account, and murdered Dr. Woods."

"With her left hand," I said.

"What?"

"She stabbed him with her left hand. Claire is right-handed. Just another nail."

Sarah chuckled again, a bubbling sound that never grew tiresome. "I'll note that detail. Anyway, the detectives will gather more evidence to exonerate Claire and charge Trisha. It has to be done correctly, though, and that will take time. The most important thing is establishing a timeline which places Claire away from the murders and puts Trisha at each murder."

"Which we have," I said.

"For the theft and for the affair with Dr. Woods. Not for the murders."

"If you think it's wise," Maya said, "I can write a piece in the *Here &* *Now*. I'm a full-time journalist there as of Friday." Maya showed her teeth, sitting up straighter in her seat.

"How long have you waited for the perfect window to announce that?" I asked.

"That wasn't even the perfect window," Maya said. "I had to blast through it."

"You can title the story *Doppelgänger Danger*," Fred said.

Maya reached across Alina and punched his shoulder. "That's perfect. I love that."

"I love our chances of Claire walking free," Sarah said, stepping through her window to right the conversation. She looked directly at me. "Thank you for your help. I couldn't have survived this case, literally, without you."

I faced Alina and Maya and Fred. "It's not me. It's never me. It's all of us working together." I shifted my attention to Zachary and Miette, who had sat invisibly quiet. "Same for you two. Those three right there deserve more credit than me for helping you."

"He's the pretty face to sell the product," Fred said. "We're the brains behind the operation."

"Speaking of operation," Maya said, clearing her throat. "Should we tell him about Operation Vacation?"

"What's Operation Vacation?" I asked.

"Well," Fred said, grinning, "we know we couldn't convince you to take a real vacation, so we're going on a hybrid vacation. To Santa Cruz."

"I don't have the time," I said.

"It's celebratory," Maya said. "To celebrate my full-time position as a journalist, and the both of us quitting our jobs at the bookstore."

"Wait, what?" I asked. "Quitting our jobs? I didn't quit."

"Well, when you didn't show up to work last night, guess who called me? That's right. Tom. Also, in my hungover state, I might have forgotten to call in sick or to show up for my shift. Anyway, long story short, I quit for the both of us."

"I needed that income," I said, massaging my temples and shaking my head.

"Well," Maya said, pouting out her lip and frowning, "you might have to get on your knees and beg. Our departure wasn't cordial. However, guess what? Vacation to celebrate!"

"Besides," Fred said, "you have the time. First, Doc said to take it easy, remember? Second, the vacation is for work. Apparently, a group of five individuals are experiencing shared nightmares featuring the same mutilated demon haunting them."

"A demon haunting people's nightmares?" I asked.

"Just like the *Nightmare on Elm Street*," Alina said. "By the way, that's one of my favorite horror movies of all time. I'm a sucker for slashers, though. Freddy. Jason. Michael. Leatherface. Even Art the Clown gets my goat going."

"Listen," Fred said. "Work vacation. Solving mysteries by the seaside. It's a write-off. We'll get paid by the clients. We have the rental home for five days, so after we solve the demon stalking dreams, we can lounge on the beach and do nothing but relax and take it easy."

"Rental home?" I asked.

"So we can all be in the same place," Fred said. "Otherwise, we'd all have to stay in separate hotel rooms. That gets expensive fast, and inconvenient to meet and discuss the case."

"He's right," Alina said.

"You're not going," I said, thinking of Alina skipping school. "You have school."

"Actually, I have next week off."

"Do you? That's convenient. So, if I called your principal, he would confirm that you have next week off?"

"Yup," Alina said. "Call him."

"We already booked the stay," Fred said.

"I'm going, too," Maya said, pumping her hands in the air. "Remember, I'm an honorary employee at Blue Moon Investigative Agency. I send you clients, you help me build stories. A demon haunting people's nightmares seems like a story worth writing. Also, celebration, baby!"

I rubbed my eyes with my right hand. My left dangled uselessly at my side. The bullet wound hurt down my entire arm.

I looked at the Verdin siblings. "What about you two?"

"We're not going," Zachary said.

"Sorry. I meant, what's next for you two?"

They looked at each other, back at me. "Cops arrested Vanessa," Zachary said.

"Arrested?" I asked, shocked. I watched her brain matter splash across the stage.

Zachary slowly nodded. "I don't know how, but she lived. I saw her, too. Hole the size of my finger in her forehead. When the EMTs arrived, though, they found a pulse and rushed her to the hospital."

I couldn't believe that. I couldn't fathom how people like Vanessa Snow survived, but those like Aaron Brooks died.

"Once the doctor's save her life," Zachary said, "the state will charge her with kidnapping, attempted murder, and three counts of murder. So, at least she'll never walk free again."

"Three counts of murder?" I asked.

"Our parents," Miette said.

"And Justin, her ex-boyfriend. Apparently, he learned the truth."

"He told him," Miette said, staring at the table. "I told him not to, but he did."

I narrowed my eyes, wondering who had told Justin. I thought I knew the answer, though.

"Miette and I will leave California. I don't know where we'll settle, but at least we'll be together."

"Miette," I said. "You okay?"

"Yeah. I'll be okay. I think for the first time in two decades, I'll be okay."

"You two have my number, yeah?"

They both nodded.

"Call me for anything. I'm here."

"Mr. Watson," Miette said.

"August."

"August, after I escaped from Norman, I didn't know where to go or who to talk to. I didn't want to call the police, because I wasn't ready to answer their questions and relive what I had only just escaped from. Honestly, I wanted my family. That was it. I stole Norman's car and drove until I ran out of gas. Placerville. He stopped to help me, and he introduced himself. Daniel Quinn."

I tensed, biting my tongue.

"He helped me, offered to put me up in a hotel and give me cash to get back on my feet. After a few days, I shared pieces of my story with him, mostly because I needed his help to locate my family. Danny, that's what he had me call him, told me everything, and he told me how to destroy the girl's life who took over mine. I refused, but he wouldn't accept that. So, he sabotaged her. I only wanted to see my parents again. To see Zach again. Danny did the rest."

"Except Vanessa murdered your parents," I said.

"Yes," Zach said. "As with everyone involved, if not more, she was confused. Vanessa had lived her entire life as Miette, and she feared this woman who had contacted her on social media, who claimed to be her. I think the same man, Daniel Quinn, contacted Vanessa and encouraged her to reach out to you. I don't know why she listened to him, but I think she feared the truth leaking out."

Miette wiped a stray tear from her face. "I thought you should know about that man."

"Thank you," I said.

The business discussions died, replaced with small talk.

Alina went on about her favorite horror movies, which included elevated horror, as she termed it, and guilty-pleasure horror, such as slashers and parodies. Maya chastised her movie taste, claiming raunchy romantic comedies were the best kind of movie.

"Heartfelt. Emotional. Funny. Often, there's action. There's always a hunk. What's not to love?" Maya asked.

Miette and Zachary kept mostly to themselves, and even that occurred in a silent, unspoken form of communication.

Fred ate, as Fred does, piling food into his mouth so his cheeks balled outward and his tongue couldn't move to speak.

I listened to them and thought about what I planned to do next, building the courage to do just that.

Walking Through the Door. Sunday, April 30th, 1722hrs.

Glacia's phone went straight to voicemail.

I almost hung up, but decided I should leave her a message speaking my mind.

"Hey. It's me again. Listen, I'm…" I trailed off, not having worked out what I wanted to say. I had mostly intended to talk to her, to hear her voice and discuss my recent cases and ask her about Oregon. I exhaled through my mouth. "I don't really know what to say, so I guess I'll say what's on my mind. I'm not much of a one-night-stand guy. I'm feeling a lot of mixed emotions right now." I ran my hands through my hair. "I'm at their front door again. Honestly, I was hoping for a boost of confidence."

I had nothing else, so I hung up and stared out the passenger window at Mr. and Mrs. Brooks' home. They had a single vehicle parked in the driveway, driving up the chances that one of them was home.

"I can't do it," I said.

"You can and you will," Vincent Dupree said from the driver's seat. I hadn't dared ask anyone I actually knew to chauffeur me around Sacramento, but I had asked Vincent, and he had jumped on the opportunity.

My phone rang, and Cambria's name showed. I closed my eyes, knowing I should take the call but not wanting to. Instead, I wanted to drive to the gym and pour my energy into a crushing workout. Unfortunately, my recent collection of wounds barely permitted me to walk, let alone work out.

"Hey," I answered.

"Hey yourself. I never heard from you yesterday."

I popped a knuckle. "You said you only went on the date to appease my mother. I didn't want to bug you."

"Would you have called otherwise?"

Why lie? It never proved a viable solution. "Probably not. Yesterday was... busy for me."

"Oh, yeah?" Maybe I imagined it, but she sounded hurt.

"Not in the typical sense, but in the sense that someone shot me right after our date."

"Shot you? What?"

"Shot me in the shoulder. I'm fine, mostly. It hurts a lot, but not as much as my stab wound. That happened yesterday morning."

"Someone stabbed you, too?"

"In the hip. Spent Friday and Saturday in the hospital. That's why I didn't call."

"I talked to your mom yesterday. She called to ask about our date, but she never mentioned that you were in the hospital."

I scrunched my face, realizing I hadn't ever taken the time to inform her of my condition. "She doesn't know."

"August, how does your mom not know you were shot and stabbed?"

"While in the hospital, it felt like a lot of energy to support her emotional distress. Now that I'm out and about, though, I honestly forgot to let her know."

"You're going to have to tell her."

I closed my eyes. "I know."

Cambria snickered. "Who gets shot and stabbed? Are you auditioning for an action movie?"

"Something like that," I said. "I spent most of yesterday in the hospital, drugged out of my mind. That's why I didn't call. If not for that, I would have, though." I coughed, hesitating to speak the next part, but wanting to. "I had a good time on our date."

"Me, too."

"Oh, yeah?"

"Until you abandoned me, that is."

"I'm sorry about that."

"You abandoned me to get shot. How do you think that makes me feel?"

"If it makes you feel better, I didn't leave expecting to get shot."

"Can I say it serves you right, or is that too mean?"

I chuckled. "It probably serves me right." My tension melted away during our banter, and the surmounting fear of knocking on Raymond and Tammy Brooks' door dwindled.

"What are you doing now?" Cambria asked.

Again, why lie? "I'm sitting in my car, parked in front of the Brooks' home, about to drive away."

"We're not driving away," Vincent muttered.

Cambria remained quiet for a moment. "Why would you drive away?"

"I can't face them."

"I know you suffered a gunshot, and I'm sure some doctor fuzzed your mind with drugs."

"Fuzzed my mind?"

"Fuzzed, yes, and I'm sure that fuzziness made you forget our conversation. You won't confront them for your sake or for their sake. Do it for Aaron, though. Yeah? You want to apologize to him. This is how you do that."

I grunted, not wanting to admit she was right.

"You're in the supernatural business to find proof of the afterlife so you can apologize to Aaron. Well, do what you can control. Apologize to his parents."

I rested my head against the passenger window, knowing I had to follow through with this. Not only for Aaron's sake either, but for his parents' and mine. So we could heal. I had to overcome my fears. I had to step forward and continue with my life.

"Do you want to go to Santa Cruz with me?" I asked, blurting out the question.

"What?"

A fire burned up my neck and into my face. Why had I asked that? "We have an investigation in Santa Cruz, but we're pretending like it's a work-vacation hybrid deal. Do you want to go with us?"

"You just want to see me in a bikini, don't you?"

I stumbled over how to respond. Saying yes didn't sound great, but saying no sounded worse.

"I'm kidding," Cambria said. "When?"

"Tomorrow through Friday."

"You know I have a job, right?"

"Yeah, of course. I didn't expect you to say yes. I kind of, just, I don't know, asked on a whim."

"I'd love to go."

"Really?"

"Really. I only had clients scheduled for two days this week, anyway, and they're regulars. I'm sure I can reschedule for next week."

"I'll still have to work."

"And while you're saving people from ghosts, I will sit on the beach, enjoy a cold drink, and read a fun book. We can spend the evenings together, if you promise not to abandon me in favor of getting shot or stabbed."

"I promise," I said.

"Perfect. Now, call me later and tell me how it went with Aaron's parents."

I stared at their front door. "I will."

Cambria ended the call.

"You're okay to wait here," I asked Vincent.

"All night, baby."

I stepped out of the car and limped to the front door. Riding the wave of confidence Cambria had plugged into me, I closed my eyes, exhaled, and knocked.

The sound my knuckles made on the stiff wood reverberated through time, echoing far too loudly. The world vibrated for a second, as if pitching my existence between time, somewhere where nothing exists.

For a second, Aaron's bleeding body flashed before me, lying on the asphalt, twitching.

I blinked, and the world crashed back into being. The sensations of vibrant life exploded around me. That image faded away, his youthful face transitioning, growing older and more haggard.

Raymond Brooks stood in the open doorway. Tammy Brooks shadowed him.

He offered a sad smile as tears slipped down his face, and the man stepped aside. "Come inside, August. Please."

The End

What's Next for August and Friends?

Nightmare Scare

There are good reasons to fear the night. August Watson is about to kick them in the pants.

Kids getting hurt by a figure in their nightmares might sound like the makings for a bad slasher movie, but for August Watson, Sacramento's only paranormal detective, it's a very real case.

He's heading to the coast for a well-deserved break, but he's soon gonna wish he'd stayed at home. That could be because his assistant sneakily invited August's entire family and the two women he is struggling to pick between.

Recovering from injuries sustained solving his last case – something he might have omitted to tell his mom – August figured the dream demon case would be easy to solve.

Not only is it anything but, all too soon he has multiple cases to juggle, and they are coming to him whether he wants them or not.

Flocks of birds attacking people, and a ghostly apparition on the coastal highway prove to be the tip of the iceberg, for lurking in the background, a self-appointed nemesis is pulling the strings.

Books by Alex Gates

Dead Awake

Dorian Miller, a private detective specializing in the supernatural, investigates a blackmail conspiracy involving the daughter of one of Sacramento's elite families who partook in a satanic ritual.

But the simple assignment soon turns un-deadly.

Zombies and golems rise around the city. The corpses of vampires are found slaughtered in a horrific manner. And rumors warn that a Revenant—the spirit of a dead Necromancer summoned back to this world—stands behind all the mayhem.

How much longer can Dorian run from Death before it catches up to him?

Inherent Magic

Once struggling to make rent, Skylar must now use her budding magic to save the world...

As a child of abuse, Skylar Neveah knows desperation and terror from first-hand experience. But nothing in her past prepared her for a date ending with her getting sacrificed to a fallen angel. By blind luck and a touch of magic, Skylar escaped with her life. To do so, she murdered two wealthy, influential men.

On the run from the police and the supernatural world, a man approaches Skylar. He offers her refuge at a secret university for humans like her with magical powers. She hesitantly accepts his offer. But her problems aren't solved... far from it.

A cosmic war has kicked off. Somehow, Skylar landed in the middle of it. And the fallen angel has fixed his attention on her. He will stop at nothing to see her killed. Will Skylar stop running, learn to control her magic, and fight back?

Books by Steve Higgs

Paranormal Nonsense

The paranormal? It's all nonsense but proving it might just get them all killed.

When a master vampire starts killing people in his hometown, paranormal investigator, Tempest Michaels, takes it personally ...... and soon a race against time turns into a battle for his life. He doesn't believe in the paranormal but has a steady stream of clients with cases too weird for the police to bother with.

Mostly it's all nonsense, but when a third victim turns up with bite marks in her lifeless throat, can he really dismiss the possibility that this time the monster is real.

Joined by an ex-army buddy, a disillusioned cop, his friends from the pub, his dogs, and his mother (why are there no grandchildren, Tempest), our paranormal investigator is going to stop the murders if it kills him ......

but when his probing draws the creature's attention, his family and friends become the hunted.

Untethered Magic

Today's tasks:

1.Escape from underground cell

2.Recruit snarky d-bag werewolf to help

3.Invade demon realm and rescue a girl

For wizard detective, Otto Schneider, magic has always kept him out of trouble. Now it's working in reverse and he's just started the fight of his life. There's an ancient secret buried in the Earth's past, and he just uncovered it.

Magical beings once ruled over us until their betrayed leader made a death curse with his final breath. Banished from the realm of man for over four thousand years, the curse is weakening, and these beings, these ... demons, are coming back to rule the Earth once more.

They are powerful, immortal, and unstoppable, but they don't know everything.

They left some of their magic behind and their return has sparked an awakening.

Heroes will rise ...

<u>**More Books By Steve Higgs**</u>

Blue Moon Investigations
Paranormal Nonsense
The Phantom of Barker Mill
Amanda Harper Paranormal Detective
The Klowns of Kent
Dead Pirates of Cawsand
In the Doodoo With Voodoo
The Witches of East Malling
Crop Circles, Cows and Crazy Aliens
Whispers in the Rigging
Bloodlust Blonde – a short story
Paws of the Yeti
Under a Blue Moon – A Paranormal
Detective Origin Story
Night Work
Lord Hale's Monster
The Herne Bay Howlers
Undead Incorporated
The Ghoul of Christmas Past
The Sandman
Jailhouse Golem
Shadow in the Mine
Ghost Writer

Felicity Philips Investigates
To Love and to Perish
Tying the Noose
Aisle Kill Him
A Dress to Die For
Wedding Ceremony Woes

Patricia Fisher Cruise Mysteries
The Missing Sapphire of Zangrabar
The Kidnapped Bride
The Director's Cut
The Couple in Cabin 2124
Doctor Death
Murder on the Dancefloor
Mission for the Maharaja
A Sleuth and her Dachshund in Athens
The Maltese Parrot
No Place Like Home

Patricia Fisher Mystery Adventures
What Sam Knew
Solstice Goat
Recipe for Murder
A Banshee and a Bookshop
Diamonds, Dinner Jackets, and Death
Frozen Vengeance
Mug Shot
The Godmother
Murder is an Artform
Wonderful Weddings and Deadly
Divorces
Dangerous Creatures

Patricia Fisher: Ship's Detective Series
The Ship's Detective
Fitness Can Kill
Death by Pirates
First Dig Two Graves

Albert Smith Culinary Capers
Pork Pie Pandemonium
Bakewell Tart Bludgeoning
Stilton Slaughter
Bedfordshire Clanger Calamity
Death of a Yorkshire Pudding
Cumberland Sausage Shocker
Arbroath Smokie Slaying
Dundee Cake Dispatch
Lancashire Hotpot Peril
Blackpool Rock Bloodshed
Kent Coast Oyster Obliteration
Eton Mess Massacre
Cornish Pasty Conspiracy

Realm of False Gods
Untethered magic
Unleashed Magic
Early Shift
Damaged but Powerful
Demon Bound
Familiar Territory
The Armour of God
Live and Die by Magic
Terrible Secrets

About the Authors

Alex and Steve met online through their mutual love of urban fantasy. Both established writers with their own successful series, they chose to collaborate on a spin-off of Steve's Blue Moon Investigation stories.

They duo hope to meet in person one day when pandemics and other global dramas allow, but one of them will need to cross the Atlantic first. Until then, they will continue to churn out thrilling fantasy tales.

Read on and enjoy.

9 781915 757364